Christina Jones has written a ~~~~ ns of Proper Jobs including factor ~~~~ r, blood donor attendant, barma ~~~~ fruit picker). She first had a short s ~~~~ when she was just 14 years old, and since then has written for teenage and women's magazines, had her own humour column in the *The Oxford Times* and contributed to national newspapers, as well as writing over 20 acclaimed romantic comedy novels.

Praise for Christina Jones

'As cosy as a goose-down duvet and bursting with sparkle and joy . . . Christina Jones is a wonderful writer' Jill Mansell

'The H.E. Bates of our time . . . The same earthy, bucolic charm' Katie Fforde

'A fun read for dull January evenings' *Sun*

'[A] feisty tale of friendship and laughter, loyalty and love . . . Engaging' *The Times*

'Bloody good read . . . A lively romp through rural England' *New Woman*

'Bubbles with more joy than a magnum of champagne' *Peterborough Evening Telegraph*

'Chick-lit with a magical twist' *Heat*

Summer
at
Sandcastle
Cottage

Christina Jones

ACCENT

First published in 2021
by HEADLINE ACCENT,
An imprint of HEADLINE PUBLISHING GROUP

1

Cataloguing in Publication Data is available from the British Library

ISBN 978 1 7861 5728 7

Typeset in 10.5/13pt Bembo Std by Jouve (UK), Milton Keynes

Printed and bound in Great Britain by Clays Ltd, Elcograf S.p.A.

HEADLINE PUBLISHING GROUP
An Hachette UK Company
Carmelite House
50 Victoria Embankment
London
EC4Y 0DZ

www.headline.co.uk
www.hachette.co.uk

For Sue Brown – my fabulous friend. To say a huge
thank you for all the years of friendship, for the laughing and
the tears, the sharing and the understanding – and also because
she worried about Vinny.

Summer
at
Sandcastle
Cottage

Prologue

It's a glorious summer in Firefly Common, the old-fashioned south-coast seaside village where Kitty Appleby (thirty-something, recently single, a bit of a Julia Roberts lookalike) and her friend Apollo – her one-time landlord and employer – and her oldest school friend Jemini (with her toddler daughter Teddy), rent the delightful Sandcastle Cottage. They moved in just before Christmas (see the snowy short story *Christmas at Sandcastle Cottage* for the story of their arrival at Firefly Common) and have enjoyed every moment of their new life so far.

But now, six months later, that life is far from being all sunshine and lollipops for Kitty (currently working as a waitress in the Silver Fish Bar, with a lot more than chips on her mind); Apollo (will he ever be able to convince Firefly Common that what it really needs is a kebab takeaway?); and Jemini (now working part-time in the estate agent's with her much-younger squeeze Connor, having found a nursery place for Teddy). The only two residents of Sandcastle Cottage without a care are Honey and Zorro, the rescue Staffies.

Because, as Kitty's neighbours, the kindly-but-overbearing Mr H and his wife 'she loves a tipple' Angelica, keep reminding her, very soon, Mavis Mulholland – the owner of Sandcastle Cottage – will return from her lottery-won round-the-world-cruise, and want her home back . . .

As Kitty, Apollo and Jemini have all been homeless once, it's not something they want to face again. Especially when that

1

would mean leaving the adorable Sandcastle Cottage – and probably Firefly Common – for ever.

And Kitty has another, very pressing reason for wanting to stay: the enigmatic, mysterious Vinny, who walks along the beach, alone. Because Kitty, recognising another lonely soul, knows there's far more to 'Vinny the Vagrant' than meets the eye.

As the scorching summer unfurls in Firefly Common, and as Zorro and Honey waggle and wobble and Staffie-smile their way into everyone's hearts; Apollo and Jemini try to make their dreams come true; Kitty tries hard not to fall spectacularly stupidly in love; and Mavis Mulholland's cruise ship nears port . . . who will end up living happily ever after? And where?

Chapter One

The thump of mail through Sandcastle Cottage's letterbox made Kitty jump. Despite living on the rural south coast for six months, she'd never quite got used to the early morning arrival of the post. When she'd lived in the centre of Reading's urban sprawl, letters had sometimes not been delivered until well into the afternoon. She blinked at her watch. Lordy – it wasn't even seven o'clock. An insane time for posties – or fish-restaurant waitresses for that matter – to be awake, not to mention up, dressed, and already getting on with the day.

Kitty yawned and stretched. No doubt the post would just be flyers and junk mail as usual. Nothing important. She'd deal with it once she'd had a good shot of caffeine.

Still yawning, Kitty reached for the coffee jar, lazily watching the sun-dancing dappled patterns through the kitchen window as she spooned granules into her mug. It was another glorious morning in Firefly Common, heralding another scorching June day. And as she still had plenty of time to enjoy it before she had to leave for work, Kitty decided she would kill two birds with one stone and take her coffee out on to the porch, picking up the mail on the way.

Pushing her tangle of auburn-ish hair out of the way behind her ears, Kitty poured hot water into her mug. Then, closing her eyes, she inhaled the aromatic steam.

Bliss. Absolute bliss.

Her shift at the Silver Fish Bar didn't start until 11 a.m., but she loved the silence and solitude of these beautiful summer mornings and always made an effort to be first up. Much as she adored her housemates, Apollo and Jemini, they were both night owls by nature and both needed noise in the mornings to get going. So, before anyone else appeared and the radio bellowed rock 'n' pop and Apollo and Jemini sang along – or Peppa Pig squawked from the television to entertain Jemini's toddler daughter Teddy – Kitty made a point of savouring her first mug of coffee in blissful isolation.

Well, almost.

Hearing a familiar thud above her, then the thundering of eight massive paws on the stairs, followed by an excited scrabble of claws on the tiles, Kitty hastily put her mug down. She reached for the dogs' food bowls, and managed to fill them and get them on the floor just as brindle Zorro and black Honey rattled to a halt in the doorway. Then, with tails going like rotor-blades, they slithered at breakneck speed into the kitchen. Giving her their best big Staffie smiles they fell on their breakfast with joyous and noisy enthusiasm.

In the time it took Kitty to pick up her mug again, the food bowls were empty.

'Gannets,' Kitty said fondly, looking down at Zorro and Honey who were snuffling hopefully under their bowls, chasing them with slobbery joy across the quarry-tiled floor. 'No, you're not getting a refill. You're spoiled rotten as it is. We're going outside. However, because I love you,' – she reached for the dog biscuits – 'you can have a treat, and' – she grabbed a packet of chocolate digestives – 'so can I. Come on . . .'

The dogs needed no second bidding, and were immediately swaying happily towards the front door ahead of her, when Kitty remembered the post. Clutching her coffee and tucking the biscuits under her arm, she rushed to rescue the mail before the Staffies got their paws on it.

She made it. Just. Scooping up the flyers and junk mail with her free hand, Kitty frowned down at the solitary envelope remaining on the doormat. It had separated itself from the plethora of unsolicited mail as if it knew its importance.

Kitty shivered. It was scary how easily a plain blue airmail envelope, liberally decorated with foreign stamps and addressed to Ms K Appleby in very curly black writing, could instantly take the warmth out of the gorgeous June morning.

She knew instinctively exactly what it was. It simply couldn't be anything else. It was the letter she'd been told to expect but had hoped upon hope would never arrive. The letter from Mavis Mulholland, Sandcastle Cottage's owner, telling Kitty when she was intending to come home.

Kitty's heart sank. She knew only too well that the letter would tell her when she and Jemini and Apollo – not to mention Teddy and the dogs – had to leave. When they'd first rented Sandcastle Cottage on a temporary basis it had simply been their refuge, but had rapidly turned into their home – just when they'd all needed one most: a home they'd fallen in love with, in a village they adored. And now, before long, they'd be out on the streets again.

It was something they'd all known would happen – and they'd all known when the tenancy would expire – but foolishly they'd all pretended the problem might just go away, and had made no contingency plans whatsoever. They'd all simply tried not to think about it. But now burying their heads in the sand had come back to bite them with a vengeance, Kitty thought miserably, truculently mixing her metaphors and clichés.

Careful not to slop coffee over the airmail letter, she pushed it into the pocket of her Silver Fish Bar tabard, then deposited the rest of the post on the hallstand. She'd read Mavis's letter later. When she was properly awake. And had had her coffee. And maybe felt a bit braver.

Outside, after having settled the dogs with water and a handful of biscuits, and placing her coffee and the chocolate digestives carefully on a rickety bistro table, Kitty sank into one of the mismatched cushioned rattan chairs that lined Sandcastle's front porch. All the porch needed to make it absolutely perfect, she'd always thought, was a rocking chair and one of those hammock swings that you saw in American films ... and maybe if Sandcastle Cottage was her permanent home, and she'd earned enough money waitressing at the Silver Fish Bar, then she'd buy one . . . but there was one huge 'but', as always, and the reason for it was practically burning a hole in the pocket of her work tabard.

She cupped her hands round her coffee mug and stretched out her long legs in their ankle-grazer jeans, as the dogs investigated new scents that had appeared overnight in every corner of Sandcastle Cottage's pretty front garden. Kitty smiled, watching them. That garden, which had been so bleak and overgrown and unloved when Kitty had first seen it, now had tidily mown grass, was edged with neatly pruned shrubs, and had borders of colourful tumbling perennial cottage-garden flowers lining the sandy path. A low, freshly painted wooden fence made the garden complete.

The mowing, pruning, planting and painting had been a shared springtime venture, overseen, helped with, and loudly advised on by Mr H next door. Which, they'd all admitted at the time, was just as well because between them they knew diddly-squat about gardening.

Mr H had been just as useful in the back garden too, which was surrounded by a tall honeysuckle-covered trellis, and had been restored from a rather tangled jungle to a neat lawn, curving shingle paths, and fruit trees. They'd discovered a large wooden patio table with folding chairs and an umbrella in the shed and, once renovated, they now took centre stage. Apollo had also built a bird table and a hedgehog house, as well as a sandpit and tree swing for Teddy, much to her delight.

Kitty savoured her coffee and the gentle early morning warmth, as on the other side of Sandcastle's newly painted fence, Firefly Common began to wake. Dog walkers from the other cottages dotted along the lanes amongst the tall pine trees smiled and waved at her; the milkman, escorted by Zorro and Honey, clattered up the path and deposited glass bottles with his usual 'gonna be a right scorcha, duck' greeting; several commuters said their good mornings as they hurried past Sandcastle Cottage en route for Firefly Common Halt and their rail journeys into Bournemouth or Christchurch, or maybe even further afield.

The dogs, deciding that they'd had enough snorting and exploring in the garden and had satisfactorily seen off the milkman, clambered inelegantly up the low flight of wooden steps that ran the length of the porch and looked hopefully at Kitty. She laughed at them, and threw down a handful of dog biscuits. With much huffing and puffing they hoovered up the biscuits at the speed of light.

If only, Kitty thought, I could join in. Oh, but not with dog biscuits, obviously . . . She eyed the packet of chocolate digestives. No, it was no good – Mavis Mulholland's unread letter had robbed her of her appetite . . . Damn it.

She took another mouthful of coffee and watched the early morning sun cast lattice-work patterns through the trees. Snaking off into the distance, the tiny shingle paths and narrow rutted lanes, dark with blackberry bushes and overhung with fern fronds, twisted away across the common towards the roads which led to the clifftop in one direction and Firefly Common's High Street in the other.

Bees and butterflies danced in and out of the gorse and heather, and the only sounds were that of birdsong and the distant hush-shush of the sea. The air was soft, and sweet with the scents of blossom and warm sandy soil. This really was the most glorious place to live.

Ah, well . . .

Taking a deep breath, she reached into her pocket for the airmail letter.

Chapter Two

'Good morning, Kitty!'

The voice stopped Kitty in her tracks and the letter remained untouched. The dogs rattled down the porch steps and sashayed side by side towards the gate, their tails whirling in synchronised greeting.

'Hi, Angelica.' Kitty smiled at her neighbour, now bending down to fuss Honey and Zorro. 'You're out and about early,' she added as she looked in some surprise at the slender dark-haired figure in the pink tracksuit, pink baseball cap and even pinker trainers. 'Oh, and are you – um – running?'

'Jogging.' Angelica beamed from behind her huge sunglasses. 'I have a new get-fit-and-stay-fit regime. I've only just started, but I think it's going to be fun. You should join me.'

Kitty laughed. 'Thanks but no thanks. I'm on my feet all day at work and I walk the dogs for miles, and that's more than enough for me. Jemini might be interested, though. She's always been more into organised exercise than I have. I'll mention it to her when she eventually manages to get out of bed . . . and – um – does Mr H not want to join in on this – um – new venture?'

'Good heavens, no!' Angelica chuckled. 'He says he gets all the exercise he needs from gardening and golf. But he's glad I have a new interest to keep me out of mischief. Anyway,' – she glanced at the slimline electronic gadget strapped to her wrist – 'I still have several thousand steps to get in – not to mention calories to burn.'

'What? There's nothing *of* you. You don't need to burn calories!'

'My wellness guru says otherwise. I may have no outward fat, but apparently inner unseen fat is clogging all my organs.'

Kitty blinked. Unless Firefly Common's cottage hospital had recently installed state-of-the-art medical equipment, Angelica's wellness guru must have had a good pair of X-ray specs as well as a Master's in dietary nutrition, if they could diagnose visceral fat just by looking.

'And to combat that,' Angelica continued, 'I need to eat clean and exercise – and, apparently, alcohol isn't helping either my calorie count or my liver, and you know how I love – *loved* – a tipple.'

Kitty did. Angelica would happily accept any drink, anywhere, from anyone, whether the sun was over the yardarm or not. This was all a massive departure. 'Mmm, yes. Well, maybe it's a good thing for your liver, but what the heck is "eating clean"?'

Angelica grinned. 'I'm honestly not too sure. I thought it was just making sure you washed your lettuce properly, you know, that sort of thing. But apparently it isn't. We're covering that in a later session, I think. In the meantime, I'll need to look at my brochure to discover exactly what it is, then I can tell you what you should be doing.'

'OK,' Kitty chuckled. 'I clearly need to know where I've been going wrong all these years.'

Too late, Kitty realised Angelica was nodding and taking it all very seriously. She quickly changed the subject. 'Um . . . and have you – um – given up drinking altogether?'

'Good god, no! The Merry Mermaid would go bankrupt! Not to mention my lovely online wine man. But I've cut down. Everything in moderation, Destiny says.'

'Destiny?'

'My wellness guru. She's amazing.'

And I'll bet any money her real name's Doreen, Kitty thought, but didn't say. 'Oh, lovely. And does – er – Destiny have a practice or a surgery or whatever here in Firefly Common?'

'In the village hall, on a Wednesday.' Angelica was now running on the spot. 'Did you not get the flyer through the door?'

Kitty hadn't. No doubt it had arrived and instantly been chewed beyond recognition by the dogs. Sorry, Destiny.

'Anyway,' – Angelica looked at her wrist again – 'I'll have to be going before it gets too hot. I've paid Destiny an awful lot for this regime – mustn't let it go to waste. Bye!'

Kitty waved and watched as Angelica's slender figure disappeared through the trees. 'An awful lot' to Angelica was probably like a lottery jackpot win to normal mortals. Kitty wondered how much Destiny was making from the wealthy, retired and bored ladies – and some of the men, no doubt – of Firefly Common. On the other hand, if it steered Angelica away from drinking too much, maybe it was worth the money.

Finishing her coffee, Kitty wondered, not for the first time, exactly how old Angelica was. In fact, it was something she and Jemini had pondered over often, playing the 'guess-the-age game' ever since they'd moved into Sandcastle Cottage.

It was so hard to gauge anyone's age these days. Mr H, lean and weather-beaten from hours of gardening and golf, looked older than his wife. So, in his sixties? Early seventies, maybe? And Angelica could be anywhere between forty and sixty. Not that it mattered, of course, but speculating on Angelica's age had always led them to wonder how old Mavis Mulholland was.

Ancient, Jemini had decided, with a name like Mavis. But Kitty hadn't been so sure. Especially now that trendy parents were giving their daughters old-fashioned between-the-wars names like Elsie and Edna and Gladys.

And Sandcastle Cottage – the much-extended home of the Mulholland family, and once run as a successful B&B, then inherited by Mavis when her husband, the last of the original Mulhollands, died – gave no clues as to Mavis's age at all. It had been let fully furnished but every last vestige of its owner had been carefully removed. There wasn't even a left-behind photo or anything personal at all.

They'd asked Angelica, of course. Tactfully.

Angelica had shrugged and said 'maybe my age, but possibly younger – no idea, sweeties. We're good neighbours but we've never been that intimate. Mavis wasn't a local Firefly-Common girl, you know? She came from up the coast a bit, I think. I can tell you one thing, though: Mavis was much younger than Clive, her husband, who had been widowed years and years earlier and had lived alone here for yonks – oh, and he was Mr H's age. And Mavis and Clive, they met online – how daring was that for Firefly Common? Mavis was divorced, I believe. And they, Mavis and Clive, hadn't been married all that long when Clive had his coronary and died – and of course, there were no other Mulhollands roaming the earth – well, not related to Clive anyway, so Mavis was the sole beneficiary and inherited Sandcastle Cottage.'

'Oooh,' Jemini had said excitedly. 'Do you think she bumped him off?'

'No!' Angelica had looked shocked. 'She was very fond of him. It wasn't a love match for either of them, but he got companionship and she got a nice home. It suited them both.'

'Was she heartbroken when he died?' Jemini had asked.

'No. Upset, of course. And sad. But not heartbroken. And I think she's enjoyed her widowhood – and then, of course, there was the enormous lottery win . . .' Angelica had sighed. 'Some people have all the luck, don't they?'

And Kitty and Jemini had tentatively agreed.

Annoyingly, Connor Lowe – the youthful estate agent who had rented them the cottage, and who was now, um, walking out, as well as sleeping in, with Jemini – was even less help. 'Dunno,' he'd said, nonchalantly shaking back his gelled quiff, when Kitty had asked him. ''Bout the same age as my mum I guess. Like, *ancient*. Well, maybe even older than my mum . . . but not as ancient as my nan . . . but older than you and Jem, or maybe not. Seriously, Kit – I dunno.'

And, Kitty thought with a chuckle, she and Jemini had on more than one G&T-fuelled evening, googled Mavis, with no tangible results. They'd assumed that as Mavis had met Clive Mulholland online, then she must be Internet savvy. However, as she may well now have reverted to her maiden name, or could easily be one of the ninety-three thousand worldwide Mavis Mulhollands who had appeared as a result of their search, but probably wasn't, they'd eventually given it up as a lost cause.

Therefore, frustratingly, Mavis Mulholland remained something of an enigma, although, whatever her age, Kitty imagined her as short, plump, blond-permed and smiley. And possibly with a London accent. And a smoker's chuckle. All in all, a lovely person – but one who'd be wanting her home back asap.

Kitty knew she'd have to read Mavis's letter before there could be any further interruptions, whether from Mr H wanting to talk runner-bean trenches and mulching, or Jemini and Apollo yawning and grizzling about the earliness of the hour, or even an appearance by Noel and Netta, the elderly and rather eccentric twin brother and sister who were their nearest neighbours on the other side of Sandcastle Cottage, as they headed off with their Nordic walking poles and backpacks for their routine constitutional.

She took a deep breath, and her fingers closed round the flimsy, crinkly envelope.

Chapter Three

'Kiiiitttteeeee!' Teddy, Jemini's mini-me daughter – all caramel skin, huge dark eyes and tumbling black curls – toddled barefoot along the veranda, clutching her favourite cuddly toy, a much-loved, chewed and sucked rabbit with no ears, and beamed at Kitty. 'Peppa . . . *Please* Kittttteeeee . . .'

'Ah, you need me to turn the TV on?' said Kitty – realising fractionally too late that she'd left Teddy out of the interruption equation – pushing the letter back into her tabard pocket and laughing. 'OK, poppet. Is Mummy not awake yet?'

Teddy shrugged, then shrieked with laughter as Honey and Zorro clambered up the porch steps and began licking her bare feet.

'Tickle toes!' Teddy giggled delightedly, stretching her arms wide and hugging both dogs.

Kitty stood up and whisked Teddy out of the reach of the Staffies' tongues and headed towards the front door just as Jemini, wearing unicorn shorts-and-vest PJs and looking almost as adorable as her daughter, appeared.

'Cheers, Kit.' Jemini pushed her mass of just-got-out-of-bed hair from her eyes, blinked sleepily and reached for Teddy. 'We were in the kitchen. I was just getting her cereal ready and asked her if she wanted yoghurt as well, then I turned round and she'd disappeared. I guessed she'd be with you – and the dogs.'

'Mummmmyyy . . . Peppa . . . please.' Teddy struggled, wanting to be put down.

'She's all yours, Jem!' Kitty grinned. 'And Peppa's, obviously. Is – um – Connor here? Will he need coffee? Breakfast? Industrial supplies of hair gel?'

Jemini shook her head, giggling. 'He didn't stay over last night. There's a board meeting at the Lymington branch this morning and his dad's called a three-line whip. Connor left me the keys to open up the Firefly Common office at nine, therefore I need to get Teddy to nursery early – which is why I'm up in the middle of the night. Again.'

Kitty laughed. Jemini was now employed part-time with Connor in the Lovell and Lowe Estate Agents office in the village. They'd all found work since arriving in Firefly Common: Jemini with Connor, she in the delightfully retro Silver Fish Bar, and Apollo as chef at the Merry Mermaid. None of them worked full time, so their various shifts meant there was always someone at home to look after the dogs and Teddy. It had all worked out so well. Until now, of course. Kitty's fingers once again closed around the thin airmail letter in her pocket and she sighed.

Jemini held out her hand to Teddy. 'Come on, madam, let's have breakfast in front of the telly and see what Peppa's up to shall we?'

With a shriek of glee, Teddy ignored her hand and headed at some speed towards the front door, rapidly followed by her mother and both the dogs, who knew they'd get to lick the cereal bowls once they were empty.

As they vanished indoors, and the lane outside the cottage seemed completely free of friends, neighbours, milkmen, postmen or anyone else who might interrupt her, Kitty sank back into her chair and pulled out Mavis's letter.

'*Kalimera*, Kitty!' Apollo, handsome and dark-eyed, with the first grey streaks appearing in his black hair, wearing jeans and a T-shirt, and clearly straight from Greek-Cypriot central casting, shouted along the veranda from the doorway accompanied by a background blast of his favourite Iron Maiden track. 'It's another nice morning, but I'd still prefer to be asleep.'

'*Kalimera*, Apollo. Good morning – still a bit early for you, is it?' Kitty raised her voice above the blast of heavy metal, and pushed the letter back into her pocket. 'Are you on lunches at the Mermaid, today?'

'Yes. Not my favourite shift, Kitty, as you well know. I like to work late into the night and see the sunrise from the other side. Anyway, do you need anything from the village?' Apollo shouted even louder over the chorus of 'Run to the Hills'. 'I'm just going to take the dogs out for a walk in the recreation ground. Oh, and I've fed them.'

'So have I,' Kitty called back, laughing. 'And they've had biscuits. And whatever they can scrounge from Jemini . . . they'll need to run for miles to burn that lot off. And no thanks, I've got to be at work by eleven too, so I'll buy whatever's on the list on the way home.'

'OK!' Apollo grinned. 'Oh, don't buy any food for tonight, though. There is one good thing about being at work early today: they've asked me to make stifado and kleftiko in bulk, ready for their Cyprus Night, and they've said I can bring some home for supper. Chef's perks.'

'Oh, wow! Thank you – that sounds fabulous,' Kitty said as Apollo vanished back indoors and Iron Maiden faded behind the closed door. Because it was fabulous. And it all worked so well. Apollo always cooked, because he loved it and was a magician in the kitchen – one of those people, Kitty always thought, who could make a banquet out of manky fridge leftovers, stale bread and a tin of baked beans – and because his job at the Merry Mermaid meant he was allowed to take home whatever wasn't needed after each shift, there was always food in the house.

Leaving Apollo in charge of the kitchen, she and Jemini shared most of the housework between them – although Apollo was always willing to step in and help out if needed. They all added to a joint list of household necessities, and whoever was in the village did the shopping. Financially everything was split three ways. Jemini had said she should pay more because she had Teddy, but as

15

Kitty and Apollo had pointed out, they had Honey and Zorro – so it was honours even.

Yes, it had worked brilliantly. And soon it would be over. Kitty knew she'd have to read the letter, then tell Jemini and Apollo how soon they'd have to pack up and go. It may only be days. She'd ask Connor to keep an eye open for any other rental properties on the Lovell and Lowe books, of course – but she was pretty sure they'd never find anywhere in Firefly Common they could afford, that would be large enough, and be willing to take children and dogs, and that was anywhere near as perfect as Sandcastle Cottage.

Apollo, now with Zorro and Honey on their harnesses and leads, interrupted her thoughts as he headed down the porch steps. 'I'll be off. Have a good day. *Antío*, Kitty!'

'You, too. *Antío*!' Kitty replied. Like *kalimera*, it was one of only half a dozen Greek words she knew. 'See you later.'

As the dogs tugged Apollo out of the gate and into the depths of the common's greenery; and as Jemini, inside the cottage, got ready for work and sang along to Westlife; and as Teddy giggled happily with Peppa Pig; Kitty, alone at last, stood up, walked down the porch steps, then along the path, through the gate, and away from Sandcastle Cottage.

Then, taking a deep breath, she turned in the opposite direction to Apollo. She knew there was only once place to read this letter in complete solitude. Her bolthole ever since they'd moved to Firefly Common. Kitty, loving the heat from the sun, and the warm, honey-sweet scents from the ferns and heather, headed along the shingle track to the clifftop.

Chapter Four

Having dropped Teddy off at nursery and enjoyed a stroll through Firefly Common's sunlit lanes on the way to work, Jemini was now sifting through the mountain of morning post in the Lovell and Lowe office and wondered, as she always had since starting work at the estate agency, why so many people still used snail mail. Surely everyone in the world had mobiles and tablets and laptops? Surely everyone in the world could just text and Instagram and upload and download and send stuff via the Internet?

Even the sales brochures and house details could be dealt with this way, she reckoned, and not, as currently, via the Firefly Common printers. Although, as Connor had pointed out, the local printers employed local people, and after the recession and the ensuing lean austerity years, jobs for the locals were scarce enough in the village as it was.

OK, fair point, she'd thought, now arranging the general post in piles on her desk and the 'private and confidentials' and things that didn't look like sales material, on Connor's, but she couldn't remember the last time she'd written or received a proper letter. Even her parents now sent their weekly family-catch-up via email.

Of course, there had been the nasty threatening letters she'd received last year when she'd spent far too much on far too little, and her life had spiralled terrifyingly out of control. But thanks to Kitty, who had been through something similarly hellish herself, being sensible and sane and calming her down and giving her the advice and help she needed to sort out her finances, they were a thing of the past. Anyway, she thought, they weren't real letters – just threats and menaces from faceless institutions. And, mercifully, over.

And now, Jemini thought, pausing to look out at Firefly Common's sleepy, sun-drenched High Street, her life – and Teddy's – simply couldn't be better.

The Firefly Common Lovell and Lowe office was small, but with large dual-aspect windows which were really handy for people-watching. Jemini loved everything about her job: she loved looking at the properties for sale or rent; she loved chatting to the customers; she loved the fact that having done business studies at college she was now, at last, putting the skills she'd learned into practice; she loved wearing pretty dresses and heels to work instead of the overall and safety shoes she'd had to wear in the supermarket in her old life; but most of all she loved Connor Lowe.

This had come as something of a shock. She certainly hadn't intended to fall in love with the 'cute boy' who had arranged the Sandcastle Cottage rental six months ago. Falling in love was a whole new emotion for her – and one she'd been pretty sure she'd never experience. She loved Teddy, of course, adored her as only a mother can adore their child. But, she knew now, she'd never been truly in love with a man. Not with any of her previous casual boyfriends and certainly not with her ex-husband. Far from it! It had never been what anyone would have considered a proper marriage, anyway. Although, that was all over and done with now. Thankfully. She'd known her husband well and oh, she'd liked him well enough, they'd been good friends, and she might even have imagined she loved him in a way. But she'd never known this glorious heady rush of giddiness . . . the smiling . . . the laughing . . . the shared glances and jokes . . . the touching . . . the understanding . . . the blissful happiness of just being together – all the things that she shared with Connor.

Since her divorce she hadn't dated anyone. And seeing as the divorce, as amicable as it had been, had sent shock waves through the family, Jemini had sworn off men for life.

Until now.

She smiled to herself as she reached the last few letters. After all the horrors, life was perfect now. She had Teddy, and Connor, and good friends, and a wonderful place to live. What could possibly go wrong?

'Oops, nearly missed this one . . .' Jemini said to herself as she frowned at the flimsy airmail letter that was caught up on the back of a large manila envelope. 'Oooh, nice bold writing. And lots of stamps. Don't recognise any of them. I wonder who it's from? No sender's address on it. Someone moving here from abroad, obviously. Oh, well, they could certainly find a worse spot to live than Firefly Common.'

It was addressed to Mr L Lowe. *Lester.* Connor's father. Co-owner of Lovell and Lowe. Her boss. As Connor ran the Firefly Common branch, Lester didn't have a desk here. His office was at the Bournemouth headquarters. Jemini looked at the letter again and decided, as it didn't say 'personal', 'urgent', or 'private and confidential', to leave it with Connor's mail. He could open it, or pass it on to his dad. Funny, though, it just proved what she was thinking earlier – if someone from abroad wanted to know about properties in Firefly Common, surely they'd use the Internet? This was the 21st century after all. Who'd risk sending a flimsy thing like this through the post? Jemini shook her head – people were so poorly informed about the modern world sometimes.

Still, as it was just a letter, it couldn't be very important, could it?

Chapter Five

Across the other side of Firefly Common's High Street, and a stone's throw from the narrow sandy tracks that led towards the cliffs and the sea, Apollo sat on a bench in the vast, pine-tree-enclosed recreation ground. Having walked twice round the perimeter, he now retrieved the dogs' bowls and a bottle of water from his backpack, filled the bowls, and watched fondly as Honey and Zorro tore around madly, chasing one another, and laughing as only Staffies let off the lead can.

In the very furthest corner of the park, mothers, and some fathers too, with babies in prams and toddlers in buggies, were gathered round the swings and slides. Children's laughter and high-pitched, happy voices echoed across the park. Apollo was always careful to keep the dogs well away from the playground. Honey and Zorro were soft as butter, and very well trained, but as Staffies they came with such a bad press. And even though the play area was fenced off, it still wasn't worth the risk of upsetting anyone.

He lifted his face to the sun. This place was gorgeous. *Gorgeous.* He liked that word. It sounded fat and fabulous. It was just right for today. And for his new life. Everything was gorgeous here: the cottage, the village, the sea, his friends, and the cheffing at the Merry Mermaid – everything. Apollo sighed. The dogs were snuffling happily in the long grass now, investigating dead leaves and bits of litter, pouncing and bouncing on each new find. They were so happy, too. And soon, maybe, for all of them, it would be over.

Only too aware that the six-month rental on Sandcastle Cottage was nearly up, he'd seen the envelope in Kitty's hand earlier. Was this a letter telling them they had to leave? Kitty had pushed it quickly back into her pocket, clearly not wanting to share the contents of the letter with him – or anyone. Not yet. He knew she would, when the time was right. It would be a sad time.

But then maybe, Apollo thought, he was wrong and the letter wasn't anything to do with Sandcastle Cottage.

Maybe it was from that rat of an ex-boyfriend of Kitty's . . . the one who had almost ruined her life . . . Apollo frowned. Maybe – what was his name? – John? Josh? No . . . ah, yes, *James* . . . Maybe James was trying to get back into Kitty's good books again. Apollo sincerely hoped not. And if the vile James showed up in Firefly Common then he'd have the wrath of Apollo to deal with.

'*Yia sou*, Apollo.'

Apollo jerked his head up and squinted against the sun at the slender woman all dressed in pink. 'Er – *yia sou* – hello, Angelica. You look very sporty. Are you – what is the politically correct term these days? *Keeping fit*?'

'That'll do.' She giggled. 'I'm jogging round the rec. Part of my new regime.' She looked at the slim gadget on her wrist, then plonked herself down beside him. The dogs rushed over to inspect her and welcome her to the bench. She fussed them, then looked at Apollo. 'Are you OK? You looked angry, just now. Very fierce.'

Apollo shrugged. 'Not angry. Not fierce. Just thinking about Kitty. And James . . . the man who treated her so badly before we came here. He almost destroyed her, and I think he might be trying to contact her again.'

Angelica pushed her sunglasses on top of her head and pulled a face. 'Really? What makes you think that? Sorry – not being nosy . . . well, yes I am, but Destiny – my wellness coach – says it's so much better for your mental health to be honest and open and ask questions and get answers and not bottle things up.'

'Your – er – wellness coach may be right.' Apollo grinned. 'But only if you ask the right questions of the right people.'

'And am I?'

Apollo watched the dogs chasing after dancing tree-shadows. 'Maybe. OK, yes. Kitty had a letter this morning. She didn't want me to see it. I'm not sure what it was about – but she knows how angry I am still with her ex-boyfriend, so I think it might be from him.'

'But you don't know that the letter was from her ex, do you? I mean, why would he send her a letter. No one sends letters any more. He'd text her, surely?'

'Maybe . . . maybe he'd already tried that and she didn't answer him. Or just deleted the text when she saw it was from him. Maybe he thought sending her a letter would mean she'd have to open it and read it and—'

Angelica laughed. 'Oh, my word! You fancy her, don't you? Go on, admit it! And who wouldn't? Looking like Julia Roberts and with that cascade of red-gold hair, Kitty is stunning even if she doesn't realise it. So, does she know how you feel?'

Apollo stared at Angelica. '*What?* No! You have it all wrong! Kitty is like my little sister. She is my friend! No way do I – fancy – her! She is lovely and funny and kind and beautiful, yes. But it is not Kitty I am in love with.'

Angelica raised her eyebrows. 'Oooh . . . so there is *someone*, is there? Do I ask who? Or shall I just ask about the letter?'

'Maybe you should do neither,' Apollo said gently, as the dogs swayed up to him, tongues lolling. He bent down and topped up their bowls with water. They slopped and slurped with gusto. 'Maybe your Destiny wellness coach should tell you sometimes not to ask too many questions.'

'Oh.' Angelica looked hurt. But not for long. 'OK. Let's assume the letter isn't from Kitty's ex. It could be a bill, or from her parents, or an appointment of some sort, and she didn't want you to see it for some other reason . . . which is all a bit boring, to be frank.'

'Maybe. But you weren't there when Kitty was so hurt back in the day. James was a very unpleasant man who caused her a lot of trouble. And because she's my friend I will not let him do that to her again. See?'

'Yes. Of course. OK, point taken. So, who *are* you in love with?'

Apollo roared with laughter. Zorro and Honey, startled, lifted their heads from their bowls and instantly dripped water and drool all over Angelica's pristine pink trainers.

'*Eugh!*'

Apollo chuckled. The dogs, heads down again, continued drinking.

Angelica shook each of her feet delicately. 'But you are in love with someone, aren't you? And if it's not Kitty, and obviously not Jemini because she has Connor, then – oh, is it someone you work with at the Merry Mermaid?'

'Angelica,' – Apollo tried hard not to laugh – 'whatever your Destiny person suggests, believe me, sometimes you simply must not ask too many questions. OK?'

'Maybe.' Angelica grinned impishly, watching Honey and Zorro who had finished drinking and were wiping their muzzles dry along the grass. She smiled at them. 'They are so lovely. I love animals. We've never had pets as Mr H is allergic to them. Such a shame.'

Apollo picked up the water bowls. 'It is. I've always had animals in my life and I've loved them all. I've always found animals to be better friends than most humans.' He sighed. 'Now then, Angelica, shall I ask *you* a question? Something I've wanted to ask for a very long time. Why do you call your husband Mr H? Surely he has a forename?'

Angelica chuckled. '*Touché*! You want the truth? OK. My poor husband's first name is Orlando. His mother had a thing for ginger cats. I hate the name and so does he. He always has. Also, and this is something I rarely mention, our surname is Huggingbottom which is of course – and this is so not a pun – the *butt* of jokes. So, he's called himself Mr H ever since he entered puberty. He thought it made him sound mysterious – like someone out of James Bond. Everyone we know calls him Mr H.'

23

'Right . . . I think I understand . . . Although, of course, now Orlando Bloom is considered very attractive by the ladies, isn't he? And Lando Norris the racing driver . . . But ginger cats?'

'Orlando Bloom is a drop-dead gorgeous Hollywood A-lister. Lando Norris is using the diminutive of the name and is a sporting superstar. No one cares what they're called. Being called Orlando in suburbia when everyone else was called Dave or Kevin was very difficult for Mr H . . . oh, and the cats – well, Orlando was the name of a ginger cat in a series of children's stories. My late not-so-lamented ma-in-law was addicted to the Marmalade Cat books and thought it was the perfect name for her only son.'

Apollo nodded. 'Ah, yes, I think I see now. I can understand. But I don't think we had the Marmalade Cat stories in our school library in Cyprus. I'm guessing you and Mr H never read the tales of Orlando the ginger cat as bedtime stories to your children, then?'

Angelica stared across the sunny recreation ground towards the swings and slides. 'We've never had children. Sadly, they never happened. And we left it far too late to do anything about it. So, yes, before you ask, that probably is why I drank too much and why Mr H spends his time gardening or vanishes to the golf course at every opportunity.'

Apollo shook his head. 'Angelica, I'm so sorry. I'd not have mentioned it if I'd known . . . I assumed your children were now grown-up and . . . again, I'm so sorry. Those things are private and I shouldn't have asked.'

'But you should! This is what Destiny was telling us. Ask questions, get answers. Free the inner demons, so to speak. I'm absolutely fine about not having kids now – Mr H and I chug along nicely together and have had a happy life. So, no damage done by asking the question – questions are just seeking the truth. Which is why you should just ask Kitty about her letter. And now,' – Angelica stood up and stroked Honey and Zorro – 'I'm going to continue with my run. *Antío*, Apollo.'

'*Antío*. Enjoy your exercise.'

'Oh!' Angelica stopped and pulled her sunglasses from the top of her head. 'I'm so dumb! I know who it is you're in love with! You're gay and it's Connor! I'm right, aren't I?'

'Angelica!' Apollo chuckled. 'Just go. And no – you're very, very wrong.'

'Seriously? *Bother* . . . Never mind. I'll get there!' Angelica readjusted her sunglasses, and with a jaunty wave, jogged away. Then stopped again and looked over her shoulder. 'One last shot – it's not me, is it? I mean, I'm very flattered and all that, and you're in great shape and very attractive, but Mr H may not approve even if I—'

'Angelica!' Apollo laughed. 'It's not you.'

'Oh . . . OK . . . *antío*!'

Apollo, still laughing, watched her go, then stood up, whistled to the dogs, fastened their leads and slowly walked in the opposite direction, deep in thought and memories.

Chapter Six

Kitty sat at the top of the steps that lead down to the beach, on the clifftop's coarse grass, and kicked off her flip-flops. The sun cast dancing diamonds across the sea, touching the wavelets with glints of gold. Below, the beach, with its soft sand and drifts of pebbles, was busy with dog walkers and pre-school children running in and out of the shallows, watched by careful parents. Seagulls swooped and screamed above the row of ice-cream coloured 1950s beach huts. The air was warm, and salty and sweet with the heady fragrance of wild campion and thrift. It was, Kitty thought as she drew her knees up, the most perfect place on earth.

She pushed her sunglasses up into her hair and squinted along the shoreline. Just in case. Not that she expected him to be there. She hadn't seen him for several months. Vinny the Vagrant. She hated the nickname but it was what everyone in Firefly Common seemed to call him. She'd first noticed him when they'd moved into Sandcastle Cottage during those dark, freezing December days, and he'd been walking along the shore: tall, lean, youngish it seemed from the way he walked, his dark hair ruffled by the biting wind, his long black coat giving him an air of mystery. Apparently, no one really seemed to know much about him: what he did, or where he lived, or why he walked alone on the beach in all weathers.

Kitty had first smiled at him in January when she'd been exercising the dogs on the beach, and he'd smiled back. He had a nice smile. And a rather gorgeous high-cheekboned face. By March, they'd got as far as 'hi' and 'good morning' and he'd always make a fuss of the dogs . . . and then he'd vanished.

Kitty smiled to herself. She missed him. Silly, of course, but she'd woven so many stories around him. And she'd almost thought of him as some sort of talisman. If he was here today then the letter wouldn't be bad news. If he wasn't . . . she shrugged. Stupid, really. There was no sign of him . . . so, hey-ho. She replaced her sunglasses and pulled the letter from her pocket.

'Hail, Kitty! Well met!'

Oh, god . . . Kitty sighed heavily. Her other neighbours, the elderly and eccentric Netta and Noel, were stomping up the sand-covered railway sleepers that formed the beach steps and heading straight for her. She closed her eyes . . . Was she ever going to get to read this letter in peace?

'Hello, you two . . .' She hoped she sounded delighted to see them, but somehow doubted it.

Dressed, as always, the same in their khaki shorts, Aertex shirts and stout walking boots, they leaned on their Nordic walking poles and beamed at her.

'Ah, this is handy! You've saved us writing an invite,' Netta bellowed. 'We're having a barbecue. Next Saturday evening. Not this week – next. It's our birthday. We'd like you all to come. Everyone. Little Teddy and young Connor Lowe as well, of course, because he's courting Jemini. We've invited his parents, too – Noel knows them from the Rotary. The more the merrier, I always say.' Netta grinned suddenly, showing a lot of large and very prominent teeth. 'What about you, Kitty? And Apollo? Do either of you have any – um – special friends whom you'd like to invite?'

Special friends? Kitty frowned. 'Oh – you mean do I have a boyfriend . . . partner? No, no I don't. And I'm pretty sure Apollo is happily single, too. But thank you for asking.'

'No worries, Kitty, dear. It's so difficult these days to know if one is saying the right thing or not. We just didn't want anyone to feel left out. Everyone is welcome. We're inviting all the neighbours. We've never had a barbecue before but this weather is so glorious and set to hold in the foreseeable, according to the weatherman, so we thought we ought to move with the times. And Noel, as our chef de partie,' – she blinked pale and almost-lashless eyes towards her brother – 'has been looking up all sorts of al fresco recipes.'

Kitty attempted to sound ecstatic. 'Oh, how fabulous! We'll all look forward to it, I'm sure. And I know it's Apollo's weekend off from the Mermaid, and I'll be finished at the Silver Fish Bar by five.' She beamed at Noel. 'I bet the Internet has some really scrummy food suggestions, hasn't it?'

'We haven't consulted the Internet!' Noel sounded scandalised. 'We don't believe in the Internet! I've referred to the no-nonsense cookery book that our dear mother always used.'

Oh, goody, Kitty thought bleakly. That had to be at least pre-war. Did they even have barbecue food pre-war? Was it even a thing?

'It sounds wonderful,' she lied quickly. 'So, yes, is there anything you'd like us to bring?'

'Just yourselves and your appetites.' Netta smiled, showing even more teeth. 'We'll be firing up the appliances ready for grub-up at seven.'

Appliances? Seriously? Kitty sucked in her breath. 'It really sounds as if it's going to be tremendous fun . . .' She stopped. Did she just say *tremendous*? She was sounding like one of the Famous Five. Very soon she'd be saying 'top-hole' or something. 'Well if you do think of anything we can add, please give us a shout.'

Netta bared her teeth again. 'Exceedingly generous of you, Kitty, but we're well equipped with everything. Noel is seeing to the eats, as I've said, and I'm in charge of the décor, and the vino – homemade, of course, and cleverly all non-alcoholic because Noel and I don't indulge, you know – and soft drinks for the kiddies. We're very excited.'

Not even any booze, Kitty thought bleakly. She decided not to share that piece of information with the others.

Then she looked at Netta and Noel and suddenly felt guilty about thinking mean thoughts. They were kind, good-hearted people who were doing a nice thing. It was their shared birthday for heaven's sake. It would be a lovely evening. She was turning into a grouch. She smiled at them. 'It all sounds fabulous and I'm sure we'll enjoy every minute. Thank you so much for inviting us. Oh, what about Honey and Zorro? Can we bring them?'

'Of course!' Noel roared. Both he and Netta had extremely loud, carrying voices. Kitty reckoned it came from them having been schoolteachers. 'Well-behaved dogs are always welcome chez nous, and we love your doggies!'

Kitty felt that Zorro and Honey may well object to being called 'doggies', but the provision of limitless barbecued food would possibly mollify them.

'That's great. Lovely. Thank you again.'

Netta wiggled her walking poles. 'And you'll pass the invite on to the others?'

'Yes, of course. Oh, do we need to RSVP?'

'Only if you're not attending,' Netta brayed. 'And then you can just shout over the fence! But of course you'll all be there, won't you? Well, toodle-pip! Off we jolly well go, Noel.'

Kitty watched them go as they stomped their way across the clifftop: an odd-ball couple who truly belonged to another era. Eccentric and gentle. And lovely neighbours. But not for very much longer . . .

Before anyone or anything else could stop her, she pulled the flimsy airmail letter from her pocket and opened it. The writing was black, small, and cursive, and there was a lot of it . . .

My dear Ms Appleby,

I think that sounds very formal, maybe I should just say Dear Kitty? Either way, I've decided to write to you personally – as well as sending a more business-like version of this letter to Lester Lowe – because yours is the name on Sandcastle Cottage's tenancy agreement, and I've thought about you a lot and feel I know you. I'm very grateful to you for renting the cottage, for living in my home and looking after it so well in my absence. My spies have told me that you and your little 'family' have been perfect tenants. Oh, just in case you think I don't trust you, I don't really have spies, that was a joke – I merely have Lester Lowe – it's in his interest, of course, that any rental properties on his books are well looked after. So, thank you for making Sandcastle Cottage come to life again. As you know, the rental agreement was for six months. My world cruise (and totally out of this world it has been, I can tell you!) terminates at the end of June. Currently, I am on a glorious Caribbean island, and it was all arranged for the water taxi to take me back to the mainland this week, and then I'd be chauffeured to the airport, and escorted to my no doubt luxurious flight home—

Between her fingers, the thin airmail paper fluttered in the warm sea breeze. Kitty stared down at the beach for a moment, watching the waves swooshing gently onto the sand and then rattling softly back out again; watching the children building sandcastles and squealing with delight as the water filled their moats; watching the people walking with dogs, or without. None of them were the one person she wanted to see. She took a deep breath and read on . . .

However, I have fallen so much in love with this particular place and the people, and have met up with some very friendly ex-pats here, too, so, to cut a long story short, I'm staying on here for a little bit longer. I have cancelled my return tickets and my lovely travel agency have arranged for me to sail home – rather than fly! – on another cruise ship (oh, the joys of having limitless funds – for the first time in my life!) in August. This is a very long-winded way of saying I won't be home in Firefly Common until sometime in September – so I do hope you and your friends will be happy to continue renting (same terms, of course!) Sandcastle Cottage for the rest of the summer. I do so hope you haven't already made plans to move out – if so, Lester Lowe will no doubt inform me asap – and please, if you have, then cancel them immediately and stay! I very much hope this new arrangement will suit you, and I do hope you will still be there when I eventually come home. I am longing to meet you all.

With all best wishes,
Mavis Mulholland

Kitty stared at the letter. Then read it again, slowly, just in case she'd made a mistake. No – no mistake. They had a stay of execution. They had just over three months to enjoy the summer, to still be in Sandcastle Cottage and Firefly Common, and could take their time over finding somewhere else to live ... Three months ... Three whole months. Not simply a matter of days, as she'd dreaded. Who knew what might turn up in that time? OK, it wasn't for ever – unless Mavis decided to stay in her Caribbean paradise, of course – and that wasn't seriously going to happen, but this was a pretty damn good outcome in the meantime. Anyway, anything was possible in three months, wasn't it?

Kitty laughed to herself. She'd always been a bit of a Pollyanna – even during that awful time with James and losing the house and everything – she'd always thought that something would turn up. And, of course, it had. And now, who was to say it wouldn't again? Oh, God love Mavis Mulholland and whichever Caribbean island had captured her heart. Not to mention her limitless funds, of course. Lucky, lucky Mavis, Kitty thought.

Having glanced at her phone and checked that there was still ages to go until she was due at work, Kitty pushed the letter back into her tabard pocket and scrambled to her feet. Then she picked up her flip-flops and, barefooted, practically skipped down the skew-whiff sand-covered sleepers towards the beach.

Goodness, it was hot. Kitty squinted against the sun as the shallow waves broke and foamed round her toes, and the ebbing tide sucking her feet squelchily into the sand. The breeze tangled her hair and she pushed it away from her face as she waded along the shoreline, unable to stop smiling. The Merry Mermaid, always looking as if it was balancing precariously on the cliff edge, was at the far end of the bay. It was Kitty's usual morning route with the dogs, as far as the Mermaid, then back again. Steps led drunkenly upwards from the beach, through the cliff's gorse and broom, towards the rickety gate that was the back entrance to the pub's beer garden. Away from the ice-cream stalls and the beach shack selling sun hats and buckets and spades and suncream and

31

vividly coloured inflatables, this part of the beach was always quieter.

At the foot of the pub steps, in the shade, there were several older people reading newspapers or dozing in deckchairs, and a very young couple on the sand, entwined and oblivious. Kitty smiled some more. Happy, contented people and young love. It gladdened her soul. Then she laughed out loud simply because she could. The breeze took the sound away and her laughter mingled with the calling of the gulls and the shushing of the waves. She was still laughing when her phone rang.

'Kit!' Jemini's voice was excited. 'Kit – you'll never guess what's happened . . . There's this letter. Airmail. And it was addressed to Connor's dad, but Connor opened it and—'

'It's from Mavis Mulholland, to say she isn't coming back yet and—'

'We can stay in the cottage—'

'For at least another three months—'

'Until September . . . *What?*' Jemini's voice rose. 'You *know*? How did you know?'

'I had a letter from Mavis, too. It arrived this morning.'

'Shit, Kitty! You knew? And you didn't tell me?'

'I didn't read it. I've had it for hours and only just opened it.' Kitty laughed. 'I was scared it was going to say we had days to pack up and get out. I knew we should have been thinking about it sooner, but I – we – had been through so much and were all so happy at Sandcastle, I think I just pretended it wasn't going to happen.'

'Me too,' Jemini admitted. 'But it's such great news, isn't it? Connor and I have danced round the office! And now he says we can all be properly sensible and look for somewhere else to live later in the year.'

'He's right. This time we really do have to be grown-up and realise that we're not going to be living in Sandcastle forever . . . Tell Connor to keep an eye out for anything at all that's suitable – however, in the meantime—'

32

'Let's make the most of every minute. Oh, and we should have a party to celebrate!'

'Funny you should say that – actually, we've been invited to a birthday party barbecue next Saturday night. We can celebrate then.'

'Oooh – fab. Whose?'

'Netta and Noel's.'

Jemini shrieked with laughter. 'That'll be like an oldies tea party, Kit! I mean, Netta and Noel are lovely and everything, but they're – well – ancient.'

'I know, and I thought the same, and then I was pretty ashamed of myself. After all, they may be totally off the wall but they're also very kind and gentle people, and they're making such an effort, and it sounds like it will be fun – and if it isn't, then we can make our excuses and leave.'

'You've already told them we're going, haven't you?'

'Um . . . well, yes, I have. But they've invited Connor – and Teddy of course – and the dogs as well.'

'OK.' Jemini giggled. 'Whatevs, Kitty, whatevs. Oh, and are you telling Apollo or shall I?'

'About staying at Sandcastle till September, or Netta and Noel's barbecue?'

'Both.'

'Actually, Jem, can you ring him, please? I'm on the beach and my phone is going to need charging pretty soon, plus the reception isn't great – you're fading in and out. He took the dogs out earlier, but he'll probably be at home now getting ready for work – he's on lunches today. You ring him, or text him, OK?'

'OK – and this barbecue better be like the headline at Glasto or I'll melt down your Beatles vinyl and be streaming Boyzone and Westlife on a loop into your headphones and phone and tablet and every other gizmo you hold dear, for ever and ever.'

'Sod that!' Kitty chuckled. 'Thanks, Jem – see you later. Bye.'

Heading back along the beach, away from the Mermaid's steps, Kitty quickly pushed her phone into her tabard pocket, and in doing so managed to dislodge Mavis's letter.

She tried to catch it before it hit the sand, but it flew from her grasp. She dived for it, but light as a feather and caught by the sea breeze, it floated tantalisingly away from her, dancing and swirling. Kitty stumbled after it, crossly realising that running through soft sand was like wading through treacle. It didn't matter really, she thought, watching the flimsy blue paper rolling along the shoreline now. It didn't have a return address on it, and Lovell and Lowe had the official version – but no, it *did* matter. It suddenly seemed vital that she was able to hang on to it, so she could read it again and again and convince herself that she hadn't dreamed it all.

As the letter tumbled over and over on its inexorable journey towards the water's edge, Kitty groaned: that glorious closely packed, black-inked, swirly writing would never survive.

She made a final stumbling dive for the letter – just as someone behind her beat her to it.

'Oh – wow! Well fielded! Thank you. Thank you so much.' Kitty turned and pushed her hair from her eyes. 'I thought it was going to be – Oh!'

'Hello.' He smiled at her. 'We meet again.'

Chapter Seven

'God – I'm sorry. That's such a corny line.' Still smiling, he handed her the letter. 'I guessed this was yours . . . I mean, I saw you chasing after it. I don't think it got wet. It might be a bit sandy, though, but I think I caught it in time.'

'You're a star. I'm just grateful to have got it back. And the ink hasn't run . . . thank you so much.'

This time Kitty pushed the letter firmly into the pocket of her jeans, happily convinced now that he was indeed the talisman that she'd always imagined him to be. He was there – and Mavis's letter had told her she'd have the rest of the summer in Sandcastle Cottage. The two things surely had to be linked by some sort of divine-interventional card shuffling or something, didn't they? Maybe Angelica's new guru would be able to confirm that this sort of thing happened . . .

She stopped and realised that he was watching her. 'Sorry . . . I was just thinking . . . um – anyway – thank you, again.'

'You're welcome. I assumed it was an important letter.'

'Yes . . . yes, it is. Very. Thanks for – well . . . er . . . I mean . . .'

They stared at one another for moment, then he laughed.

He had a nice laugh. And fabulous blue eyes. And his longish dark hair was layered and silky. He was wearing faded jeans, a grey T-shirt with some ancient band logo, and sand-scuffed trainers.

Pretty sure she was blushing from her toes upwards and convinced that he must now think of her as some sort of bumbling, mumbling, tongue-tied idiot, Kitty tried to appear nonchalant. 'Er – right. Thank you again. Um – I ought to be going.'

He nodded. 'Of course. Me too. Actually, I expected to see you with the dogs in tow. They're wonderful. Are they both OK?'

'Oh, yes. They're fine. Still living in luxury – as befits two rescue Staffies, of course – but Apollo's walking them today.'

'Apollo?' He nodded. 'That's a cool name.'

'It is. He's Greek Cypriot . . . he has brothers called Raphael and Vangelis.'

'Seriously? I think he might have got the best deal with Apollo.'

'Yep, maybe.' Kitty laughed.

'He must be the guy I see down here with the dogs sometimes, then? They always come and see me. He – obviously I didn't know his name was Apollo – says they always know a dog lover.'

'They do. Definitely. And yes, Apollo usually takes them to the recreation ground for a run – but I know he comes down here to the beach sometimes. Anyway, we take it in turns to walk the dogs depending on our shifts, because we live together, and he owns Honey, the black one. Zorro, the brindle, is mine . . . um . . .'

Kitty stopped talking and briefly closed her eyes. She was babbling. He didn't want to know about her domestic arrangements or the ins and outs of Apollo's family names, for heaven's sake! What was wrong with her? She opened her eyes again. He was frowning slightly. He seemed to have withdrawn from her somehow.

She pushed her hair away from her face again. The breeze blew it back. She sighed. 'Anyway, I really must be going – I'll be late for work if I don't.'

'At the Silver Fish Bar?'

Kitty gaped at him. He knew that? Seriously? Had he been stalking her? 'Yes, but . . . I mean . . . How did you know where I worked? Are you psychic?'

'Ah, yes. Vincent Cassidy, International Mind-Reader and Clairvoyant – that's me.'

So, he really was called Vincent. Vincent Cassidy . . . Nice . . .

He indicated her tabard. 'Actually, it's on the logo on your pocket.'

Kitty blushed even more. 'Oh, god – of course – I'm such an idiot . . . you must think—'

'I think you'll probably be late for work.'

'Oh, yes . . . I will . . . um . . . thank you again. And – er – I'll maybe see you around.'

He smiled briefly. 'Maybe.'

'Goodbye, then.' She smiled at him again, then before she could make any more of a fool of herself than she already had, she turned quickly and walked away.

Kitty hid her delighted grin until she was halfway along the beach, then turned to wave at him – just in case he was watching her go. But Vinny was far along the shoreline, past the Mermaid's steps now, head down, shoulders hunched.

Enigmatic! That was the word, she thought. Vinny Cassidy: enigma. She smiled to herself again. He was back – but from where? And where did he live? And what did he do? Where did he work? And if he had a job, why was he always walking on the beach? And if he didn't, then maybe he was a rough sleeper . . . And was he married or involved with anyone? And, if he was, why did he walk along the shoreline alone? And if he wasn't, why did he walk along the shoreline anyway? And did he know the locals called him Vinny the Vagrant? And why the hell hadn't she asked him some of those things while she had the chance – or turned the conversation in the right direction, at least?

And now she was probably going to be late for work – but she'd seen him! And spoken to him! They'd had a proper conversation! Well, almost proper. And tomorrow morning – and every morning to come – she'd be on the beach with the dogs, just in case. And now, because he knew where she worked, maybe – just maybe – he'd call in for lunch or something.

Still smiling, Kitty happily climbed the wide wooden steps away from the beach two at a time.

Chapter Eight

Halfway into the hectic lunchtime service at the Silver Fish Bar, with the hum of a dozen conversations competing with the whirring of the ceiling fans, Kitty was deftly carrying a tray loaded with two servings of cod, chips and mushy peas, with extra bread and butter, across the restaurant. She managed to slalom neatly between the full house of occupied tables without disturbing a single diner or an inch of the red-and-white gingham tablecloths.

When she'd first started working as a waitress, she'd been amazed at how busy the Silver Fish Bar's small restaurant was. Even in winter, when the opening hours were shorter, the dozen tables were always occupied, and sit-downs were twice as popular as takeouts, with locals and visitors alike. Mind you, Kitty had thought, it really was like stepping back in time: fish (cod, haddock, plaice – or the new and rather daring addition of skate wing) and chips, bread (brown or white) and butter, plus a pot of tea (coffee by request, cold drinks for the children, iced tap water in a jug – free) on the menu, nothing else. It was snug and cosy in the cold weather, and cooled by the overhead fans on hot days like today, and always friendly and welcoming. As if the 21st century had passed it by. Like most of Firefly Common, really.

'There we go,' she said and carefully placed the heaped plates on the table. 'And a pot of tea for two coming right up.'

'You're so good at this, young Kitty.' Jessie Riley from the retirement bungalows just past the recreation ground, beamed at her. 'It's like you've been working here for ever. You're the best waitress they've ever had here. Me and Norm have always loved coming here for our lunch once a week, ever since we moved down from Brum, haven't we, Norm? And we've said Kitty is the best, haven't we, Norm?'

Norm, a man of very few words, nodded.

'But sometimes the service has been slow and sometimes they've had some right surly lasses waiting on,' Jessie continued. 'But not like you, love. You're always polite. You're always smiling. And that's a lovely big smile you've got on today, isn't it, Norm?'

Norm, already digging enthusiastically into his cod and chips, paused momentarily and nodded again.

'Thank you.' Kitty, who was pretty damn sure she'd be wearing her Cheshire Cat grin for the rest of the day, smiled even more widely at them. 'I love working here – and I'm very happy.'

'It shows, duck.' Jessie shovelled up her mushy peas with some alacrity. 'It shows.'

Kitty, whisking back behind the takeout counter and into the kitchen, then making the return journey armed with a tea tray – a fat Brown Betty teapot, two white earthenware cups and saucers, teaspoons, hot water, tea strainer (no teabags in the Silver Fish Bar), milk jug and sugar basin – actually wondered if she'd ever stop smiling.

She'd be spending the summer in Sandcastle Cottage – *and* Vinny was back! And well, surely, they'd moved their casual acquaintance on to a friendship footing, hadn't they? Well, at least they'd chatted now – and they could chat some more . . . just as friends, of course. Not that she was thinking of him romantically – of course not. After what had happened with James, that would be insane . . . and she didn't even know Vinny. But . . . oh, but . . .

She put the tray carefully on the table and dispensed the tea-for-two. Jessie and Norm, mouths full, nodded their thanks. Still beaming, Kitty whirled round a couple of nearby recently vacated tables, collecting up empty crockery and cutlery and then heading back to the kitchen.

'No idea what you're on.' Mrs Gibby, the Silver Fish Bar's

owner grinned. 'But I wouldn't mind having some of it. You haven't stopped smiling since you started this shift – and you're working like a little dervish. It must be love, eh, Kitty?'

'I couldn't possibly say.' Kitty laughed, sliding the dirty dishes into the appropriate slots of the massive dishwasher. She straightened up and stretched. 'We're really busy today.'

Mrs Gibby nodded. 'I should have asked Rhonda to come in for a couple of hours to help you out.'

Rhonda, who was one of Mrs Gibby's many distant relatives and a mum of four, worked part-time in one of Mrs Gibby's other shops, shared the Firefly Common shifts with Kitty and helped out wherever and whenever she was needed.

Kitty shook her head. 'It's fine. I'm coping well. Don't bother Rhonda on her day off. Oooh – customers in the shop – shall I . . . ?'

'No, you've got more than enough to do front of house, love. I'll go. And Rhonda's not on a day off, she's – oh, hang on.'

Mrs Gibby moved her considerable bulk towards the rank of fryers, and deftly flicked baskets of chips, which were hissing and spitting in the boiling lard (no oil for the traditional frying in the Silver Fish Bar), and almost simultaneously used the tongs to place golden battered cod and haddock into the glass-fronted warming cabinet.

'Fish and chips three times, love? Salt and vinegar on all three? There you go – ta, lovely . . .'

Kitty watched her boss as she moved smoothly between the fryers and the counter, dishing up the fish and chips, then wrapping them deftly, and smiling and chatting to the customers as she did so, as if she was choreographed. Mrs Gibby, who owned a chain of Silver Fish Bars, managed by members of her vast extended family, all along the south coast, was probably in her late seventies. She was short, round, had frizzy hennaed hair, was always cheerful – and she'd been in the fish-and-chip business all her life.

Early on in Kitty's employment, at the time when she and

Jemini had been trying to work out Mavis Mulholland's age and what she looked like and if there was any chance at all, while cruising the world, she might get snaffled up by some lonely, handsome widower who would whisk her away to his Scottish castle or something, she'd thought Mavis and Mrs Gibby might well be contemporaries. So Kitty had casually asked Mrs Gibby if she knew Mavis. But it had been another dead end. Mrs Gibby didn't live in Firefly Common and said she couldn't recall any local customers called Mavis. So Mavis had remained an enigma. A bit like Vinny . . .

At the thought of Vinny, Kitty smiled even more.

'There, that's a few more tums filled and a few more coppers in the bank.' Mrs Gibby grinned. 'Where was I?'

'Saying why Rhonda wasn't on her day off.'

'Ah, yes. No, Rhonda's working in our Christchurch shop today. It's closer to where she lives and I know how well you cope single-handedly here. I didn't think we'd need her. Sorry if I'm knackering you, love. Maybe we need more staff all round. But people don't seem to want to work in a chippy these days. If they want to work at all, they either want to play football, be on *X Factor* or what have you, work on YouTube, or be a Kardashian.'

Kitty laughed. 'That's so true. But honestly, after working in Apollo's kebab shop, this is paradise. Oh, Apollo was a lovely boss, and he's one of my dearest friends, and he saved my life – literally – by giving me a job and a home, but the area wasn't like this . . . and the customers weren't like yours . . . I just love it here. I love that it's old-fashioned. I love the customers – and you're a dream to work for.'

Mrs Gibby snorted with laughter. 'Get away with you! I'm a dragon and a slave driver!' She stopped laughing and sighed. 'Mind you, I'm getting to the point where I think I should be taking it easy. Maybe take a bit of retirement before I pop me clogs . . . Oh, customers looking for a seat in the restaurant, Kitty, and a little group in the takeaway . . . Off we go. No rest for the wicked.'

Mrs Gibby swayed away into the shop, and Kitty fixed her

best-ever waitress smile as she approached the eat-inners. 'A table for four? Yes, of course. Follow me, please.'

And as she negotiated the table-maze, she hid her grin in the sheaf of menus she was holding and wondered, not for the first time that day, if she'd be showing Vinny the Enigmatic Vagrant to a table anytime soon.

Chapter Nine

June scorched its way into July, and early on the Saturday morning of Netta and Noel's birthday barbecue, Apollo fastened the harnesses on Zorro and Honey, clipped on their leads and attempted to get both dogs pointing in the same direction.

'Hang on!' Kitty appeared at the door. 'Are you just going out? Down to the beach?'

Apollo nodded. 'Before it gets too hot or too crowded, yes.'

'Wait a sec, then, and we'll come with you.'

'We?'

'Me and Teddy. Jemini's working until lunchtime so I'm on child-minding duties until I start in the chippy at one o'clock and we do handover. And I've already had two hours of *Peppa Pig* – I need a break.'

'Yes, that I understand. But haven't you also had enough of the beach? You're never away from there.'

'I'll never ever have enough of living on the coast. Oh, and you know . . . gorgeous weather . . . sea on the doorstep . . . where else would I go? Hold on, and I'll make sure Teddy has her sandals on and a sun hat and some factor fifty.'

'It's hard work this parenting business,' Apollo said, but Kitty had already darted back inside the cottage for Teddy, so he looked at the dogs. 'Though, I doubt I'll ever know for real.'

Zorro and Honey snuffled happily round him at that point. He bent down and fussed them and they rewarded him with big slobbery Staffie kisses. He chuckled. 'And why would I want to have

43

human babies anyway, eh? I've got you. You're the best kids, ever. I love you very much. You love me unconditionally – and you don't want to watch *Peppa Pig* at dawn.'

'No, they just want feeding every five minutes and then sleep on top of you and snore.' Kitty jumped down the porch steps with Teddy in her arms. 'But I love them, too. OK, let's go . . .'

Apollo looked at her. 'Have you just got changed? Were you wearing that when you went indoors just now? You look very pretty, Kitty. Oh, I mean, you always look very pretty, but now, this morning, you look – better – nicer – more glamorous – um – different . . . oh, *sod it* – is that what you say?'

'When Teddy's around, yes.' Kitty grinned. 'Keep digging!'

'I know when to stop.' Apollo laughed. 'Maybe then, you're all ready for the party tonight? This is your outfit?'

Kitty, who was wearing white shorts and a pretty pink vest sprigged with blue rosebuds, and had put on mascara, and run some of Jemini's hair product through her wayward auburn curls – just in case – tried to look nonchalant. 'Goodness, no . . . I've got an afternoon of waitressing to come yet . . . no – I just chucked this on because it's so hot.'

'Well, you don't look "chucked on".' Apollo stopped. 'Am I allowed to give you a compliment, by the way? Is it politically correct these days? It's a minefield.'

'I love a compliment – so, thank you. Other women may not – they'll probably not understand your motives. They'll think you're attempting to chat them up, or worse. I agree it's a very tricky area these days, so maybe it's best not to say anything – especially to strangers. Anyway, ta from me.'

'Thanks for the thirty-second lesson on acceptable social behaviour in the twenty-first century.' Apollo laughed. 'I'll never compliment any woman, of any age, on anything, ever again.'

'That's probably the best plan,' Kitty agreed.

And chuckling together, they set off across the common, surrounded by the scent of heather and honey-sweet pollen, ducking beneath the trees, with the ferns brushing their legs, and with the dogs managing to stay more or less in a straight line all the way to the clifftop. From there, Teddy, her much-chewed one-eared fluffy rabbit under one arm, carefully manoeuvred her way down all the sandy steps holding Kitty's hand.

It was early morning blissful. Quiet, apart from the gentle breaking of the wavelets on the shore, and the occasional cry of the gulls. The beach huts and shack-shops were still closed, and no families had yet ventured down onto the sands. As there were no children to be frightened of the dogs, Apollo let Honey and Zorro off their leads and he and Kitty watched them tearing along the water's edge, turning in dizzying circles before rushing off again, chasing shadows and imaginary dragons, splashing in and out of the shallows, smiling their biggest Staffie smiles.

Teddy handed the chewed rabbit to Apollo, smiled prettily at Kitty, and pointed towards the dogs. 'Kitty – paddle – now – please. With 'Pollo.'

'OK, as long as Apollo doesn't mind,' Kitty said. 'Which I'm sure he won't – no, look, he's smiling. Right, let's have your sandals, keep your sun hat on and make sure you hold Apollo's hand all the time.'

'Yes, Kitty.'

Kitty watched them go, hand-in-hand, crossing the warm sand towards the sea. Then she started to walk slowly along in the same direction, looking up and down the beach.

He wasn't there.

She wasn't sure whether she was glad or not. Apollo was right, she'd been haunting the beach every day since she and Vinny had spoken, with the dogs or without . . . just in case. And on a couple of occasions, she'd spotted him in the distance and waited for him to catch up. Then she'd smiled and raised her hand – because the beach had been crowded and she didn't know if he'd seen her or not – but he'd simply nodded in her direction by way of acknowledgement and walked on.

Enigmatic or not, she'd thought his behaviour was – odd? Rude? Maybe he had issues he didn't need or want to share; maybe he was ill; maybe he actually thought she was too silly for words; maybe he just didn't fancy her; maybe he was married with half a dozen kids and adored his wife . . .

Kitty kicked at the sand as she walked along. She really was acting like a moody teenager with a crush on the fittest lad in the local football team. Surely she'd learned her lesson after James. Surely . . .

Then she saw him.

And maybe Vinny was all those things, but Kitty still thought he was the most devastatingly gorgeous man she'd ever set eyes on – and possibly the loneliest, too. And until he told her otherwise, she wasn't going to give up on at least being his friend.

He was walking towards them, barefooted, on the shoreline. His jeans were old and faded, and his T-shirt was pale blue. The dogs, splashing ahead of Apollo and Teddy, saw him, and recognising a friend, bounced off towards him in fountains of spray. Apollo called them back but they chose not to hear him and took no notice. They jumped up and danced around Vinny and he fussed them and laughed.

Kitty hurried across the beach to join Apollo, and took Teddy's hand. Apollo whistled to Honey and Zorro, and this time they heard him, stopped bouncing round Vinny, paused, looked over their shoulders, and then raced back again.

By which time, Vinny was merely yards in front of them. He and Kitty stared at one another. He looked away first.

'Hi. Sorry about the dogs – as usual,' Apollo said. 'They tend to get a bit excited when they see a friend.'

'It's nice to see them again. It's a mutual appreciation society. You know I think they're pretty amazing,' Vinny said, turning away from Kitty and watching the dogs as they bounded in and out of the water again, snapping at the tiny foamy white waves. Then he smiled down at Teddy. 'And are they your dogs, too?'

Teddy went suddenly dumb and giggly, then, clinging more tightly to Kitty's hand, quickly nodded her head.

Kitty, who'd simply had no idea what to say, just looked from

Apollo to Vinny and back again. 'So – are you two friends? You know one another?'

'We've passed the time of day when we've met on the beach – because of the dogs,' Apollo said. 'They always know when they've met another dog lover.'

Vinny pushed back his hair and looked at Kitty. 'I did mention seeing him with the dogs, I think, when we spoke. I just didn't know then that he was Apollo.'

Apollo frowned. 'You know my name?'

'She . . .' he nodded towards Kitty. 'I'm sorry – that's very rude of me – but I don't know your name.'

'Kitty.'

He paused for a moment and almost smiled. 'Thank you. Well, yes, Kitty told me your name was Apollo.'

Apollo frowned some more, this time at Kitty. 'Why on earth would you do that?'

Kitty took a deep breath. This was all getting weird and bizarre and silly. 'I mentioned you, the other day . . . It was the day I got Mavis's letter. I was reading it down here. It blew away, and – um –' She looked at Vinny, not sure what she should call him. She went for the safest option, the name he'd called himself. 'Er – Vincent – saved it and we were – um – talking about the dogs – and I mentioned your name. I mean, at the time, I had no idea you and – um – Vinny,' – *oh, sod it!* she groaned inwardly – 'er Vincent, had even spoken.'

'Vinny?' Apollo frowned even more. 'The same Vinny that—'

'Yes!' Kitty said quickly before the conversation became any more embarrassing. 'Small world, eh?'

Vinny looked at her again but she couldn't read the expression in his eyes. Then he looked at Apollo and finally at Teddy. He smiled. 'Nice to have met you. All of you. And the dogs, of course. You're very lucky. Very lucky indeed.'

And he turned and walked away.

Kitty's heart sank. That was it, then. He wasn't interested in her. Not even as a friend. Nice one, Kitty, she thought miserably.

Apollo didn't appear to notice anything wrong. 'He's a nice chap, Kitty. He loves the dogs. We've met a couple of times down here. I didn't realise that he was the one who walked the shoreline who you talked about when we first moved here. He doesn't seem like a – a vagrant to me.'

'No I'm sure he isn't,' Kitty said quickly. 'I think that's just a cruel nickname some of the villagers gave him; like a joke, because he's – well – non-conformist. And you know what people are like about anyone who's different.'

'Only too well,' Apollo said with feeling. 'I hope he doesn't know what his nickname is then.'

'Me too.' Kitty tried to sound normal but it didn't quite work. 'Well, I guess we ought to be getting back. You whistle the dogs and I'll dry Teddy's feet – oh, I know, poppet, I promise not to make the sand rub . . .'

Ten minutes later, with the dogs on their leads and Teddy on Apollo's shoulders, they were all trudging back towards the wooden steps. It was definitely time to leave. It was already very hot and the beach was rapidly filling up with families. The sand was covered with towels and sunloungers and brightly coloured umbrellas, and the earlier silence was now punctuated with screams and shouts of excitement and the dull undulating whisper of splintered conversations.

'You know, Kitty,' Apollo said once they'd reached the clifftop and they'd bought Teddy an ice lolly and paused to let Honey and Zorro have a much-needed drink of water. 'Look at all those people down there. All families. All different. But all happy. It's not always mum and dad and two kiddies any more, is it? But that doesn't matter – they're family.' He chuckled. 'And they probably look at us and think we're a family . . . you and me, with a little girl and two dogs.'

Kitty sighed. 'They probably do. We all live in our little bubbles don't we? We know nothing about anyone – all we do is assume.'

'Are you OK, Kitty?'

'Me? Yes . . . I'm fine. Absolutely fine.'

Chapter Ten

The blisteringly hot day had mellowed into a gloriously warm, still evening. Just before seven o'clock, the inhabitants of Sand-castle Cottage joined the steady trickle of people heading along the lane to Noel and Netta's house.

'They must have invited the entire world!' Jemini said. 'How big is their garden?'

'Bigger than ours, I think,' Kitty said, 'because they have the bend in the lane. But as we've never been invited there before, and because their hedges are so high, I've never seen what the garden is like.'

'Neat, I bet,' Jemini said. 'All parks-and-gardens universal planting, no doubt. So boring – and we'll have to stand around with a plate and doily and a napkin and a plastic beaker and not know where to put anything or how to balance everything at once and . . .'

Kitty laughed. 'That reminds me of when we first came down here – our little gang from school, all organised by I'm-Still-Head-Girl-Amy, for Miss B's memorial service. And we had that snack thing afterwards in the Mermaid, and there were no tables, and when I tried to eat something I had no idea what to do with my plate or the coffee.'

'And neither of us were telling the truth about our lives that day, were we? We were both pretending everything was hunky-dory, when it was far from it.' Jemini smiled. 'And neither of us would have dreamed that we'd actually end up living together here in Firefly Common.'

Kitty groaned inwardly and really wished Angelica would stride off to join Mr H. 'No. Not a secret one, or a non-secret one – I was just smiling – um – because I'm happy.'

Angelica nodded. 'And so you should be. It's a glorious evening and we're all going to have some lovely neighbourly villagey fun.'

Kitty tried hard not to laugh. 'Are we? I'm not really sure what to expect tonight, to be honest.'

Angelica shrugged. 'No, well, none of us are, obviously. This is the first time Noel and Netta have entertained in their entire lifetime, as far as I can recall. But it's a lovely excuse to dress up for once, isn't it? And you look stunning, Kitty, as does Jemini. Such pretty dresses you're both wearing tonight. Are they from Frocks in the village?'

'Thank you,' – Kitty shook her head – 'and sadly not. Neither of us earn enough to be able to afford their prices.'

'Oh, I don't find them too expensive. I always try and buy something from there every season. Keep the local businesses in the black and all that. Mind you, I still love Harvey Nicks for my shopping sprees when I go up to town.'

Kitty sighed softly. It was like they lived on different planets. Still, it would be a boring world if everyone was the same. Somehow she doubted she'd ever be popping up to town to buy designer clothes in this lifetime. 'Angelica, you look fabulous, too – but then you always do. And Harvey Nicks is also way out of our price range. Actually, Jemini found tonight's dresses online, very cheaply, from somewhere abroad I think.'

'That's very daring of you.' Angelica raised her exquisite eyebrows. 'I mean, you never know what you're going to get online. Or if you're even going to get anything at all.'

'No, you don't – but these arrived, and they're exactly how they looked in the photos, and they fit, so we're delighted with them.'

'Well they don't look cheap, I must say!' Angelica didn't flinch as she doled out one of her back-handed compliments. 'Actually, I did wonder if Jemini would wear one of her gorgeous saris tonight.'

'She thought it was probably better not to.'

'Oh? Did she think Netta and Noel may not approve? Because they may be throwbacks to the land that time forgot? But they read the *Guardian* and vote Labour you know. And they used to go on the CND marches and knew Bertrand Russell. They're very broad-minded, really.'

Kitty chuckled. 'I'm sure they are. I think it was more that Connor's parents are going to be at the barbecue tonight, and while Jem gets on really well with Lester, his mum is another matter.'

'Ah.' Angelica tapped the side of her nose. 'Say no more. Well, we'll have to make sure the lovely Mrs Lowe doesn't upset any apple carts tonight, won't we? Oh, and,' – she indicated the tote bag in Kitty's hand – 'have you brought boxed gifts for Netta and Noel? Does anyone do boxed gifts any more?'

'We do.' Kitty laughed. 'We're old school like that. We pooled our resources – it's their birthday after all, and they're even more old school than we are. We thought they'd like a present to open, but as we know nothing about their tastes – apart from the walking, and we're sure they have all they need for that – we were a bit stumped. So we went to Locktons.'

'Really?' Angelica frowned. 'Did you? And did you manage to find anything? It's all so messy and higgledy-piggledy in there.'

Which was the whole joy of the place, Kitty thought. But she doubted that Angelica, even though she had lived in the village for years, would find any pleasure at all in a shop that had been trading since the late 1800s and had atrophied somewhere around 1958. Locktons, the first shop on Firefly Common's High Street, was an Aladdin's cave, a Tardis, that stretched back into little dimly lit alcoves, and round corners, and up little flights of uneven wooden stairs. It was crammed with shelves piled high with books and toys and gadgets and things you never knew you wanted or had forgotten how much you needed.

'So, what did you buy from Locktons, then?' Angelica frowned. 'We never bother with presents, as such, these days. I mean, we got them a gift voucher – we always do gift vouchers; it's so much easier.'

'We bought books.' Kitty held up the tote bag. 'Enid Blyton books. Famous Five and Secret Seven books. Locktons had several of the titles in hardback, and all with the original jackets, tucked away upstairs.'

'Seriously?'

'Seriously. We all loved them and still have them. Jem is going to read hers to Teddy as soon as she's old enough to forego *Peppa Pig* – and they've been some of my comfort books since childhood.'

Angelica wrinkled her nose. 'Well, yes, sweetie, of course – I read them too, back in the day, but *children's books*? For Netta and Noel? Why on earth would you . . . ? No, don't bother – I'm sure Netta and Noel will be polite. Anyway, I can see Mr H hovering, so I'll catch you later – oh, and I'm being allowed some alcohol tonight – Destiny, my wellness coach, says it depresses the inner spirit if you deny yourself a modicum of pleasure.'

'I'm sure she does,' Kitty said, straight-faced. 'And I'm sure she's right.' And Angelica hitting the booze that night after abstaining for so long could be quite amusing . . . oh, but Netta had said it was only non-alcoholic homemade plonk, didn't she? Totally harmless, then. Fruit and herbs . . . which, all things considered, and knowing Angelica's propensity for plain speaking when tiddly, was probably just as well.

And, of course, Angelica – lovely as she was – would no doubt never understand why they'd chosen those particular books for Noel and Netta. But even Apollo had read them as part of his English lessons, and loved them at school, and they'd all agreed they were the embodiment of the 1950s – as were Noel and Netta. And probably this entire grey, austere make-do-and-mend-era evening.

'OK.' Jemini slipped her arm through Kitty's. 'One tiara found and fastened; one child happy again – so, let's go.'

They followed the other Firefly Common residents round the bend in the lane, with the foxgloves and shepherd's purse brushing against their bare legs, and the heady scent of wild garlic filling the air.

'Here we are, then,' Jemini said as they reached Netta and Noel's willow-weave gate. 'In we go – let's see what delights await us, then let the fun commence . . .' She stopped walking and gaped at Kitty. 'Oh – holy crap on a cracker, Kit – just look at this!'

Chapter Eleven

'Oh wow! It looks just like *Bake Off*!' Kitty stared in delight at the pastel paradise that was Netta and Noel's garden. 'They've even got a marquee!'

Softly painted pink, pale-green, blue, and yellow tables and chairs were dotted across the lawn, all adorned with matching candles in glass flutes, flowery napkins and pastel plates and cutlery. Pretty flower-sprigged bunting festooned the garden and fluttered overhead; the marquee was a fully functioning bar area; and there were long gingham-covered tables all along the far hedge, laden with picnic food.

Jemini grabbed Kitty's arm. 'Look! They have picnic baskets! Up there – by the food! Noel's cooking things on that great big oven contraption – it must have come out of the ark, but it looks like it could cook for hundreds of people, which is just as well. Ah, Kit – look at him in his big chef's hat and apron, love him.'

Kitty laughed. 'He really looks the business – and so does Netta, handing out the picnic baskets in her pretty pinny and her Prue Leith necklace! Oh, and they've got loads of salads and flans and bread and things all laid out and – oh, wow! You help yourself to hot and cold food, and pack your picnic basket and take it back to your table . . . Oh, Jem, you've got to hand it to them – this is such an original idea.'

Connor, Apollo and Teddy, with the dogs on their leads, had arrived beside them and were also gazing around the garden in amazement.

'Bloody hell!' Connor shook his head. 'Never in a million years would I have thought the Old Ns would have dreamed up something like this. It's really, really cool.'

'And the food!' Apollo was already peering across the heads of the crowd at the trestle tables. 'I can see so many old-school recipes on show there . . . flans and pies and ah, masses of the party food all old English people love – things on sticks! Cheese and pineapple, and little sausages, and cocktail onions! And salads and dips and big chunks of bread and proper butter pats. Oh – the puddings! Look at the puddings! Proper trifles! And big lemon meringue pies! And a Black Forest gateau! And fruit of all sorts. Kitty – this is bliss!'

Kitty laughed. Because it was. And because everyone in the garden was reacting in the same dazed and delighted way.

It was another Firefly Common miracle.

As they threaded their way through the chairs and tables, they greeted friends, neighbours, villagers, and various customers they recognised, who were all wearing the same beaming smiles of stunned happiness.

There was music playing from speakers in the trees: a mix of ancient and modern tunes, loud enough to hear but low enough not to intrude on conversations.

'Jemini! Hi!' A tall girl in a flowing Laura Ashley-print frock, emerged waving from the crowd. 'And Teddy. Hello, sweetheart. Look at you, in your tutu and tiara! Aren't you gorgeous?'

Teddy chuckled and nodded shyly.

'Hello, Ruby.' Jemini greeted the owner of Teddy's nursery.

'Jem, I wondered if Teddy would like to join us in the nursery area? All her friends are here – and we have suitable food, plus games. And all the nursey staff are here on duty tonight, too.'

'I'm sure she would. She'll have more fun with them than sitting with us oldies. But I had no idea that Noel or Netta had organised a play area for the children.'

'They've organised everything you can think of,' Ruby said. 'Left nothing to chance at all. Brilliant idea to entertain the

56

kiddies, though. The children have got a Peppa and George picnic on the go.' She held out her hand to Teddy. 'Do you want to come and see what's going on, sweetheart? All your besties are here – Imogen, Summer, Stanley, Dexie-Rae and Jenner and . . .'

With a squeal of delight, Teddy freed herself from Jemini's grip and hurled herself at Ruby.

'OK, Peppa wins – as always. I can see I'm not needed.' Jemini grinned, and bent down and kissed Teddy. 'See you later, poppet – have a lovely time with your friends – and I'm only just over there if you need me.'

'Come and collect her when you're ready – we're over in the far corner, under the willow trees. Bye then.'

Teddy gave a regal wave in Jemini's direction, straightened her tiara, fluffed her tutu, and trotted off with Ruby without a backward glance.

'Blimey,' Connor said, fondly watching her go. 'The Old Ns have covered all the bases tonight, haven't they? So, shall we grab a table then take it in turns to get food and drink?'

They grabbed a pale-blue table for six on the edge of the lawn. Honey and Zorro, having been walked off their paws earlier in the afternoon, immediately dived beneath it, slobbered their way through the bowl of water Kitty put down and subsided with happy Staffie sighs.

'Connor and I'll get drinks,' Jemini said. 'Then we can leave the dogs here to guard the table while we nip up and stuff our picnic hampers.'

'OK – but I don't think they're serving anything alcoholic,' Kitty warned. 'You may have to get drunk on dandelion and burdock, and the atmosphere alone.'

'And love.' Connor winked. 'We're always high on that.'

'Yeurgh!' Kitty pulled a mocking face. 'Clear off and get the drinks!'

Half an hour later, with their hampers open on the table, remains of their picnic piled on their plates, and their glasses topped up from the jugs of fruit cordial from the bar, Kitty and co were having a wonderful time, and the dogs, under the table, were lazily snaffling any leftovers that came their way.

Several couples, including Angelica and Mr H, were dancing to some rather seductive Latin American music.

While they were up at the food table, they'd even managed to find time to give Netta and Noel their birthday present – and at the same time compliment them on the genius of their barbecue. Netta and Noel had literally squealed with delight over the birthday books.

'Oh, my word! We love these! Oh, you're so clever!' Netta beamed, hugging them all in turn. 'We had all these when we lived at home, didn't we, Noel?'

'Our favourite books of all time,' Noel confirmed. 'And our nanny used to read them to us in the nursery before bedtime – and then, later on in life, we'd pack them in our trunks and take them to boarding school and they helped with the homesickness.'

Netta nodded. 'And then they all got lost somewhere along the way – and we've always talked about them and the adventures in the stories, and our own childhood escapades chasing imaginary spies and having picnics with lashing of ginger beer. Thank you – thank you all so much, you couldn't have found anything we'd enjoy more.'

Kitty and Jemini had grinned soppily at each other as they'd made their way back to their table.

'Blimey, though,' Jemini said, 'they must have come from a posh family. And been very rich. A nanny . . . a nursery . . . and boarding school. All very Enid Blyton in real life.'

'Another world – again,' Kitty said. 'I'm just so glad the books were the right thing to give them. Oh, look – Connor's parents are sitting at our table.'

'Bugger!' Jemini frowned. 'I'd really hoped to avoid the parentals tonight. Hey ho – here I go.'

She strode up to the table, beamed at Connor and at Lester Lowe, then held out her hand to Deidre, Connor's mother. 'Hello, I'm Jemini. I've been so looking forward to meeting you.'

Deirdre Lowe didn't miss a beat. 'And me, you, of course. I've heard so much about you from my boys.'

'They don't like one another, no?' Apollo whispered in Kitty's ear.

'First meeting – but I'm sensing no,' Kitty whispered back. Then she raised her voice and beamed at everyone. 'Hello, Lester and, Deirdre, is it? Isn't this a fabulous barbecue? Oh, good idea, Connor – move those chairs round a bit, there's plenty of room for us all.'

Oh lord, Kitty thought, now *she* was sounding all jolly hockey sticks – exactly like Amy, the domineering and overbearing leader of Miss B's Girls.

'I'll go and get some more drinks,' Apollo said quickly. 'Another jug or two?'

'Two at least,' Kitty said, hopefully managing to tone down her slightly too-bossy voice. 'It's so hot and they go down really well. Although, I must admit, for soft fruit cordials they do seem to have a bit of a kick.'

'Dad and I were just saying that.' Connor chuckled. 'I feel like I've had several pints, a spirit or three, and a couple of shots, already.'

Kitty looked around her. The laughter seemed louder, there were more shrieks than earlier, the dancing was wilder, and several people had stumbled, giggled, and carried on. Maybe, she thought, knowing Netta and Noel were only serving non-alcoholic drinks, people had brought their own booze.

However, even she felt slightly light-headed, and all she'd had were several glasses of rhubarb and elderflower cordial. Maybe it was the heat . . .

Maybe.

Connor, rather unsteadily, had finished rearranging chairs and sat down beside Jemini, kissed her cheek and held her hand.

Good for you, Kitty thought, don't be fazed by your mother.

Deirdre Lowe beamed at Jemini with a bared-teeth smile. 'My husband tells me you're invaluable in the office, Jemini. We're clearly very lucky to have you.'

'Thank you. I think I'm very lucky to be working in a really interesting local business with local people. And I have qualifications in business studies' – Jemini smiled sweetly – 'so it's been a pleasure to be able to put some of them into practice.'

Connor smiled proudly. Kitty winced at the very obviously rehearsed-for-the-occasion words.

'Of course, Firefly Common is the smallest of our branches' – Deirdre studied her gel nails – 'and therefore much quieter. I can't see that you'd be very stretched.'

Connor squeezed Jemini's hand more tightly. 'Mum . . .'

'It's OK.' Jemini smiled at him, then turned to Deidre. 'Oh, I find more than enough to keep myself busy – especially when Connor or Les – er – Mr Lowe are out with clients. Even without customers in the shop or on the phone, there are always plenty of online enquiries to deal with and brochures to send out – then there's the correspondence to answer.' Jemini chuckled. 'And the filing system was in a bad way. And the IT stuff on the computer was from the dark ages. I've updated all the systems and—'

'That was my job while I was working with Lester,' Deidre said icily. 'I put those systems in place.'

Connor cleared his throat. Kitty shook her head.

'Ah.' Jemini swallowed. 'Um . . . yes, well, of course, in your day they were no doubt the dogs' bol—I mean the epitome of up-to-date business practice – but things change so quickly and—'

'In my day,' Deidre broke in, 'wasn't that long ago. I'm not *that* old, you know.'

'Mum!' Connor brushed angrily at his quiff.

Jemini closed her eyes 'No – no, of course you're not. I wasn't meaning to suggest anything of the sort.'

'Here we are!' Apollo said cheerfully as he returned with a tray and several jugs of pale-amber-coloured liquid. 'I thought it was a good idea to get plenty – although the barrels in the tent are enormous.'

'Barrels?' Kitty said quickly, needing to find anything to divert attention away from Jemini and Deidre's spat. 'Netta and Noel have homemade fruit cordial in barrels?'

'And proper casks, as well,' Connor added. 'Rows of them. Like Apollo says, they're massive. You just help yourself from the taps. Noel and Netta put the marquee up round them for tonight – apparently they've been brewing the stuff for years. Noel was telling us they use all their own fruit from the garden and throw it in and just add a bit of water and some sugar to take the edge off and leave it. Cool, eh?'

Kitty giggled. Fruit and sugar, left to ferment in casks for years – they were clearly drinking extremely potent alcohol. Everyone at the party had been glugging it back as if it was the fruit cordial Noel and Netta believed it to be. Oh, joy.

'As I was saying,' – Deirdre Lowe leaned across the table towards Jemini – 'in my day – oh, my god! What's that noise?'

Apollo laughed. 'It's the dogs. They're under the table asleep – and snoring.'

'Oh, really?' Deirdre pulled a face. 'You've brought your dogs to a party? Goodness me . . . Who wants dogs anywhere near them at a party? Or near food? Or indeed, anywhere?'

'We do,' Apollo, Kitty, Jemini and Connor chorused.

Deidre shuddered and drew her skirts more closely to her. 'I don't like dogs. I'm going to have to move in a minute – they probably have fleas . . .'

A fuming Apollo opened his mouth, then, seeing Kitty's warning glance, shut it again as Deirdre continued.

'Anyway, where was I . . . ah, yes . . . in my day . . .'

Connor slid his arm round Jemini's shoulders. 'Mum, the dogs are fabulous – you really should get to know them – and we're all aware that you were a superstar in your day. We all know the business would never have got off the ground if it had been left to Dad. But I don't want to talk shop tonight, and I'm sure Jem doesn't either.'

Oooh – brownie points to Connor, Kitty thought.

'And I certainly don't want to talk shop either,' – Lester Lowe stood up, steadying himself on the edge of the table – 'Deirdre, darling, let's leave the children and the dogs – come and dance with me. Listen, they're playing our song.'

Kitty blinked. Jive Bunny and the Mastermixers? Really?

Apparently so, as Deidre and Lester swayed off into the wildly dancing throng.

'Thank f-flip – for that.' Jemini sank back into her chair and looked at Connor. 'That went well, then?'

'Yeah . . . Sorry, Jem. Mum can be a bit—'

Mr H suddenly loomed over the table at that moment and clapped Apollo and Connor on the shoulders. 'Just the men I want! Noel's organising a poker school in the marquee. He's a demon player – learned to play at his exclusive boarding school, he says – for matchsticks then, but tonight the stakes are apparently high! I need help! Come along – no excuses!'

And he's a little drunk, Kitty thought. As are we all.

'Go.' Jemini smiled at Connor. 'You love playing cards. Go on – and you, Apollo – have a boys' night out in the marquee.'

'I will follow in a moment,' Apollo said. 'When I have finished my drink.'

Kitty bit her lip. Apollo was suddenly sounding very Cypriot. She really should tell them all not to drink any more. But on the other hand . . .

'OK – I'd love to play – if you're sure you're OK, Jem?' Connor stood up and swayed slightly.

Jemini grinned at him. 'I absolutely swear not to run across the lawn and spear your mother with a cocktail stick. Will that do?'

'I guess.' He leaned down and kissed her. 'See you in a bit, when I've won a fortune.'

'Ouf . . .' Jemini said as soon as Connor had followed Mr H towards the marquee. 'She hates the dogs and she hates me. His mother hates me. Is it because I'm brown?'

Kitty laughed. 'Jem, sweetie, the divine Mrs L is at least three shades browner than you are – and I reckon hers must cost a fortune and then some. And I don't think she hates you at all. She may dislike you for various reasons – but none of them are because you're brown. Dear Deirdre would *love* to look like you.'

'Really?'

'Yep, really – now, I reckon that firstly, she dislikes you because she thinks you're a cougar.'

'A what?'

'Cougar. You know – older woman, younger bloke.'

'Oh, that. That's crap.'

'Whatever. Secondly, she also dislikes you because she's a clinging mother who can't accept the fact that her son loves another woman more than he loves her.'

Apollo nodded and said nothing.

Jemini shrugged. 'OK. Maybe.'

'Thirdly,' Kitty continued, 'she also worries that her only child is about to be snaffled by a gorgeous woman who is not only ten years older than her only son, but has been married and divorced, and has a child of her own, and however glorious that child may be, she could, if things get serious between you and Connor, be about to become a grandmother – or at least a step-grandmother. In other words, you are making her feel her age.'

'Good,' Jemini grinned.

Apollo filled their glasses again. 'Yes,' he said, 'like Kitty says – it's an age thing. Jemini, you are young and very beautiful, and the Deirdre woman – who is not going to be one of my friends because she doesn't like dogs and she was rude to you – was also obviously once young and very beautiful. She is still a beautiful woman but no longer so young. Some women don't like to accept that they must age.'

'That's daft,' Jemini said. 'You can't fight getting older anyway, and she – Deidre – looks stunning for her age.'

'She does, however, fourthly and finally,' – Kitty stretched – 'Deirdre dislikes you because she thinks you're a gold-digger.'

'What? How?'

'The business, Jem, the family business. The Lowe half of it will be all Connor's, one day – she thinks that's the attraction.'

Jemini laughed. 'You reckon? Well, she's wrong on that front, isn't she?'

'You know that; Apollo and I know that – and Connor knows that. Deirdre – maybe not so much.' Kitty laughed. 'Oh, look, change of subject – Angelica is heading our way.'

In a flurry of pastel-pink layers and a cloud of Chanel, Angelica subsided into the seat that had been so recently vacated by Deirdre Lowe. 'Well! What a wonderful evening this is, isn't it? Who'd have thought Netta and Noel could pull off something like this? So, what are we gossiping about round the table? I need some gossip – Mr H has gone off to play poker in the tent and left me to my own devices. And I've had a drink or two – albeit non-alcoholic, which is such a disappointment seeing as Destiny gave me the green light for tonight, but then, what can you do? So, here I am, and I'm ready to gossip the night away.'

'Um, just a thought, but maybe you should stick to the soft drinks from the children's tent from now on?' Kitty said. 'As you're obviously out of practice.'

'Darling!' Angelica shrieked. 'I've been drinking that divine cordial of Noel's all evening, so no alcohol has touched my lips – although I do feel rather gloriously intoxicated.'

And no wonder, Kitty thought.

'Yes, well, maybe stick to the kiddie fruit squash or bottled water for now. Just in case? After all, you don't want to undo all Destiny's good work, do you?' Kitty looked across at Jemini. 'And maybe you should do that too, Jem. Because you've got a child to take home, remember?'

'Oooh,' Angelica shrieked with laughter, 'is Connor staying over at Sandcastle Cottage tonight?'

'Teddy,' Jemini said through a forced smile. 'She means Teddy.'

'I knew that!' Angelica chuckled. 'I was just being funny. Some people have no sense of humour. Anyway, back to more entertaining things. Now we've got Apollo here – and presumably before he joins the rest of the testosterone in the beer tent – shall we do a sort of Truth, Dare, Kiss or Promise game?'

Slightly less risky than the more modern version, Kitty thought, although it wasn't a game she'd ever enjoyed. 'Um, probably not . . .'

'No, listen.' Angelica held up her hand; diamonds sparkled. 'Don't stop me now, as dear Freddie used to say. Destiny, my wellness guru, says we have to ask questions and seek answers to free our inner turmoil, so—'

Apollo shook his head. 'Not again, Angelica. Please, no.' He shrugged at Kitty and Jemini. 'We met in the recreation ground one morning. Angelica did her Twenty Questions on me. I said too much, probably. I'm not playing again.'

'Oh, don't be a spoilsport.' Angelica's eyes sparkled almost as much as her diamond jewellery. She beamed across the table at Kitty and Jemini. 'Because I know that Apollo has a secret love . . . and I think we should find out who it is, don't you?'

Chapter Twelve

The still, warm July evening was gently melting into dusk. Magically, as the sun began to set, hundreds of multi-coloured fairy lights started to glow from the trees and bushes and hedges until everywhere was surrounded by a twinkling, dancing rainbow. Then, intertwined with the bunting overhead, dozens more lights appeared, waxing and waning, and giving Netta and Noel's garden a kaleidoscopic canopy of stars.

'Wow,' Kitty breathed. 'How beautiful and how clever. Noel must have worked his socks off to produce this. You'd never think, would you . . . seeing him yomping off with his walking poles . . . just goes to show . . .'

'Never judge on appearances, no.' Apollo nodded. 'Always a mistake, I've found. But for Noel – a tremendous success, yes?'

They all nodded, still gazing at the delightful and totally unexpected homemade miniature aurora borealis.

For a moment, the whole barbecue crowd stopped, the laughter quelled, and the dancing halted, as they stared at the lights. Then, after a few seconds silence, everyone started clapping and cheering.

Jemini, like all the partygoers, simply stared at the light show in total wonderment. 'And to think I thought this was going to be boring . . . It's without doubt the most incredible barbecue I've ever been to.'

'And me – I'm gobsmacked too. I love it,' said Apollo. 'It's all very spectacular, but now,' – he attempted to stand up – 'if you'll excuse me, ladies, I have a poker hand waiting for me.'

Angelica, Kitty and Jemini raised their eyebrows in unison and looked at him.

'I think not,' Angelica said archly. 'There's the little matter of your secret love. Remember?'

'Yes – we're dying to know, now. Have you been holding out on us all this time?' Jemini chuckled. 'You sly fox, Apollo – who is she? Or he, of course.'

'She,' Angelica said quickly. 'I ruled out the gay possibility at our previous encounter. So, we know it's a woman.'

Apollo sat down again and slowly poured out another glass from the jug. 'OK – you win. If it makes you all happy and keeps you quiet.' He laughed. 'I'll tell you – but, I must warn you, it's a disappointing story – and then I'm going to play poker.'

Kitty was slightly concerned that they may be treading on dangerous ground and, having never heard Apollo even hint at having a lover, touched his arm. 'Seriously – you don't have to. I was only joking. It's none of our business.'

'Kitty's right.' Jemini nodded. 'Sorry, we really shouldn't pry. Your private life is just that, Apollo. Don't listen to a bunch of slightly inebriated women who should know better.'

'It's OK.' Apollo raised his glass. 'This has loosened my tongue. And who knows, maybe Angelica – and her Destiny person – is right. Maybe it's good for the inner soul or whatever it was she said . . . sorry, I think I may be a little intoxicated, too.'

Kitty sighed. 'Yes, maybe. Um – I think the fruit cordial is a little stronger than we anticipated. But, honestly, you don't have to tell us anything you don't want to.'

Apollo smiled slowly. 'Twenty years ago, I met a girl. We fell in love. She was the one and only love of my life. She left me. I never heard from her or saw her again. The end.'

'Nooo!' Angelica shook her head. 'Nooo! Not like that! That's awful – I mean, that's so sad – but that's no way to tell us the story. There's got to be more to it than that! You cannot have been in love with this . . . woman – and no one else, ever – for twenty years!'

'A girl, yes, as she was then,' Apollo said. 'A woman now, obviously – and yes, I have.'

Kitty shook her head. 'Angelica, leave it at that, please. I've known Apollo for ages and I had no idea about any of this – and it really is none of our business. I don't think we have any right at all to make Apollo go back to things he finds painful.'

'But we should!' Angelica insisted. 'This is what Destiny says is holding us back. We're all repressed because we don't face our inner pain.'

'Then Destiny's a daft cow who obviously likes nosing into things that don't concern her,' Jemini said. 'Hurt is hurt, and painful memories are sometimes far best left buried – as we all know.'

Kitty sighed. 'And maybe we don't need to be washing our dirty – or sad – laundry in public, either. I'm not sure your Destiny person knows what she's talking about.'

Angelica bridled. 'She most certainly does! You come along with me – the next Wednesday that you're off – and see for yourself!'

'OK, I will. But don't expect me to get sucked into some faux hocus-pocus nonsense.'

'Destiny is the real deal, Kitty, I'll have you know. She knows all about how to have a healthy mind, body and spirit, and—'

'Twenty years ago,' Apollo said quietly, 'I was twenty-two years old and a waiter in my parents' taverna restaurant in Cyprus.'

Kitty, Angelica and Jemini all stared at him.

'You want me to continue, yes?'

'Yes!'

'It was a coastal village, not one of the big resorts, but favoured by British holidaymakers looking for the real Cyprus. We were practically on the beach . . . we were open from mid-morning until the last customers had gone – maybe in the early hours . . . My mum and dad both cooked – we just did traditional Greek-Cypriot meals back then, very popular with the tourists . . . we were always busy – I, with my brothers and two sisters, waited on tables.'

'It sounds idyllic.' Kitty leaned forward. 'But you've never been back, have you? You must miss your parents? Your family? Oh – did they not approve of this girl? Or did she marry someone you knew and you couldn't bear to see her with someone else and—?'

Apollo shook his head, laughing. 'Nothing like that, Kitty. I left Cyprus because my heart was broken, yes. I hoped I could find this girl. She was English, you see, on holiday.'

'Oh.' Angelica nodded. 'A holiday romance! And the old cliché – naïve English girl falls in love with handsome foreign waiter. All hearts and flowers and promises of eternal devotion under the seductive Mediterranean sky – until it's time to go home, then it's farewell and on to the next one.'

'Not for me, it wasn't,' Apollo said quickly. 'Nor, I think, for her. I don't know. I thought her feelings were the same as mine. She was young – was staying in a villa with her parents. Not just for a week – for a month of the summer. They were very posh . . . rich people. They didn't approve of me.'

'How young?' Jemini sipped her drink. 'I mean, *how young*?'

'Seventeen. Nearly eighteen. She'd just finished her school exams and her parents wanted her to go to university.'

'OK. Not that young, then. Old enough to fall in love,' Jemini said. 'And she didn't want to go to university?'

Apollo smiled. 'Not then, no. She wanted to stay in Cyprus and live with me and walk barefoot along the beach and serve tourists with moussaka and halloumi and vine leaves and olives.'

'Oh, wow . . .' Kitty sighed. 'So romantic. So, she fell in love with you, too?'

'Yes. I honestly think she did. Anyway, after a little while, when I'd saved some money, I came here, to England, and tried to find her. I started working for other Greek family members who had restaurants in the south of England, and they taught me to cook properly, and time went on – and then I bought my own shop in Reading because the only other thing I knew about her was that she lived in Berkshire. I thought Berkshire was a small place. It wasn't, of course.'

'Oooh,' Angelica said. 'You had your own restaurant? Goodness me – so, if you sold it before you moved down here, surely you had enough money to—'

Apollo and Kitty both laughed.

'Not a restaurant. I owned a small kebab shop,' Apollo said.

'Eeeewww.' Angelica pulled a face. 'Really?'

'Really.' Kitty grinned. 'And very fabulous it was, too. It – and Apollo – saved my life and my sanity.'

Angelica still looked disbelieving. 'But a *kebab shop* . . . ?'

'Yep. It was in a rather run-down area, too,' Apollo said. 'And I was very proud of it – and I cooked all the extras myself, made my own pittas, koftas, souvlaki, gyros, tzatziki . . .'

'And out of this world they were, too,' Kitty added. 'But the shop – all the shops in the row – were compulsorily purchased to make way for housing. Apollo got peanuts and we were homeless.'

'This is exactly it. Very little money for many years of work – and a place I loved and people I knew . . . all gone in the name of progress.' Apollo sighed. 'Anyway . . . in answer to your earlier question: no, I've never been back to Cyprus – although my family have visited me sometimes over here. And I never found her – the girl – either.'

'Was she very beautiful?' Kitty asked.

'To me – yes – the most beautiful girl in the world. I have a picture . . . just one picture . . . my brother took it of us together . . . it has been with me for twenty years and it got creased and faded a little . . . so I photographed it on my phone to keep for ever – see?'

He flipped through his phone then held the screen towards them.

Kitty looked at the photo – it wasn't very clear at all: a much younger Apollo in jeans and T-shirt, with his arm round a tall, slim dark-haired girl wearing a huge floppy hat, shorts and vest, and sunglasses. It was all slightly fuzzy and out of focus, and they were both smiling at the camera with the taverna and the sea in the background.

'You were very good-looking,' Angelica said, adding quickly, 'not that you aren't now, of course . . .'

Typical Angelica. Kitty and Apollo exchanged smiles. But yes, months into his busy Firefly Common lifestyle, Apollo had lost weight, looked fitter – and didn't appear very different from his younger self in the photo.

Angelica peered more closely at the phone screen. 'We can't see much of your girl. We can't really see her face at all.'

'I don't need a photo to remember her face. I will never forget her face.' Apollo gazed at the picture for a moment then put the phone away. 'I'm only sad that this is the only photo I have. If I'd known what was going to happen, I'd have borrowed my brother's camera and taken a thousand photos of her.'

They all sighed.

'But why didn't you write to her? Phone her?' Angelica frowned. 'Surely, if you and she were that smitten you'd have exchanged details? I know there was no social media like there is today – I mean, today it's a breeze to keep in touch or find someone, back then it was like the dark ages, but even so . . .'

Apollo took a swig from his glass and sighed. 'She'd gone before I knew it. Before she was meant to. We didn't even get to say goodbye. The day before she was due to leave she didn't come to see me at the taverna. So I walked up to the villa – crept around in case her parents saw me – but it was locked up, empty, shutters closed. The cleaners were there – they said the family had all gone in the middle of the night. Packed up. Left early.'

Kitty, Jemini and Angelica all looked at him. He concentrated on his drink and stared at the table.

Kitty touched his arm. 'God, Apollo, I'm so sorry. We should never have pushed you into talking about it. That's just so sad. What horrible parents they must have been.'

He shrugged. 'Maybe they were good parents. They didn't

71

know me. They were protecting their daughter. I couldn't blame them for that.'

'But you must have known her name?' said Angelica. 'And the villa people must have been able to give you the family's details. There wasn't much, if any, fuss about data protection back then, was there?'

Apollo shook his head. 'No one was going to give me any information at all. Why should they? I might have been planning some sort of crime. I tried so hard to find out where she'd gone, where she lived, but no one could or would help me. The villas were owned by a company based abroad. The staff who worked there knew nothing about the people who rented them, they just cleaned them and restocked them all through the season.'

'So,' – Jemini sighed – 'you had no idea where to start looking, apart from somewhere in Berkshire? She didn't tell you her surname?'

'No. And I didn't tell her mine. That would have been formal . . . we were anything but formal . . . Anyway, we thought we'd be able to do all that on the day she was going home. She was just May – that's what I called her. My girl, the month of May – there was an old song called that, it was playing on the radio the first night she came into the taverna with her parents and I waited on their table and fell in love with her at first sight. My girl, the month of May . . . I used to sing it to her – very badly I think.'

They all sat in silence for a while. The barbecue party had roared back into life and people were dancing and singing and laughing.

'But,' Kitty said, 'she knew where you worked. She could have contacted you there. Written a letter to the taverna. Maybe, it was just a holiday romance for her?'

'It wasn't! And I would bet you a million pounds that any letters sent from abroad and addressed to the taverna would have got lost in our postal system. We didn't have a street name or were even part of a village. Twenty years ago was another world – both here and in Cyprus – for technology. Back then, if you lived off the beaten track but the post guy knew your grandmother's aunt's husband's cousin then you could more or less rely on getting your mail through, otherwise – nothing.'

'It was much the same here,' Angelica admitted. 'Still is, in some parts. Some of the lanes in Firefly Common have never appeared on any map or grid and yet people have lived there for generations. Deliveries to several places in the village have always worked on who you know lives where, for years.'

'So,' – Jemini poured more drinks – 'we're assuming that May did try to contact you, but when she didn't receive a reply she thought that it was exactly how Angelica said – a holiday romance, and that she was already forgotten, and that you would be ready and waiting for the next young impressionable English girl to walk into the taverna and fall for your charms – oh,' – she laughed – 'don't look at me like that, Apollo! I know that wasn't the case for you, but . . .'

'Yes, I think that's it, exactly,' Apollo said. 'May must have thought it meant nothing to me. I had had girlfriends before, of course. Local girls, girls from school, but I'd never fallen in love. She was my first love – and my last. No one can understand this. My parents, they thought I'd find a nice local girl and marry her and have half a dozen kids like my brothers, but there was no way I could ever marry anyone else. My heart already belonged to May. So, instead, I searched for her, failed to find her, learned to cook, helped rescue and rehome abandoned animals . . . and have dreamed about her nearly every night.'

They sat in silence again. Kitty sighed. It was all so sad, but she really didn't see how they could help him. They'd never be able to find her – not even with the help of social media – there simply wasn't enough to go on. And anyway, maybe May didn't want to be found after all this time. She was presumably married and probably had children by now, but even if she didn't, then she wouldn't remember – or maybe even want to remember – her holiday romance of two decades earlier with anything more than a happy smile of reminiscence: it had been young love; a holiday romance; something to tell the mythical grandchildren one day. Nothing more.

Apollo stood up. 'Now, I'm going to play poker. And Angelica, maybe your Destiny woman was right . . . maybe talking about it has released some of the hurt . . . who knows. And thank you for listening – and for being my friends.'

They watched him weave his way, slightly swaying, through the crowds towards the tent.

'Blimey,' – Angelica topped up the glasses again – 'that was full-on. I'm all wrung out now. How flipping emotional was that? And who knew there was so much pent-up heartache in there? Damn this May woman – she broke the heart of a really decent man.'

'She did. I hate her.' Kitty nodded. 'And Apollo is just gorgeous. He deserves to have someone in his life to love him.'

'He does.' Angelica sighed. 'He's an extremely attractive chap, but he's clearly a one-woman man. Oh, what a mess!'

Jemini blinked. 'I feel a bit squiffy – so, please tell me that this is mad – but what if . . . what if May is actually short for Mavis . . . And what if . . . ?'

'Nooo!' Angelica shrieked. 'No way on god's earth! I do believe in coincidences – Destiny said the heavens and portents and spirits all move like a massive game to arrange and rearrange our lives – but that's going too far!'

'Jem,' Kitty said softly. 'It's mad – and so are you.'

'I know, but stranger things have happened – you read about them online all the time. Maybe May was called Mavis after her gran or something and didn't want Apollo to know what an old-lady name she had, so she shortened it to May and—'

'No,' Kitty said. 'Just no.'

Jemini pulled a face. 'Spoilsport – but I'm going have a search online . . . you know . . . Mavis, May – we kind of know how old she'd be now and where she came from because Apollo told us, don't we?'

'We've tried with Mavis Mulholland and failed. There's still not enough to go on – and anyway, Apollo is very tech-savvy – do you not think he's tried all this himself?'

Jemini groaned. 'I suppose so. But isn't it all so sad? And such a waste? Oh – I know! Why don't we pinch Apollo's phone, send that picture to our phones and post that photo everywhere – or, better still, copy it and get it enlarged so we can see more of May's face, and then—'

'Jem.' Kitty laughed. 'No! And again, I guess Apollo has already been down that route. I think we'll just have to accept that they'll never meet again.'

'Oh, that's so sad!' Jemini shook her head. 'Life's so short – I just think if you have any chance of meeting someone and being happy together then you should grab it, don't you, Kitty? Kitty . . . ?'

Kitty, who had been momentarily lost in a brief and fuzzy daydream of walking hand-in-hand along the shore with Vinny, blinked. 'What? Oh, yes . . . without doubt. Everyone should have the chance of falling crazily head-over-heels in love at least once – even if it breaks your heart in the end.'

'I'm kind of guessing you're not talking about James-the-bastard-ex, here, are you?' Jemini said.

Kitty smiled and shook her head.

'Oooh,' – Angelica raised her eyebrows – 'Kitty Appleby, you dark horse. Is this a real or hypothetical once-in-a-lifetime lover?'

Kitty grinned and, smiling giddily, got to her feet. 'That would be telling, wouldn't it? Now, come on, girls – let's go and strut our stuff on the dance floor while we can still stay upright.'

'No one struts their stuff any more.' Jemini chuckled. 'Oooh, I think I might be feeling a little bit drunk . . . and, yes, even "throwing shapes" is way back in the dark ages, Connor says. And you certainly never "boogie on down". Nowadays, you just dance.'

'Move and groove!' Angelica laughed shrilly and possibly a little too long. 'That's what I do – a-movin' and a-groovin' . . . Oops, I do feel inebriated though. How very peculiar.'

Giggling, they clung to each other.

'Actually, I'd better pop over to the nursery corner,' Jemini said. 'I'm just going to check on Teddy. It's getting late and she might be overtired and wanting to go home. I know Ruby said she'd tell me if she needed me, but hang on, don't go dancing round your mythical handbags without me – I won't be a sec.'

Kitty and Angelica fondly watched her weave her way across the garden towards the nursery area.

'Oh!' Kitty yelped suddenly. 'It's not just Teddy who needs checking. The dogs! We've forgotten the dogs!'

She bent down and peered under the table. Honey and Zorro, their heads close together, their big Staffie feet all of a tangle, were soundly and blissfully asleep, snoring in unison.

'Bless them. They're out for the count.' She stood up. 'No doubt filled to the gunwales with picnic food. And I can see Jem's on her way back without Teddy, so I guess all is well there. So, are we going to dance or what?'

'We're going to dance,' – Angelica threw her arms dramatically into the air – 'wildly, like Isadora Duncan, but not until you tell us about *your* secret lover.'

'Hahahaha,' Kitty laughed as she headed towards the gyrating throng, and suddenly hiccupped into some mis-remembered version of 'Secret Love'. Then she stopped and giggled. 'And that's exactly how he'll stay . . . Hahahaha . . .'

Chapter Thirteen

Everyone in Firefly Common said it had taken them days to eventually shake off the post-barbecue hangover – which surprised
them all, as everyone knew Noel and Netta were teetotal. The
majority of the partygoers had turned out the following morning
and groaned through their muzzy heads to help with the clearing
up. Despite the skull-crushing after-effects, several people had
asked for the fruit cordial recipe, apparently, and Netta and Noel
and been completely overwhelmed by the huge amounts of thank-
you cards and gifts that had arrived at their cottage. Afterwards,
most people fetched up at Nellie's Café on the High Street for a
restorative full English. Nellie said it was the best Sunday-morning
takings she'd ever had.

In fact, everyone agreed, Netta and Noel's birthday barbecue
was the most amazingly magical night anyone in the village could
ever remember. It would go down in the annals of Firefly Common history along with the lopsided beacon and the iffy fireworks
for the Queen's Silver Jubilee, and that Christmas when Santa's
Round Table sleigh caught fire in the middle of the High Street
because one of the elves lit up a crafty cigarette too close to the
papier-mâché Rudolph.

It was three days after the barbecue when Kitty next took
Zorro and Honey down to the beach. Apollo, headphones plugged
into the best of Black Sabbath or Iron Maiden or some-such
similar heavy metal, had been taking them to the recreation
ground each morning for their first run, very early because of the

heat, he said – but Kitty and Jemini both thought his unusually early starts were more likely because he was embarrassed about how much he'd told them about May and wanted to avoid them as much as possible.

This, of course, meant that unless Kitty suddenly professed an urge for a dawn swim before work, or suggested that Teddy might enjoy building sandcastles before nursery, she'd had very little reason to head seawards. Not that she needed a reason, really. She could head off towards the cliffs and the beach any time she wanted, with or without the dogs or Teddy, just because she wanted to be there. But somehow she felt that if and when she next saw Vinny, it had to be because she was there for a reason and not as some sort of sad and lonely stalker.

Vinny may have perfected the moody solo shoreline walk, but Kitty wasn't convinced she'd be able to do the same. She always felt that, without the dogs or child in tow, she'd simply look somehow, well, furtive.

But, that aside, Apollo's lost-love story had made her determined not to waste time, and to discover, as discreetly as possible, more about Vinny, and if the attraction she felt for him was reciprocated, and whether there was any chance of anything developing between them – before she made even more of a fool of herself.

But then, even if he *was* interested, what would happen if he turned out to be another lying love-rat like James? Was she even brave enough to venture into falling in love again? Look at Apollo – what good had love done for him? And Jemini, divorced already, and OK, happily in love with Connor now, but surely he wasn't going to stay the course, was he?

Oh, why on earth did relationships have to be so complicated?

Today, the dogs behaved impeccably on their harnesses and leads. They pulled and panted in the same direction, decided to pee on the same patch, stopped and snuffled at the same scents in tandem, even paused together at the top of the beach steps to allow Kitty to unfasten them at the same time, then waddled, side by side, down towards the beach in a very sedate fashion. Kitty smiled at them. They always sensed her mood – or Apollo's – they were clever dogs. And today she felt – what? Fey? *Wow – get a grip!* She laughed to herself. Maybe not *that*, then, but happy and excited in a sort of hazy, not-knowing-why way. Like when she was very young and it was nearly her birthday, or Christmas . . . when the bubbling anticipation was almost as good as the event itself.

Dear lord! Kitty chuckled to herself as she followed Honey and Zorro down the sandy sleeper-steps. *For pity's sake, woman – get a grip.*

It was early, and there were very few people on the beach, but the temperature was already soaring. This really was turning out to be a record-breaking summer. In her white shorts and thin yellow vest, Kitty could already feel the sweat prickling her scalp, and she attempted to bundle her curls into some sort of topknot before the humidity turned them into candyfloss. Maybe she should have her hair cut? Wasn't she getting too old for long hair? Or was that not the case these days? She really should try harder to keep up with the trends and – oh . . .

She stopped on the steps. Vinny was walking along the shoreline. Unbidden, her heart did a bit of a flip – which surprised her. The dogs, sensing that she'd stopped, also came to a halt and looked over their shoulders.

'It's OK. Go on. I'm right behind you.'

And she was. Because if she walked across the sand in a straight line, once she'd reached the bottom of the steps, she and Vinny would be more or less in the same spot. A sort of organised accidental collision-course.

Now or never, Kitty thought.

The dogs tumbled down the last few steps and ran, smiling, towards the sea. The tide was just coming in, and Honey and Zorro attacked the tiny wavelets with huge enthusiasm. Kitty, giving up trying to control her hair and hoping that her face wasn't too shiny, took off her flip-flops and walked slowly across the beach.

The collision-course worked brilliantly well.

'Hi!' She smiled at him, shielding her eyes from the sun with one hand. 'Gorgeous morning, isn't it?'

There, she thought, that sounded OK. Friendly. Nothing more.

He nodded. His faded jeans were sea-soaked to above the ankle and his feet were bare; today's T-shirt proclaimed he'd lived and loved in the summer of '69.

The dogs, abandoning their attack on the ocean, gazed at him adoringly for a nanosecond, then bounded splashily towards him.

'Oh god – sorry!' Kitty pulled a face as both Honey and Zorro leapt up and down.

'They're fine.' Vinny laughed, trying to make a fuss of them both at the same time. He looked over her shoulder. 'Are you on your own today? No Apollo – and no cute little girl? Your daughter?'

Kitty blinked at him, then laughed. 'Apollo is probably asleep – he was on lates last night – and Teddy isn't mine. She's Jemini's daughter. Jemini lives with me. And Apollo. And the dogs. And actually, I don't mean that Jemini and I are a couple – and Apollo isn't my other half . . . he's not Jemini's other half, either, or Teddy's father . . . Jemini's other half is Connor – he isn't Teddy's father either . . . We're friends and we just all share a house.' She stopped. 'Probably way too much information, there.'

Vinny looked confused, as well he might. 'Yeah, maybe, just a bit . . .' He laughed. It was a nice laugh. 'But once you got to the house-share bit I was OK. I just assumed the little girl – Teddy – was yours. Sorry.'

'Oh, please don't apologise. I do that all the time,' Kitty said cheerfully. 'Assume, I mean. I'm usually wrong. Sod's law.'

He grinned. Kitty's heart did another little bounce.

The dogs, rotor-blade tails wagging, decided Vinny had passed muster, and turned their attention to snapping at the incoming waves again.

'So,' – Kitty looked out across the sea, watching the sun's reflection dance on the gentle tide before looking at Vinny again – 'do you live here, too? In Firefly Common?'

'No.'

Argh. Idiot, Kitty thought crossly. Never ask a closed question.

James's unspeakable father had drummed that into her years earlier, when she'd been working on the sales side of his business. Now where was she going to go with the conversation? Where do you live, then, was obviously out of the question, so . . . She took a deep breath.

'We moved here just before Christmas,' she said, raising her voice slightly above the shushing of the waves frothing round their feet, and the calling of the gulls floating on the warm thermal currents above them. 'We hadn't planned on living here, it just sort of happened.'

Vinny nodded. The breeze blew his dark hair across his face and he brushed it back. Kitty watched him, sighed, and looked away.

'I guess you have to be mega wealthy to live in Firefly Common these days,' he said. 'I grew up round here, but there don't seem to be many of the locals left in the villages now. It's either retirees with overflowing pension pots, or the nouveau riche – not that there are many of them left since the last recession.'

Kitty laughed. 'We're not rich, nouveau or otherwise. And pension pots are non-existent in our world, I'm afraid. We rent Sandcastle Cottage – do you know it?'

Damn! She held her breath. She probably shouldn't have said that, should she? Just in case he was an axe murderer. Or thought she was desperate. Or both – but more likely desperate . . . sod it . . . too late now.

'Lucky you.' Vinny grinned. 'Yes, I know where that is. Millionaire's Row – very exclusive and right in the middle of the common. It's a beautiful part of the village.'

'It is. We love it. We got the cottage really cheaply,' Kitty continued, 'because the owner only wanted short-term tenants and . . .' She tailed off. *Stop talking. Way too much information.* 'Sorry – I tend to babble.'

He laughed. 'If that's babbling, then please babble away. It's nice to have someone to talk to.'

Oooh, Kitty thought – that had to mean he lived alone, surely? Bonus!

Honey and Zorro decided the waves had been chased enough and decided to concentrate on the seagulls instead. They bounced off through the shallows in the direction of the Mermaid steps, hopefully snapping at fresh air.

Kitty nodded towards the dogs. 'I'll have to walk along with them in case any children run up to them. They're soft as butter, but we're always careful. Are you – um—?'

'Going the same way? Yes.'

Phew. And good. It was all OK – so far. Unless he was an axe murderer of course.

They walked slowly, side by side, following the dogs along the shoreline. Strands of Kitty's hair had fallen from the haphazard topknot and blew wildly in the salty air, probably corkscrewing into a zillion red ringlets like Disney's Princess Merida only nowhere near as pretty of course, and she didn't care. She hadn't been this happy in – well – forever.

The beach was gradually coming alive. The summer visitors and holidaymakers, having had their B&B breakfasts, were now setting up deckchairs and sunloungers and huge vibrant parasols for the day. Several of the rented beach huts halfway up the cliffs were beginning to show signs of life too, with their doors being pegged back, chairs being placed in the sun, and buckets and spades and rubber rings and lilos being piled outside.

Kitty called to the dogs who were lagging behind, playing tug o' war with a long strand of glistening seaweed. They galloped through the shallows, still holding their dripping and rather-chewed prize.

Vinny laughed. 'They're fabulous – and so lucky to have found a home with you – and Apollo, of course. Anyway, is this their exercise before you head off to dish up fish and chips to the tourists?'

Kitty gave a little mental whoop. They were having a proper conversation – and he'd remembered where she worked!

'Luckily, I'm not working today.' Now or never, she thought. 'What about you?'

He shook his head. 'Not this morning. Later, maybe, depending on the tide and the weather and – people. My work is seasonal and I'm self-employed, so it may be short-term but at least there's no one on my back.'

Whoa, Kitty thought. Lots of information there – but again, all enigmatic. So, should she ask? Was he a fisherman? A day-tripping boat owner? A lifeguard? A deckchair ticket-seller? A beach photographer . . . ?

As befitted such a wonderfully retro coastal village, there was still a beach photographer in Firefly Common. Angelica and Mr H had said the family business had been going since the first lot of post-war holidaymakers arrived, when Kitty had asked them about the brightly coloured kiosk at the top of the steps by the ice-cream shack. She'd laughed when Mr H said you could pick up your photos within two hours of them being taken. Because surely, nowadays, with everyone having mobile phones with excellent camera facilities, no one would actually need the beach photographer, would they?

But it seemed, like buckets and spades, lilos, sandcastle flags and fish and chips, they *did* – all were part of the vintage-feel holiday, and the beach photographer seemed to do a steady trade in happy family-holiday snaps.

So, was Vinny the beach photographer? Is that why he walked the shoreline? Looking for likely customers? Nah . . . she shook her head. She'd never seen him carrying a camera, or a satchel, or leaflets, or any of the other things she assumed a beach photographer would need to ply his trade.

So, whatever he did depended on the tide and the weather – and people . . . and was seasonal. Which was why he'd disappeared during the winter months. Anyway, she thought, why not just ask him?

'So, what exactly do you . . . oh, bugger!'

Zorro and Honey, still clinging on to their long seaweed banner, had cannoned directly into a paddling toddler who had immediately sat down in the shallows with a whump and a wail.

Honey and Zorro pranced happily round the screaming bundle while its mother – all piercings and tattoos and blisteringly angry – kicked sand at the dogs.

'I'm so sorry . . .' Kitty dragged at Zorro's harness, while Vinny did the same with Honey. 'It was an accident. They're only playing. They tend to get a bit boisterous, but they're quite safe.'

'Safe! Should be put down!' The mother snarled, snatching up her still-bawling and now-dripping offspring. 'Shouldn't be let off the lead! Should 'ave muzzles! Look at 'em! Great big things! Bloody dangerous animals, they are!'

Kitty knew there was no point arguing.

'Kitty, give me the leads,' Vinny said quickly. 'I'll take them both further up the beach.'

Gratefully, she threw the dogs' leads to Vinny, and once they were both securely fastened, he steered Honey and Zorro and their seaweed away from the shoreline.

Kitty smiled at the mother and now-silent-but-glaring child. 'Again, I'm really sorry – but they're very gentle, they wouldn't have hurt him. Is he OK now?'

The mother's nostrils flared. This, Kitty thought, was pretty impressive, considering the amount of metalwork adorning the nose.

'*Her*!' the mother snarled. '*She*! She's a girl!'

Oops.

Kitty stretched her smile. 'Of course . . . she's lovely . . . And I apologise again, but she's OK, isn't she?' She looked hopefully at the child who was still mercifully no longer crying. 'Can I buy you an ice cream or something – um . . . ?'

The child brightened.

'No you effing can't!' The mother roared. 'You ain't going to bribe my Nirvana with no ice cream! I want proper compo, I do!'

Nirvana . . . *Nirvana*? Seriously . . . ? Kitty clamped her lips together before she giggled or snorted or did something that could only make this entire situation far, far worse.

Nirvana, sensing the promise of ice cream suddenly being snatched away, burst into tears again.

'Now look what you've done.' Nirvana's mum glared at Kitty. 'I brings her on holiday, and you scares her shitless with your dogs and then says the "i" word to 'er! I'm trying to bring her up proper and cut back on the e-numbers and then you go and – oh, is that your hubby on 'is way back? He's a bit tasty, ain't 'e?'

Kitty squinted against the sun. Vinny, looking drop-dead glorious, was anchoring the dogs' leads with an abandoned Paw Patrol spade. Zorro and Honey, meanwhile, sat placidly side by side, their thumping tails creating a miniature sandstorm, happily chewing their seaweed trophy.

'Er, no – he's just a friend,' Kitty said, as Vinny made sure the dogs were secure and headed towards them. But oh, how I wish, she thought, as her heart gave another little cartwheel of unbidden lust.

Clearly sensing an opportunity to flirt, Nirvana's mum placed the still-snivelling Nirvana on the sand, patted her own wind-blown hair into some sort of shape, pushed her sunglasses on top of her head, and wriggled down the front of her bikini top. Kitty blinked at the emergence of colourfully multi-tattooed bosoms. Blimey – that must have hurt . . .

'Hello.' Vinny smiled.

Kitty smiled back; Nirvana's mum did a sort of bared-teeth shimmy; Nirvana just sat on the sand and howled even more hysterically.

Vinny squatted down in front of the bawling child, said something quietly, and started scooping sand with his hands. Nirvana, still hiccuping and slightly snotty, watched with growing interest. Vinny spoke quietly to her again and grinned. She laughed. And sat down on the sand beside him.

'Stone me, he's got the magic touch, hasn't he?' Nirvana's mum said admiringly. 'You can always tell when a chap's got kiddies, can't you?'

Kitty was horrified at the wave of dismay that suddenly engulfed her. Of course he must have children! Of course he was married or partnered or something! Of course!

'Nirvana's dad did a runner the minute he knew she was on the way,' Nirvana's mum said matter-of-factly. 'Blokes are bastards, ain't they?'

Kitty nodded, thinking again of her own lucky escape. 'Yes, well mine was.'

She and Nirvana's mum exchanged a look of sisterly solidarity.

However, she thought, watching Vinny and the now beaming and happily gabbling Nirvana, playing in the sand, Vinny and James were definitely chalk and cheese, and it was obviously patently unfair to label all men as feckless bastards.

Although, now fairly sure that Vinny had a family, maybe he wasn't *that* different . . .

Another one bites the dust, Kitty thought miserably. Vinny was a family man, adept at building sandcastles and knowing exactly what to say to wailing toddlers – and therefore definitely off limits. Sod it.

Mind you, she told herself, that was what she'd intended to find out, wasn't it? Whether there was any chance of a future relationship? At least she knew now . . . She sighed and kicked at the sand.

'There!' Vinny sat back and smiled at Nirvana. 'Your own princess castle.'

Nirvana clapped her chubby hands in delight.

Nirvana's mum just mouthed, 'Bloody hell – look at that! He made that in a flash! That's amazing. His kids must love him – he's a right clever dad!'

And Kitty just went, 'Wow.'

The little sandcastle was pure fairy tale, all perfect turrets and towers and spiralling minarets.

'And this is a moat,' Vinny said seriously to Nirvana. 'And I've made a little channel out towards the sea just here, look, so when the tide comes right in, it'll fill with water . . .'

Nirvana laughed and jumped up and down.

'And now,' – Vinny stood up, wiping his sandy hands down his jeans and looking at Kitty – 'we have to be going, don't we?'

'Er – um – yes, we do . . .' Kitty nodded, still looking in awe at the miniature masterpiece on the sand. 'Nice to have met you – um . . .'

'Charlene-Louise.'

No longer Nirvana's mum, forever Charlene-Louise.

'And I'm really sorry about the dogs and everything.'

'No worries.' Charlene-Louise beamed. 'The sandcastle's more than made up for it. And he,' – she jerked her head in Vinny's direction – 'can come again any time.'

Vinny grinned and headed towards the waiting Zorro and Honey. Kitty, knowing exactly how Charlene-Louise felt, sighed. 'Well, you've certainly got a fan for life there – oh, and quite an audience.'

As Vinny handed her the dogs' leads and they headed away from the sea, they both looked back at the growing crowd now admiring Nirvana's fairy-tale castle.

'I'm not surprised people are looking at it. It's a stunningly beautiful castle,' Kitty said, puffing slightly as she slipped and slithered through the toe-scorching soft sand.

Goodness, it was searingly hot. Her face was no doubt shiny, there were rivulets of sweat trickling down her back, and her masses of escaping curls, she was sure, were no longer Disney Princess, more Very Bad Perm. And here, even further up the beach, the sea-breeze offered no respite at all. She wanted a long, cold drink, a room with air-con – and yes, Vinny.

Ugh . . . she groaned. Still, however bad she felt at having to accept that Vinny was definitely off limits, she was determined that he would never, ever know that her feelings for him had ever been anything more than passing-acquaintance/casual-friend.

Wending their way through the sunbathing families, they reached the base of the cliffs. Kitty forced a cheerful smile. 'I've no idea how you built that sandcastle so quickly – and just, well, out of nothing. You know, I reckon you must be an architect in your real life. That's one heck of a talent . . . oh, hang on, let me just give the dogs a drink.'

Turning on the standpipe tap at the base of another of the

snaking wooden cliff-steps and letting the water gush into the trough beneath, Kitty waited until Honey and Zorro were drinking noisily and messily, then, without thinking, she echoed Charlene-Louise's assumption. 'You must build fantastic sandcastles for your children.'

Hell, Kitty, she shook her head. Blatant fishing or what? She instantly sensed, rather than saw, the change in him. One question too far, Kitty.

'Child. Singular. And not any more.'

Oh, god. Kitty went cold. She swallowed. This was even worse than her clumsy attempt to discover his marital status. Far, far worse.

'I'm sorry . . . none of my business . . . I didn't mean to . . . *bugger*.'

She closed her eyes. Of course. That's why he walked the shoreline alone. That's why he looked like a forlorn and lonely soul. Poor, poor man. His heart was irretrievably broken. He'd lost a child . . . his only child . . . the worst thing that could happen to anyone, ever.

The shushing of the waves on the sand, the cry of the gulls, and the cocktail of happy holidaying voices deafened her. What an idiot she was! Oh, god . . . when would she ever learn? Again, she'd been crass enough to blurt out her usual burbling speak-don't-think nonsense. She wanted to cry, scream, apologise, sink into the sand and vanish without trace.

She opened her eyes. 'Vinny . . . I'm so sorry.'

He shrugged. 'It's fine.'

It so clearly wasn't. He looked blankly at her. She looked away.

Honey and Zorro lifted their heads from the water trough, dripping droplets over her feet. She grabbed their leads. 'Um – right, well, I think I'd better get the dogs home before it gets any hotter . . . um . . .'

For pity's sake, shut up, Kitty she told herself. Just shut up!

'Of course, if you need to go now . . .' Vinny frowned at her, then nodded. 'Yes . . . it's probably best to get them into some shade.'

The ensuing silence was even worse than their stilted words.

'OK then . . . um – yes . . .' She turned away. 'Um – well – goodbye . . . er . . .'

And without waiting for any reply or looking back, Kitty, flanked by the heavily panting and slightly bewildered dogs, hurtled up the sandy sleeper steps, two at a time.

Chapter Fourteen

It was a week later, not quite 10 o'clock, on another scorchingly hot July morning. The air conditioning was already whirring non-stop in the Firefly Common branch of Lovell and Lowe Estate Agents.

'How's Kitty?' Connor perched on the edge of Jemini's desk as she typed up property details.

'Still mortified, heartbroken, embarrassed, disgusted with herself, and not going anywhere near the beach, or into the village without a disguise, or anywhere out in daylight, or talking to anyone ever again in her entire lifetime.'

'Not got over it yet, then?' Connor grinned.

'Nope.'

'And has she told you yet what really happened?'

'Nope,' Jemini said again, her fingers flying over her keyboard. 'Well, not the details . . . nothing new. Just what I've already told you.'

'She said the worst thing you could ever say to anyone, to Vinny? And then she ran away?'

'Yep.' Jemini shrugged. 'Well, possibly not quite like that – but yes, that's the gist. And no, I haven't asked her anything else.'

'But she's not permanently locked away in the attic or somewhere? She's still going to work?'

'Yes, of course – and she takes the dogs out, but via the recreation ground now, not on the beach. Whatever she said was clearly very insulting but also totally unintentional. Look, however clever she tried to be, I know she was growing very fond of Vinny – and they were becoming friendly – and now she says she's blown it. End of story. She's told me, in the nicest possible way of course, that I should keep my nose out and back off.'

Connor shrugged. 'It all sounds a bit OTT to me. After all, she hardly knew the bloke, did she?'

'Like that matters!' Jemini snorted. 'They'd met, they were getting to know one another. She really liked him. She thought – hoped – he liked her too. She's had a crap time in the past – getting closer to Vinny was a big deal for her. What's not to understand? Men! Huh!'

Connor grinned and slid from the desk. 'OK. I get the sisterly solidarity bit. So, why don't we try to help her? Why don't we take Teddy down to the beach and look for Vinny and tell him that—'

'No way! Never! Ever!' Jemini stopped typing and shook her head. 'We can't interfere in this. Seriously, we'll just have to leave them to work it out for themselves. But being honest, I guess Vinny must have been pretty hurt by whatever she said, because Kitty says he knows where she lives and works and hasn't been in touch.'

'Why would he?' Connor frowned. 'They hardly know each other. He's hardly going to chase after a woman who he meets sometimes casually on the beach and who insults him and runs off, is he?'

Jemini groaned. Put like that . . . And both she and Kitty had earlier had a big 'back off' from Apollo over their abortive online attempts to find his lost love, too. No, there was no way Kitty would thank them for any meddling – however well-intentioned.

She was just about to say so, even more forcibly, when the office door opened and several sunburnt holidaymakers hurried in and gasped blissfully beneath the air-con. She and Connor exchanged 'lookers-only – no commission here' grins.

The business was doing OK, but browsers such as these were never going to purchase or rent a property. The day-trippers and holidaymakers, people who had delighted in the throwback

91

'No – it's so strange how things turn out,' Kitty said. 'And no doubt Amy will be in touch soon about the next Miss B's Girls' get-together. Have you heard from her since we moved?'

Jemini shook her head.

'No, me neither,' Kitty continued. 'So, she's going to get one heck of a shock when she finds out I've left Reading and you're no longer in the Midlands – which I *think* is what we told her last time – and that we're sharing a house down here.'

'Mind you,' Jemini said. 'If she hadn't done her bossy-boots thing and organised our Miss B's Girls' get-together down here for the memorial service, then none of this would have happened, would it?'

'Blimey, no. I hadn't thought of it that way – but you're right. Maybe we have an awful lot to thank Amy for, then.'

'We definitely do – oh, hang on . . .' Jemini looked over her shoulder. 'Teddy's lost her tiara and neither of the men have noticed. Stay there a sec, Kit, and wait for me.'

Jemini darted back to where Teddy was toddling along between Connor and Apollo, flanked by the dogs.

Kitty stood still and sighed. She'd pretended everything was wonderful all those months ago when she first came to Firefly Common – and she was doing something very similar tonight. Oh, damn it, she thought crossly. Get over it – he doesn't fancy you. He's probably weird anyway – forget him. It's not like you've got a really great track record with men anyway . . . slap on the happy smile, Kitty, forget Vinny and knock 'em dead tonight.

She was still practising smiling cheerfully to herself when Mr H harrumphed a greeting and strode on past. Angelica, expertly made-up and dressed in long layers of floaty pink chiffon, also en route to the barbecue, didn't.

'That's a lovely smile, Kitty – were you daydreaming?'

'Er – no.' Kitty quickly stopped smiling. 'I mean . . . well, yes, I suppose so, sort of.'

'Eloquent!' Angelica trilled with laughter. 'That was a "Secret Love" sort of smile. So, do you have one?'

seaside village charms of Firefly Common and thought it would be an idyllic place to live, came in their droves, browsed the racks of properties, and left with their chosen house details and their hopes and dreams, but never returned.

Nevertheless, Connor went into full estate-agent selling mode with the latest shorts-and-sandals brigade, and Jemini smiled to herself and continued to enter details of new retirement properties further along the coast, which offered, at an exorbitant price, 'sea views and lifts to all floors'.

She'd completed the purple-prose details on the retirement properties, printed off a sales sheet comparing current prices from other south-coast estate agents, and was just about to check the new customer-enquiry list and email it to Dire Deidre, as she and Kitty called Connor's mother, when her phone pinged, heralding a text.

She glanced down at it in case it was Ruby from the nursery to say there was a problem with Teddy.

It wasn't from Ruby.

Jemini scanned quickly through the message and smiled.

Hello Jem. Just catching up. We've moved on. We're in Thailand now. We like it. It's very us. We may stay. Very happy. You? You still in the seaside place? Don't tell anyone where we are, obvs. Not that I guess it's likely that you'll see anyone from back then anyway. I hope you're enjoying your new life. I am. Stay safe. With big love, Krish.

'And just who the hell is Krish?' Connor asked coldly.

'God! You made me jump! Why did you sneak up on me like that?' Jemini turned quickly in her chair. 'And why the hell are you reading my texts over my shoulder?'

'The browsers buggered off with their brochures, the shop is empty, you were smiling and looking beautiful – I was going to creep up and kiss the back of your neck . . .' He sighed. 'I didn't even know you were on the phone.'

'But you read the message anyway?'

'No! I just saw the "big love" sign-off – that's all.'

'And you don't trust me?'

Connor sighed. 'Bloody hell, of course I trust you, Jem. Please, don't blow this up out of all proportion. Sorry – no, OK, I shouldn't have even looked at your phone, but it was there and I saw it . . . it's not like I nicked your phone to find out who you were in touch with, is it?'

'If you ever did that, we'd be over, believe me. However, it still really isn't any of your business, is it? Do I ever ask who you speak to or text?'

'No, but . . .'

'Exactly. I trust you. I also accept that you have friends I've never met, know people I don't – you have parts of your life that don't involve me, and that's as it should be. We don't live in one another's pockets. I'm not an insecure kid, Connor.'

'And I am? Because I'm so much younger than you?'

'No.' Jem exhaled crossly. 'That's not what I meant at all and you know it. Our age difference has never been an issue – it never will be an issue. Trust has never been an issue, either. Oh, for heaven's sake – here –' She thrust the phone at him. 'We've never fallen out – and we really can't fall out over this. Read the rest of it. Go on.'

Connor shook his head. 'No way.'

'OK then' Jemini smiled. 'Shall I read it to you?'

'No!'

'Seriously – there are things you should know . . . things I should have told you.'

'Jesus, Jem – now you're scaring me,' Connor said. 'What sort of things?'

'All sorts of things – especially this.' Jemini indicated the phone. 'No, don't say anything, Connor – trust me, and if you won't read it yourself then just listen, please.'

Jemini read the text message out loud. 'There you go.' She smiled at him. 'Oh, and because it wasn't clear – Krish is my ex.'

'Wow.' Connor straightened up. 'Your ex-husband?'

'Yes.'

'And you're still in touch?'

'Yes.'

Connor nodded but didn't speak. He frowned. 'Oh, right. He's in touch because of Teddy? But he's never been to see her, has he?'

'Never. Because he doesn't know she exists.'

'What? Now you've lost me.' Connor frowned. 'So Krish isn't Teddy's dad?'

'Oh, yes he is – he just doesn't know it.' Jemima shook her head. 'Look, shall I make some coffee, then we can talk? Unless you want to leave it until after work? I mean . . .'

'Christ, no. Let's get it all out in the open now.'

'OK. I know I should have told you all this months ago, but somehow we were so happy and I was scared to spoil it, and then there was never really the right time – and then, well, the longer I left it and the happier we were, the less important it seemed.'

'Hold on . . . I'll get the coffee,' Connor said. 'If the phone rings, let it – this is far more important than selling houses.'

'For god's sake don't let your mother hear you say that.'

Jemini watched Connor go through to the tiny kitchenette at the back of the office, and exhaled. Bugger. She really should have told him months and months ago.

But then, when they'd first met, she was still reeling from the escape that Kitty had offered her, an escape from her life in the Midlands where she was hopelessly in debt and struggling as a single mother. Just moving into Sandcastle Cottage, sorting out her finances, being part of a family again, being happy. And then she'd fallen in love with Connor – and Krish and her marriage and her past life simply hadn't been important . . . until now.

'Thank you. You'll make someone a lovely wife.' Jemini smiled as he placed her Winnie-the-Pooh coffee mug on a coaster. 'So, shall I start? Oh, should we lock the door first?'

Connor, pulling up a chair beside her, shook his head and looked mock-shocked. 'What? Lock the door during business hours? Even I'm not that brave. Phone enquiries we can call back; customers in the flesh can't be ignored: so speaks my inner Mother. OK,' – he lifted his Kylo Ren beaker – 'I'm not sure I want to hear this, but I'm pretty sure I need to.'

Jemini took a deep breath. 'Krish and I more or less grew up together. Our parents were friends and neighbours. It was always assumed that we would marry.'

'An arranged marriage?' Connor's eyebrows rocketed. 'In this day and age? Wow, but surely—?'

'Don't interrupt.' Jemini smiled at him. 'I've hardly got started. And no, it wasn't like that – not really – but yes, with Asian families, you know, if you have children who would make suitable matches, then . . . Anyway, that's how it was for me and Krish. We were friends from babyhood. We went to the same primary school, eventually went to the same college and both did business studies, were invited to the same parties and family ceremonies, always moved in the same circles.'

'Cosy,' Connor muttered.

'Claustrophobic. So, the idea from our very respectable and honourable and devout respective parents, that we should get married, became more of a reality as we grew older. I'd had boyfriends while I was at school and college – but nothing very serious. We both had huge extended families who married and inter-married – and we were expected to join them. It just became a thing: me and Krish would toe the party line, get married, have babies, link two dynasties, almost, join the merry throng . . .'

'And so you did?'

'No . . . well, yes . . . but not like that. This is where it gets a bit complicated. Krish was in love with someone else. Someone his parents would never approve of. I was modern, non-religious, rebellious, had been to a fabulous girls' school which, as I told you early on, is where I met and became best friends with Kitty and the others. I just wanted to get my uber-strict, traditional parents off my back. Krish and I were best friends, we shared everything, we each knew the other wanted freedom and we reckoned we had one chance of escaping the perpetual "when's the wedding going to be?" crap. We got married.'

'Bloody hell!' Connor spluttered over Kylo Ren. 'That was a bit drastic!'

'It solved the problem. We knew as long as we were married, we'd be left alone to live our lives the way we wanted – and then, eventually, we'd get divorced. We were aware that the divorce would mean we'd more than likely be disowned by our families. We agreed it would be the final part of our joint escape route. So, after the wedding, we rented a nice apartment and lived platonically as friends. Krish was free to see his real lover, and I had discreet casual boyfriends. We still went to enough of the family get-togethers as was necessary to convince them that we were a typical in-love couple. We both worked full-time and blamed our careers over the years for the lack of a child. No one had any idea at all that we weren't – well – a happily married couple. It worked.'

'But . . . Teddy . . . ?'

'Yes, Teddy . . .' Jemini grinned. 'Shall I cut to the chase? OK – we had to have grounds for divorce before we could go through with it. The law is changing again now, to make divorce easier, but even back then, as long as you'd been married long enough, and if both parties agreed the marriage had irretrievably broken down, and one of the parties had, say, committed adultery, then the divorce went through pretty quickly.'

'OK – so, obviously, Krish had committed adultery and . . .'

'That wasn't how we played it. I admitted adultery, because – well – because Krish couldn't . . . Oh, look, we did this – all of it – because Krish is gay. His lover was a man. And white. They'd been together since college. His family would have made his life hell. Yes, they'd be angry about the divorce and kick him out of the family circle and tell everyone he was a bad lot and everyone would have felt sorry for his parents and closed ranks round them, but they'd still have kept their good-standing in the community.

They'd never, ever have coped with him being gay. It would have destroyed them – and neither of us wanted that.'

'Blimey – it's like something out of the dark ages.'

Jemini smiled. 'It's just tradition – and the honour thing. Respect for your forbears . . . I think a lot of families have moved on – but ours hadn't. Anyway, Krish's family – like my lot – were, are, hideously old-fashioned. To have a gay son with a white lover would bring eternal shame on their family name and all that malarkey. Divorce, with me as the guilty party, was the easy way out.'

Connor laughed, still looking slightly shell-shocked. 'Right . . . and you were prepared to do that for him?'

'Yes. He'd been my rock all my life. But it was for *me* as well. Getting divorced after our fabulous wedding would mean my parents – and the rest of the clan – would have me down as having dragged our family name into disrepute, and other stuff, and I'd be a dishonourable daughter and persona non grata . . . It meant I'd be free at last, so, it suited us both. The divorce went through. I was a scarlet woman. Krish, allegedly heartbroken and needing to get away to cope with his devastating loss, headed off happily with his lovely Matt for pastures new . . . they've been working their way round the world – currently in Thailand, as of today's message . . . and I moved north, miles away from Berkshire, found a bedsit and a job in a supermarket, floundered a bit, got into debt – which is probably all you knew about me, I suppose – oh, and discovered I was pregnant.'

Connor squinted at her. 'Now, biology wasn't one of my best subjects at school, but I kind of remember that you had to be more than best friends, or housemates or whatever, and not sleeping in separate rooms, to get pregnant. So, unless there was someone else in your life, the marriage wasn't totally platonic?'

'Oh, there wasn't anyone else at that time – hadn't been for ages. And the marriage was never consummated. Our relationship was absolutely platonic.' Jemini looked down at the desk, fiddled with her coffee mug, then looked at Connor. 'However, on the day the divorce came through and our respective families were incandescent with rage and disgust, Krish and I got madly, happily, hysterically drunk on champagne to celebrate the plan working, and somehow ended up in bed together . . . Next morning, we both had cracking hangovers and no real recollection of what had happened . . .'

There was silence for a moment.

Connor leaned back in his chair. 'But – you didn't tell him? When you knew you were pregnant?'

'No! Krish is a lovely, decent man. He'd have come back immediately and supported me and the baby, if he'd known. That would have broken his heart – and Matt's – and made us all unhappy forever. We'd been through so much to gain that freedom – he deserved not to know.'

Connor placed Kylo Ren on the desk with a crash. 'But he's Teddy's dad – they both need to know that, surely?'

'And they will – when the time is right. Which it isn't yet. And he's her biological father – never her dad. There's a huge difference.' She leaned forward. 'She has me – and you, and Kitty and Apollo, we're her family now. We're all she knows and needs. Until she's old enough to understand.'

They stared at one another. The air-con hummed.

'So,' – Jemini looked at him – 'I'm really sorry for not telling you all this earlier, but I promise you, I've just unpacked every bit of my baggage. Do you *understand* now?'

'About Krish? Yes. About not reading your private texts and leaping to insanely jealous conclusions? Yes. About why I love you . . . ?' Connor pulled her towards him. 'Oh, definitely, yes . . .'

He kissed her. Jemini slid her arms round his neck and kissed him back. Winnie-the-Pooh and Kylo Ren clattered across the desk and fell to the floor. Coffee dregs snaked across the details of the retirement apartments.

The air-con continued to hum to itself. For quite a while.

And then the door opened.

'Holy crap on a cracker!' Jemini wriggled away from Connor,

watching the newcomer, armed with a towering pile of boxes, back slowly into the estate agency. 'Oh, for pity's sake, Connor!' Jemini giggled. 'It's your sodding mother with the stuff from the printer's!'

'Bollocks.' Connor's snort of laughter was smothered by his attempt to push his quiff back into shape, re-button his shirt and find his shoes under the desk. 'I knew we should have locked that bloody door . . .'

Chapter Fifteen

'And this,' Kitty muttered, searching for a missing trainer in the depths of Sandcastle Cottage's avalanche cupboard under the stairs, 'is probably the third most stupid thing I've ever done in my life. And given that my life so far seems to have been full of stupidity and misunderstandings, that's some going.'

Angelica, limbering up on the porch, raised her enormous designer sunglasses and watched Kitty through the open front door with amusement. 'Third? Only three? You're such an amateur, Kitty.'

'I said *most* stupid,' Kitty mumbled from the depths of the cupboard. 'I wasn't counting the rest of my haphazard life choices . . . ah! Got it!' She backed out of the cupboard waving the recalcitrant trainer. 'Although, why I need to be dressed for jogging when we're just going to the village hall, I'm not sure. Is there something you're not telling me?'

'Nooo.' Angelica, in candyfloss-pink leggings and a matching racer-back vest, executed some pretty impressive stretches. 'I said it's just advisable to be – well – comfortable.'

Kitty snorted in disbelief, pulled on the second trainer, and joined Angelica on the porch. 'Sometimes, I wish you hadn't become all fit and healthy and boringly virtuous. The old Angelica was easier to cope with.'

'Give her a glass of something and wait until she falls over?' Angelica chuckled. 'I know – it's a miraculous transformation, isn't it? Mr H is delighted.'

Kitty shut and locked Sandcastle Cottage's front door, hoping against hope that she wasn't about to be regaled with intimate details of just how delighted Mr H was.

'Right,' – she adjusted her own sunglasses, equally large but more Poundland than Prada, and looked at Angelica – 'I'm wearing leggings and a vest. I have matching trainers on my feet. My hair is sort of secured in a scrunchie. All as suggested by you. Therefore, I'm ready. And if I hate it, I won't stay, OK?'

'Whatevs, sweetie.' Angelica jumped nimbly down the veranda steps. 'Whatevs. And you look super, by the way. This is going to be so much fun.'

It was Wednesday. Late morning. Once again scorchingly, deliciously hot. Jemini was at work with Connor; Teddy was happily ensconced in Ruby's nursery; Apollo, Honey and Zorro were no doubt enjoying a ramble and scramble along the clifftop with the sea breeze in their respective hair.

And Kitty was off to meet Destiny.

She actually had no idea why she'd agreed to join Angelica in this wellness nonsense . . . she was pretty sure it was all hokum anyway . . . but maybe, just maybe, it might give her the path to positivity – one of Destiny's mantras, apparently – that she needed. Because, Kitty thought miserably, she sure as hell needed something.

'So,' Angelica continued, high-stepping along the common's narrow sandy-dusty pathways, 'three big goof-ups, you said. The awful James was one, this is another – although, this isn't stupid at all, as you'll soon find out – so what's the last?'

'It's private,' Kitty said.

'Oooh, is it why you've been shutting yourself away from the world for the last two weeks? Only venturing out to go to work, with your head down, hair up – and no make-up? We haven't exactly been spying, but it's difficult not to see these things. Mr H and I couldn't help but notice that you seem to have gone into purdah, never going out, huddled beneath the trees in the garden, listening to sad songs on your headphones.'

101

'You can't possibly know what I was listening to.'

Angelica smiled. 'OK . . . well, I know you love the Beatles – but I'm pretty sure they didn't record any real dirges. Some sad songs, but . . . no, not the Beatles.'

'It wasn't the Beatles.'

'What was it then?'

'Coldplay.'

'Bingo.' Angelica smirked.

Kitty shook her head as they continued across the common, the tall fern fronds brushing against their legs, sending clouds of small blue and golden butterflies fluttering upwards and away towards the tangle of brambles and gorse and heather. The air was full of heat and sea salt and sweet wild honeysuckle.

'It's a man, then,' Angelica said as they left the common and single-filed through one of the many shingle alleyways, ducking beneath the overhanging purple buddleias, emerging onto Firefly Common's High Street between Locktons and Mr Merry's the greengrocer. 'Or *was*. You've been dumped?'

'No, it isn't, wasn't, and I haven't.'

'Pants on fire!' Angelica sang out as they avoided both shoppers and traffic, and skittered across the road.

Kitty growled to herself as she followed Angelica's pert rear along another snaking, sandy alleyway shortcut on the other side of the road: this time running between Tim and Toni, Unisex Hairdressers, and Lovell and Lowe Estate Agents. She had fleetingly wondered if she could detour in there and throw herself on Connor and Jemini's mercy.

She'd decided not. And it had absolutely nothing to do with them still smarting over last week's sudden and ill-timed appearance of Dire Deidre. They'd all laughed about that – eventually.

No, they'd only ask awkward questions about why Kitty had even agreed to do this Destiny-nonsense thing anyway. And Jemini was pretty astute, they'd known each other too long; she'd *guess* it was something to do with Kitty's Vinny-hiatus and start asking even more questions – and then say, as she'd been saying for the last two weeks, that Kitty was making a mountain out of a molehill, that she hardly knew Vinny, that if she'd insulted him that badly then why didn't Kitty just go and stalk him on the beach like she usually did, and apologise.

They'd nearly fallen out over the word 'stalk' . . .

Kitty sighed and quickened her pace slightly. This shortcut alleyway had pretty pastel-coloured bungalows on either side, and towering pine trees as a backdrop. The sun flickered through the branches throwing dancing patterns across the shingle track. Goodness, Kitty puffed, it was hot. The Firefly Common residents, well used to the soaring temperatures away from the coast, were already completing their essential shopping and heading home to drawn curtains, whirring fans and iced drinks in the garden. The holidaymakers, still just emerging from their full English breakfasts, all strappy tops, sun hats and sweat, were heading for Big Sava Express to stock up on tanning lotion and bottled water.

Kitty wondered fleetingly where Vinny was.

'Come on, slowcoach!' Angelica was waiting at the end of the track where a zig-zag stile led to the village green, the village pond and the village hall, none of which had belonged to the original village but had been added immediately post-war and, as in all rural locations, was still known as 'the new bit'.

Kitty clambered inelegantly over the stile.

Angelica, practically jogging on the spot, chuckled. 'I thought I'd lost you. I thought you'd chickened out and gone home.'

'Me? Chicken out? Of a glorious hour with Doreen?'

'Destiny,' Angelica said tersely.

'No one is ever christened Destiny. It's as unlikely as – um . . .' Kitty tailed off. Yes, she was going to say 'Nirvana' – and then was totally engulfed by the memories the word immediately conjured up. She swallowed. 'Well, it's just a daft name.'

Angelica peered at her. 'Are you OK? I know I've been teasing you, but you look so sad. You should tell me to mind my own business . . . oh, Kitty – what's the matter?'

'Nothing.' Kitty shook her head. Her scrunchie fell out. Her hair tumbled across her sticky face. Irritably, she pushed it away and her sunglasses slipped off. She sighed heavily and attempted to get everything back into place. It wasn't wholly successful. She sighed again. 'Please ignore me. You should know by now that I'm just an idiot who doesn't think before she speaks. I've upset someone I shouldn't have. That's all.'

'Ah.' Angelica did calf-stretches against the stile. 'Yes, sorry always is the hardest word, as Sir Elton frequently tells us. Which, as we all know, is nice in a song but a bit rubbish in real life. So, swallow your pride, go and say sorry – and all will be well . . . or not? Unless of course . . .' She stopped stretching. 'This isn't the secret-love chap that we heard all about at Netta and Noel's barbecue that you've upset, is it? Oh, Kitty – it is! Bugger!'

Despite everything, Kitty laughed. 'Well done, Miss Marple. Now, before I really do decide to do a runner – not literally, in this heat, obviously – let's get this wellness nonsense over, shall we?'

Chapter Sixteen

The village hall – dark and blissfully cool thanks to a battalion of whirring ceiling fans – clearly catered for every social, educational and recreational Firefly Common group and activity known to man.

Kitty lifted her sunglasses and blinked at the many, many posters and flyers on the walls. She'd never ventured into the village hall, and therefore had no idea any of these existed. Clearly no-one in Firefly Common ever needed to be bored.

Along with Wellness with Destiny, there was Slimming with Molly; Quilting with Brian; Pilates with Raj; Zumba with Steffi; Watercolours with Mary; Vegan Cookery with Larry; Crafting with Janet; Rock Choir with Sheelagh; Over 60s Keep Fit with Sue; Flower Arranging with Sunita. Not to mention Scouts and Guides and Brownies and Beavers and the WI and TWG and . . . the activities were endless.

Not, Kitty thought, as she glanced nervously at the circle of stacking chairs in the middle of the hall, that she'd be partaking of any of them, because a) she wasn't a natural 'joiner' and b) she really wouldn't be in Firefly Common for much longer.

The realisation hit her with a jolt. They'd still done nothing at all about finding alternative accommodation. And it'd soon be the end of July – there'd only be another month before Mavis Mulholland came home and reclaimed Sandcastle Cottage. The summer was racing away from them and by the autumn they'd be homeless. Again.

Just one more thing to worry about . . .

'There we are.' Angelica bounced up alongside her. 'I've signed you in as a guest for today. It's free, by the way. For guests. Shall we find a pew?'

Kitty looked over her shoulder. Apart from the elderly woman sitting at the card table in the doorway, where Angelica had obviously done the signing-in, there wasn't another soul in the hall.

'Is that Destiny?' Kitty whispered. 'Because, if it is, then her name is definitely Doreen and, unless she's a hundred and three, the wellness hasn't worked.'

'That's Mrs Plover.' Angelica chuckled. 'She's the keeper of the village hall. Rumour has it, she was appointed in 1947 when the hall was built, and she hasn't missed a function yet.'

Kitty nodded in approval. Someone with staying power. Impressive. She indicated the circle of chairs. 'Why are we the only ones here? Are you Destiny's only customer?'

'Honestly? I fudged the time a bit to make sure we got here. I thought you'd make all sorts of objections. I wasn't expecting compliance, obviously. So I factored in some stubborn time so that I could explain gently why I thought this, today, would be a good idea.'

'Nice thinking, and kind of you – but not needed. If I hadn't wanted to be here, I would have refused to budge out of the cottage this morning. I may be a bit down, but I am still able to make my own decisions.'

Kitty snorted to herself. What absolute tosh that was! Since the Vinny debacle, she'd hardly been able to decide on anything at all. She was here because – well, because today was her day off and she was just fed up with hiding away in the garden, gorgeous though it was, and moping. And because something in all this wellbeing nonsense might just lift her gloom and boost her flagging confidence. Maybe.

Having expected Destiny to have addressed her followers from some sort of podium, with seats in rows in front, Kitty looked more closely at the circle of chairs in the middle of the village hall. And then peered even more closely.

'Oh my god!' Kitty grabbed Angelica's arm and pointed at the floor in the centre of the circle. 'There's a *pentagram*! Is this some of – well – cult thing?'

'What?' Angelica frowned at her. 'No, of course not. It's just a star, isn't it?'

'Nooo – it's a pentagram – a symbol – not a star.' Kitty continued. 'Pentagrams have meanings – OK, yes, some are good, but some are far from it – but why on earth would someone who spouts about positive lifestyle changes and wellbeing want to have a *pentagram*?'

'I still have no idea why. It's no big deal, surely, it's just a thing for decoration, isn't it? Have you got some sort of pentagram phobia? Like spiders or – goodness . . . are you OK, sweetie? You've gone quite pale.'

'If you'd had the sort of upbringing I've had, you'd go pale too,' Kitty said. 'My parents have always embraced the odd and the weird and the plain barking . . . no, no jokes – I was, and always will be, a massive disappointment to them – and pentagrams featured hugely in their leisure-time activities.'

'Mother of god, Kitty! Were you raised by Satanists?'

'Nooo . . .' Kitty managed to giggle. 'However, they were devotees of Denis Wheatley and all that sailed in him so to speak. They mainlined all the old films of his books – there were always pentangles – and devils and a lot of screaming and—'

'Your parents made you sit through *that stuff*?' Angelica was horrified. 'What on earth was wrong with *Mary Poppins* and *Bambi* – oh, well, no, possibly not *Bambi* – that traumatised me . . . but horror films? For a child?'

'Oh, they didn't know I saw them. They watched them after I'd gone to bed, but our house was quite small. The noise used to wake me up and I'd sneak down and see what all the screaming was about . . . My childhood nightmares were really the stuff of nightmares. So,' – she shrugged – 'pentagrams have never been a good thing in my little world. And that one,' – she indicated the centre of the circle of chairs with her head – 'is bringing back all sorts of things I hoped I'd forgotten.'

Angelica hugged her. 'Oh, Kitty – you poor love . . . look, let me reassure you that this pentagram is definitely not intended for anything unpleasant. Quite the opposite, in fact. Destiny uses the star – um – pentagram as a symbol of good, a tool simply to illustrate her five points of positivity and happiness. You'll see later – and in all the Wednesdays I've been here, I've never once seen her conjure up Lucifer or any of his minions – promise. Although, come to think of it, there's a woman who lives in Stratton St Lacey who very well might . . . no, no, I'm just being bitchy.'

'You? Surely not?' Kitty chuckled. But she still felt shaky and her heart rate was only just subsiding. She hadn't thought about the pentagrams or the horror films or her parents' odd lifestyle choices for ages. Funny how one small trigger could bring all the memories – good and bad – flooding back. Maybe she needed some sort of therapy, after all . . . perhaps Destiny was the answer to her prayers?

'If you're feeling OK now, let's find somewhere to sit, shall we?' Angelica said. 'I think I can hear the hordes arriving – yes, we can sit anywhere. The seating circle is Destiny's idea of democracy. She says rows of chairs mean the shy ones hide at the back and the pushy confident ones are at the front – this way, everyone is equal.'

'Blimey,' Kitty muttered as they sat down. 'Egalitarianism is alive and well in Firefly Common. Who'd have thought it?'

Avoiding looking at the pentagram, instead she craned her neck and looked at Angelica's aforementioned 'hordes'. There were probably less than two dozen of them, all women, all much of an age, and all dressed in leisure wear of some sort, as they queued to sign in with Mrs Plover.

Angelica waved at them. They waved back and found seats. Kitty recognised several of them as customers from the Silver Fish Bar. She smiled at them, and they beamed back. It was all very chummy and cosy and not at all scary. Kitty began to relax.

Then, to a fanfare of 'Simply the Best' from some hidden speaker, Destiny arrived.

Kitty blinked at the apparition who strode into the centre of the circle. Nothing, but nothing, could have prepared her for Destiny.

'Are you giggling?' Angelica hissed, jabbing her sharply with an elbow. 'You are! Shush . . .'

Kitty giggled more quietly and hiccupped a bit.

Destiny stood – legs astride in the old Theresa May power stance – lifted her arms and clapped along to the beat. The hordes clapped too. Another jab from Angelica reminded Kitty that she was supposed to be joining in.

Kitty clapped.

Destiny was a big girl. She was wearing a black leotard with a waspie waist-cincher corset, and fishnet tights with Blood Rose High Tops. Her hair was very black and very long and very clearly not actually all hers; ditto her tarantula eyelashes and her massively pouty lips. She was ageless and looked a bit like she'd escaped from RuPaul's Drag Race meets Madame Cyn, on the way to Ann Summers.

It cheered Kitty up enormously.

The music stopped and so did the clapping.

'Hiya, ladies!' Destiny waved.

'Hiya, Destiny!' The hordes waved back.

Any thoughts Kitty may have had that this session was going to be an hour of whale music and humming, had already gone straight out of the window.

Tina Turner was resurrected. The noise level was incredible.

'Stamp those feet!' Destiny yelled.

Everyone stamped. It was quite bizarre, Kitty felt, to be exercising this energetically sitting down.

'Now, hands in the air and clap!'

They all did.

'Let's get the blood flowing! Heads down and up again! Quickly! That's it! And clap! And stamp!'

Everyone was upping and downing and stamping and clapping like billy-o. Kitty, feeling pretty dizzy, realised why Angelica had insisted she wore some sort of sportswear. This was hard work.

'Okaaaay.' Destiny silenced Tina Turner and tossed back her mane of someone else's hair. 'Fabulous, ladies! Fabulous! Now, relax back into your chairs. Push hard into your chairs, ladies. That's perfect. Now, feel your body's happiness. Feel the tingle. Feel the energy flow.'

Kitty puffed out her cheeks. To her surprise, she felt slightly numb and quite out of breath. Almost as if she'd just completed a proper gym workout. She wasn't sure she could feel very much at all. However, this was far more amusing than she'd imagined. She couldn't wait to tell Jemini and Apollo when she got home.

'And relaaaaax.' Destiny smiled round the circle. 'A lovely warm-up into the zone this morning, ladies. Lovely. Well done. Your bodies are now free of all that nasty tension and inhibition – so, what do we have to do to achieve total happiness?'

'Free our minds!' The cry was unanimous.

Kitty blinked. She still felt warm and more relaxed and slightly heavy-limbed – a bit like she did after a long swim. But surely the mind-freeing part was going to be trickier? Presumably an ear-shattering belt of Tina Turner wasn't going to be any use in relaxing the mass of cerebrums and cerebellums in Firefly Common, was it?

No, it clearly wasn't.

Tina had been replaced by wavering Mongolian nose flutes.

Destiny, standing on one sturdy leg like Ian Anderson of Jethro Tull – another of Kitty's parents' dubious tastes, musical this time – had already done the hands-thumbs-fingers thing and was humming.

Everyone was humming.

Kitty chuckled to herself: she'd just *known* there'd be almost-whale music and humming. Alongside her, Angelica had her eyes closed, her elbows in, her hands uplifted and her thumbs and index fingers touching. And she was humming.

110

On the basis that if you can't beat them, do the other thing, Kitty joined in. It was fun. Silly but fun. And she realised that it was actually quite difficult to concentrate on anything else while you were doing it. Was she actually in the midst of mass-meditation? Was Destiny sneakily going to send subliminal messages about not eating chips and doughnuts and shovelling down a family-sized Ben and Jerry's while binge-watching *Real Housewives of Wherever*, and drinking lots of prosecco, ever again? Is that how it had worked with Angelica?

'And ladies,' Destiny's voice purred through the nose flutes, 'relaaaax.'

The nose-flute notes fluttered away. Destiny was now orches-trated only by the rhythmic whirl of the overhead fans. She smiled round the circle. She even had very large teeth, Kitty noticed. They probably weren't all hers either.

'Wonderful effort, ladies, thank you.' Destiny had a sexy growly gravelly voice. 'Now, shall we take our virtual walk through the five points of the pentagram? Shout out with joy to each element! Feel them all around you, becoming part of you, charting your course through life! All together now . . .'

As Destiny strode from one point to the next, pausing dramati-cally each time, the hordes – including Angelica – all chorused 'Space! Air! Fire! Water! Earth!'

Kitty thought it might be getting just a bit too cultish – however, as this particular pentagram didn't seem about to be used for any-thing that would cause a screaming Beelzebub atop a red-eyed, fire-breathing horse to gallop past Mrs Plover and into the village hall, she began to really relax.

'Lovely!' Destiny beamed at them. 'Now, are we all feeling refreshed and renewed and in touch with our inner-being?'

The hordes apparently were.

'Now – before we have a cosy chat – a little reminder about looking after our bodies. What do we have to do each day, ladies?'

'Eat the rainbow!' The hordes chanted. 'Eat the rainbow!'

Kitty pulled a face. That was hardly ground-breaking, was it?

In fact, that was lifted from every healthy-eating regime known to man, woman or child. She gave a snuffle of contempt.

Angelica heard the snuffle, stared at her and administered another elbow jab.

'Ow!'

'Shush!'

Destiny appeared not to have noticed, and clapped her hands. 'Eat the rainbow! Good! Well done, everyone! Now – is there anyone who'd like to start the discussion off today?'

Silence.

Kitty stared at the floor, praying that Destiny wouldn't single her out as the New Girl and ask her to stand up and confess her peccadillos to a room of comparative strangers. 'Audience' and 'participation', were, as far as she was concerned, two of the most heinous words in the entire English language.

'Don't tell me we've all beaten our inner demons? Don't tell me we've all adjusted our lives to forever shun the things that were negative to the mind and harmful to the body? What are we going to do on Wednesdays in the future, ladies? You'll have no need for me . . .'

The hordes roared that they'd always have need for Destiny. Several ladies then took it in turns to stand up and admit to slipping back into 'the old ways' – only a little bit, you understand, not full on – without being too specific, which, Kitty reckoned, was a bit of a cheat. It was always amusing to discover that one woman's sinfulness was another's good night out.

'Ah, yes,' Destiny purred, 'but as we always say, life's for living, moderation in all things, ladies. Nothing is banned or barred. Simply listen to your body and know your limits. Nothing to worry about there. Well done.'

So far, so predictable, Kitty thought. But Angelica, who had surely been on the way to rehab when they first met, was now still able to enjoy the occasional drink, and seemed to embrace the whole mind-and-body wellness thing if her new-found exercise programme was anything to go by. Maybe Destiny had found the holy grail of the wellness world and truly discovered a way to channel into the inner psyche, and right wrongs.

Maybe . . .

Kitty looked round the circle of faces. They all looked relaxed and happy. She hadn't felt relaxed and happy since her faux pas on the beach.

She stood up.

Angelica gasped.

Destiny smiled. Her big, white teeth twinkled. 'Hiya – you must be Kitty.'

Kitty blinked. Was the woman clairvoyant as well?

'Not a trick.' Destiny chuckled. 'I looked at Mrs Plover's book on the way in and saw you were the lovely Angelica's guest. I hope you have enjoyed the session so far?'

Kitty mumbled that she had, thank you, and then wished to god she could just sit down. Why the hell had she stood up in the first place? This was so unlike her, for pity's sake . . . even at school, as one of Miss B's Girls with Jemini and the rest, she'd never ever volunteered to make the first move, the first comment.

'Good.' Destiny nodded her approval. 'So, was there a reason you came here today? Did Angelica twist your arm? Did you think a wellness session might help in some way? Or were you merely curious?'

'Yes, no, yes and sort of,' Kitty said, aware that every pair of eyes in the circle was fixed firmly on her. She took a deep breath. 'I want to know if there's any way I can stop making monumental mistakes in my life before I get too old to care. I want to know if there's some sort of positivity programme that will make me say the right things, do the right things, and make the right decisions. I seem to lurch from one blunder to the next. The bits of my life in between the gaffes are lovely – but I want to know what I can do about the rest.'

The hordes cheered.

Kitty sat down with a clatter. Angelica patted her.

Destiny pouted, but not aggressively. 'Oh, my love . . . if I had the answer to that one, I'd be making a fortune and be miles away from Firefly Common – preferably in a hammock on a Barbados beach, swigging piña coladas from coconut shells and being massaged by a phalanx of gorgeous young men with ripped bodies.'

The hordes roared with laughter.

Destiny held up her hands. 'Actually, Kitty – what you've described is life. Just that. There are good bits and bad bits and lots of OK bits in between. You are no different to the rest of us – I promise you. We all make massive bloopers . . . we all make the wrong choices . . . but the trick is – well, it's not a trick, really – to recognise this and accept it and move on and enjoy the positive parts. Does that make sense?'

'Yes, but . . .' Kitty sighed. 'I seem to get overwhelmed by the rubbish parts.'

'Oh, don't we all, my love – or at least, we used to, didn't we ladies?'

The hordes nodded.

'And this, Kitty, is where the wellness theory comes into its own.' Destiny's large lips peeled back to flash the sparkling teeth again. 'The routine we've been through this morning – the exercises, the relaxation, the mindfulness, the positivity – all works to combat the negativity we all carry around with us. You may continue to come to my meetings – I hope you will, but if you don't, then try to do those routines we did at the start of the session, every day. Yes . . . Angelica?'

Angelica was on her feet. 'Kitty is my neighbour and my friend, she's kind and generous and funny and hard-working and cares about other people a lot. I think she may have made big mistakes in past life choices, and I know she's unhappy about more recent – um – errors, but you, Destiny, have worked wonders for me. I want you to do the same for Kitty.'

She sat down again. Everyone clapped. Kitty glared at Angelica, and blushed and groaned and wished she was anywhere other than the village hall.

Destiny nodded. The coal-black tumble of someone else's hair took on a life of its own. 'OK then. Kitty, what I will say is stock

114

up with my wellness and positivity theories. Get rid of the negatives – let go of that which you can't control. Eat the rainbow. Make the exercises part of your routine and . . .'

'But not while you're serving our cod and chips!' One of the Silver Fish Bar's regulars shouted.

The hordes sniggered.

Destiny clapped her hands. 'Ladies! Please! Kitty – to continue . . . yes, concentrate on your inner body and inner mind in the way I've demonstrated today, bring them to prime positivity and, if you think you've made a mistake, then – and this is the big step forward – have the courage to face it head on, be brave and do what's right to correct it. Nothing ventured – nothing gained. Just. Do. It. How does that sound?'

'Lovely, thank you,' Kitty said.

'Lovely?' Angelica hissed. 'Destiny has just given you the best-ever lifestyle advice to sort out whatever is wrong with your non-existent love-life and you make it sound as if she's dished up your favourite pudding.'

'My bad,' Kitty muttered, chuckling to herself.

Destiny seemed unfazed. 'Now – ladies – how are we all doing with the Steps to Happiness puzzle I set you last week? Any problems . . . ? OK – let's take them one at a time . . . Nadia, you go first . . . yes, put your hands down, ladies – I'll get to you all . . . Nadia, off we go . . .'

The hordes, it appeared, had not found the Steps to Happiness puzzle a cakewalk.

Ten minutes later, having said goodbye and thank you to Destiny – who was actually apparently called Denise according to one of the Silver Fish Bar regulars, so Kitty felt she'd at least been proved right there – and smiled a farewell at Mrs Plover, and avoided most of the hordes who were still puzzling over the Steps to Happiness, Kitty and Angelica stood outside the village hall.

The sun scorched and spiralled through the pine trees, and somewhere in the distance was the evocative seaside sound of crying gulls and shushing waves.

'We usually all head down for a chat about the meeting, and manage to include some lunch and an iced spritzer at the Mermaid after Destiny's sessions,' Angelica said. 'So, how does that sound?'

'Pretty good.' Kitty grinned. 'And thanks a million for today, I thought I'd hate it – but I didn't. I really enjoyed it – and thank you for saying all those nice things.'

'It's the truth, and I hope you've found something that'll help you feel more – well – zippy . . .'

'I can assure you, I've never felt zippier in my life.'

'Wonderful – then shall we take a gentle stroll to the Mermaid?'

Kitty shook her head. 'It sounds great – but no, I won't be joining you.'

'Oh? You don't have to get back for anything, do you?'

'No.'

'So . . . ?'

Kitty smiled. 'I'm bursting with Destiny's wellness and positivity mantras. I know what I have to do – I'm going to grab the bull by the horns, so to speak, before the get-up-and-go has got-up-and-gone. I'm off to the beach to put right wrongs.'

Chapter Seventeen

In fact, well into the following week, and despite her recent oh-so-casual routine of an early morning swim and a late-night beach walk with the dogs, Kitty had still not seen Vinny.

Nothing ventured, nothing gained, as Destiny had said, and Vinny had disappeared before and come back – so, with her new-found positivity, Kitty still hadn't given up hope of meeting up with him and apologising. As for anything after that, well . . . she wasn't even going to think that far ahead – even her burgeoning positivity knew its limits.

Now, on a hot late-July evening, as Alexa softly played the Beatles on a loop, Kitty, Jemini, Connor and Apollo were sitting round the big wooden table under the trees, enjoying a supper of one of Apollo's famed Cypriot mezzes in the garden of Sandcastle Cottage.

As the temperature was still in the high twenties, they'd all opted for shorts and vests and bare feet. It was a very relaxed party.

Citronella candles flickered, keeping the wasps and mosquitos at bay, and Kitty thought it was all very *Darling Buds of May* as they drank frosty-cold Keo and helped themselves from the enormous platters of meatballs, feta, dolmades, sardines, grilled halloumi, olives, salads and dips, and a mountain of warm pitta bread with butter pats on ice.

Kitty reckoned Destiny would be delighted – they were definitely eating the rainbow tonight.

Teddy, in her second-best Peppa Pig swimsuit and with a pitta bread in one hand and a sardine in the other, was tearing round the garden, jumping in and out of the paddling pool and dashing beneath the diamond droplets of the rotating lawn-sprinkler, squealing with delight. Honey and Zorro, not squealing but Staffie-smiling, raced around after her, splashing miniature tidal waves from the pool and slipping and sliding under the sprinkler.

Kitty, forking up Greek salad and tzatziki into her pitta, watched them with something akin to happiness.

'So, are you going back to this Destiny, again, Kitty?' Apollo leaned across the table to spoon up some more hummus and add another dollop of skordalia to his plate. 'You said you liked her, no?'

'Yes, she wasn't at all what I expected – I doubt that Destiny would be anything like anyone would expect, to be honest. Still, despite being very sceptical, I did like her methods, even if they were a mixture of the outrageous and the blatantly nicked, and she did give me some good and much-needed advice . . . but, no – I won't be going back again.'

'Really?'

'You know me. I'm not a natural joiner. I'm happy in little bubbles of friends but I really don't enjoy big gatherings or organised group things. And I did only agree to go once because . . . well, because Angelica kept nagging me, and because it had made such a difference to her – Angelica, I mean – I thought it might help the way I was feeling.'

'Which it did?'

'It did. I think – no, it *did*. Definitely. There, see, the power of positivity!' Kitty laughed. 'Anyway, we'll have to wait and see if Destiny's methods come to fruition if I ever – well – you know.'

Apollo nodded. 'I know, Kitty. I know. Without you telling me much, I know. I've been there, as they say – having a hopeless lost love – I hope it's not the same for you.'

'So do I.'

They smiled at one another with a deep understanding.

'Anyway, changing the subject – although not really lifting the mood – sorry.' Kitty heaped another slice of flaky spanakopita onto her plate and looked across the table. 'While we're all together, what on earth are we going to do in September? It's not too far away now – and we know Mavis Mulholland will be back then and we'll have to leave here. Connor – are you still keeping an eye out for anything else that might be suitable?'

Connor nodded. His quiff, melting in the heat, flopped across his forehead. He pushed it back. 'All the time. Jem and I always check and re-check everything already on the books and anything that comes in to the office. There's nothing like Sandcastle Cottage at all – which we all knew was probably going to be the case. And the prices round here for private rentals are sky-high anyway.'

'Right,' – Kitty nodded – 'but you, being the son and heir to the Kingdom of Rentals, would have good insider knowledge, wouldn't you?'

'It certainly gives me an edge. I'd make damn sure we got first dibs at anything at all likely that came in – it would never see the walls of the Lovell and Lowe offices or appear on any mailing lists, I can assure you. But seriously, Kitty – it's not looking likely that we'll ever find anything like this.'

'We', Kitty noticed. Connor included himself in their little family. A nice touch.

'No, I know. Sandcastle Cottage is something very special.'

Teddy, flanked by Honey and Zorro, appeared at the table then, dripped over everyone's feet, helped herself to three chunks of halloumi, and scampered away, with the dogs in hot pursuit. With an almighty splash, all three sloshed untidily into the paddling pool, sat down in the resulting ebb and flow, and shared the cheese.

'Ah, bless them. This is paradise for them, isn't it? The dogs are so happy – and Teddy is so lucky.' Apollo chuckled. 'To be so young and free of worries. Those were the great years, no?'

'I can't remember that far back,' said Kitty, who actually could and preferred not to. 'But seriously, we have to think about Sandcastle . . . we've been pretty cavalier about having to leave here, haven't we? We got the stay of execution, and just thought – again – something would turn up – and now the time is disappearing and—'

'Bloody hell, Kit!' Jemini frowned. 'If you'd paid Destiny for the Positivity Plus thingy you'd have to ask for your money back. Where's your glass-half-full attitude? You were always the one we all relied on. You always knew what to do, and how to do it. Who's stolen the old Kitty?'

Kitty laughed. 'I think I was a reasonably sensible grown-up back then, and actually believed that life was what you made it, and that if you worked hard enough and thought things through, things came right – and that people were mostly basically honest and trustworthy, and that bad things didn't happen to good people and – well – we all know what happened to that little bit of ideology, don't we? Sadly, I think I'm more of the glass-half-empty frame of mind now.'

'Well, don't be,' Jemini said. 'It doesn't suit you. I love you being funny and silly and a bit ditzy – but I also like to know that when my life goes tits up, I can rely on you to know exactly what to do.'

'No pressure, then.' Kitty grinned.

'When we have to leave here – if we haven't found somewhere we can all live – we'd have to split up, wouldn't we?' Apollo looked anxiously over the rim of his Keo glass. 'And would we find anywhere that would let us have the dogs, anyway?'

'Goodness knows.' Kitty shook her head. 'I definitely think we'd have to face up to leaving Firefly Common and the south coast altogether, because it's so expensive. Our part-time jobs would never cover the rent of anything else round here, would they? So, yes, we'd probably have to split up.'

It was an awful prospect. They looked sadly at one another. The Beatles were rather dolefully singing 'Nowhere Man' in the ensuing silence.

The silence was broken by Connor's mobile ringing.

'Sorry – might be work . . .' He looked at the screen. 'Ah – it's Mum . . . might be work . . .'

120

As Connor excused himself and wandered off towards the paddling pool to talk to his mother, Kitty and Jemini exchanged 'Dire Deidre' looks across the table and tried not to giggle.

'Right.' Connor sat back down again, pushed his quiff away from his eyes and smiled at Jemini. 'I think this may be the biggest olive branch to be offered in the history of olive branches. My parents are hosting the annual Lovell and Lowe summer lunch party next week. It's a big deal business-wise. I mean it's either them or the Lovells hosting, obviously, and this year it's our turn. They close all the offices and invite all the movers and shakers of the house-selling and rental world – do we still have movers and shakers in the twenty-first century, by the way? – to join them. It's a sort of networking, schmoozing sort of event and—'

'Ooh goody,' Jemini said happily. 'A day off.'

'Not exactly. They've invited you, too. They want you to be there.'

Jemini erupted with laughter. 'After the state your mother last saw me in, she'll only want me there as the stripper for the half-time entertainment!'

'She – no, actually, both of them want you there as my partner. And not as in business.'

Kitty and Apollo watched on with some amusement and not a little interest.

'Sounds like a perfect opportunity to suss out what other properties there are for rent round here,' Kitty said. 'You never know – someone might know something – and if it's a schmoozing do, no one will object if you ask questions, will they?'

Jemini shook her head. 'I guess not and I'll do my best, promise. But blimey, Connor! An invitation to Lowe Abbey at last!'

'It's not an abbey. I keep telling you that. It's just a normal detached house.'

'I know. I googled it when we first met – and don't look at me like that.'

'Were you checking me out?'

'Yeah, sort of.' Jemini giggled. 'Nah – I just fancied you and

121

wanted to know if you were married. It was kind of reassuring to find you were young, free and single and lived in the luxury of Lowe Abbey with your parents.'

Connor laughed and shook his head.

'Anyway,' Jemini continued, 'actually, I'm very touched that they've offered the olive branch. I'd love to go, and I promise I won't embarrass you or your parents. I think it's very kind of them to include me. When is it?'

'Next Thursday.'

'My day off, anyway, which is handy and – oh, bugger!'

They all looked at her.

Teddy, Honey and Zorro, sensing drama, stopped splashing. The Beatles simply ignored the silence and wafted 'In My Life' dreamily through the summer evening.

'What?' Connor frowned.

'Thursday. I can't do Thursday! It's my day to be a minder.' Jemini sighed. 'You know. At the nursery. Ruby's.'

'Well, cancel it, then. Change it to another day. Swap with someone. It must be easy enough to get one of the other mums to step in and—'

'No,' Jemini interrupted. 'It's not easy at all. It's not minding at the nursery. It's a trip out. Coach journey thingy. They take the kids on various jollies every so often, and there aren't enough staff or available parents to keep an individual eye on the little – um – angels, so the parents take it in turns to be a minder. Each adult has two children to – well – mind.'

'So?' Connor said. 'I really don't see the problem, Jem. Same thing applies – get one of the other mums to swap and—'

'My word, you so don't know the viciousness of the mums-world hierarchy, do you?' Jemini grinned. 'It's all been written in stone since the beginning of the year. Most of the mums work full-time, hence the nursery, and we all got together and sorted out a rota ages ago. I can assure you that only death would excuse you from doing your minding duty. I'm really sorry. I'll have to make my apologies to your parents and they'll hate me for ever-more, I know.'

'I could do it,' Kitty said quickly, aware of a potential relation-ship thunderstorm brewing. 'I'm off on Thursday, and I've been DBS checked and cleared as someone who is authorised to collect Teddy from nursery when you're at work, and—'

'Kitty Appleby, I love you!' Jemini scrambled round the table and gave Kitty a massive hug. 'You're an angel! Are you absolutely sure?'

'Yes. Well, as long as the nursery say it's OK, and I don't see why they shouldn't. Who – um – is Teddy being paired with? Do you know? Is it some mini-thug that I need to be aware of?'

'It's Teddy's best friend, Imogen. She's very sweet – not an ounce of thuggery in her. Oh – you're a lifesaver, Kit. I owe you one big time.'

'Too right you do.' Kitty chuckled. 'You can stand in for me on a Friday when everyone and their dog wants a fish supper.'

Honey and Zorro, hearing the words 'dog' and 'supper', scram-bled clumsily out of the paddling pool and trundled, tongues lolling, across the lawn, followed by a soggy Teddy.

'I'm not sure I love you *that* much.' Jemini pulled a face and scrolled through her phone to find Ruby's number. 'I've seen the sort of ruffians you get in the chippy – they're scary.'

'Only if we don't have skate wings.'

'That's OK, then. Oh, Teds – you're very wet. Connor, wrap that towel round her, ta . . . oh, hi, Ruby . . . about next Thursday . . .'

The dogs muscled their way in between Kitty and Apollo.

Apollo pushed a plate towards Kitty. 'Here, give them some more halloumi. They love it and it makes their coats shine.'

'Does it?' Kitty sliced off chunks of cheese and posted them into two excitedly gaping Staffie mouths.

'No idea – but my mamma always said so. Like carrots make you see in the dark and bread crusts make your hair curly. Uni-versal mamma-talk. Your mamma did the same, no?'

'Not really . . . She wasn't much into that sort of thing.'

Apollo looked at her with sympathy as he stood up. 'I know you've not had a proper happy life. You deserve to be happy, Kitty. I can't change your past, and I doubt I can wave a magic wand over your future – but I can go and get the dessert.'

'I've been OK – but yes, ta, that'll do nicely for now.' Kitty smiled at him. 'You know me so well.'

'There. All sorted.' Jemini put her phone down and snuggled up to Connor on one side and a much-drier Teddy on the other. 'No probs at all, Kit. Thursday, eleven o'clock kick-off at the nursery – Ruby will have the indemnity forms and all that ready for you. Oh, and everyone has to have a packed lunch. I'll do yours when I do Teddy's.'

'I'll do the lunch boxes,' said Kitty. 'I know you hate getting up early – I'll see to it all, and you can have a bit of a lie-in and then spend time making yourself even more gorgeous for your appearance at Lowe Abbey.'

'It's not an—' Connor started.

They both gave him 'a look'.

'You're even more of a star,' Jemini said to Kitty. 'Oh, there are rules about no chocolate or oranges or peaches or messy fruits, or anything with nuts in, for the lunch boxes, oh, and no fizzy drinks – just plain bottled water, otherwise I think you're OK.'

'Boring – but understandable.' Kitty smiled. 'Actually, I'm looking forward to it. I've always loved a coach outing. Where are we going?'

'No idea. They never tell the kids until they get there. It's always local-ish on these little jaunts, though. Mind you, they've had whole-day trips to the adventure maze at Highcliffe Castle, they've done Marwell Zoo and,' – Jemini dropped her voice to a whisper – 'Peppa Pig World.'

'I bet that one was a winner.' Kitty grinned. 'Oooh, is that where we're going on Thursday? I think I should be forewarned in case Teddy has an excitement-overload meltdown. Not to mention me, of course.'

'Sorry, your luck's out. Thursday's trip is only a few hours or so in the middle of the day – not an all-dayer. Oooh – wow, Apollo, that looks amazing! I don't know if I've got room for pudding . . . but heck, I'll give it a go.'

'I'm sure you will, Jemini. You manage to eat much and stay so slim, always. You should sell your secret to Angelica's Destiny.' Apollo laughed as he put the massive platter of mixed baklava, and warm figs, accompanied by honey and yoghurt, on the table.

'Yeah, we always hated her for that at school.' Kitty chuckled, filling a bowl with figs and honey. 'She assured us then it was simply good genes and a fast metabolism. Of course, in later life, the fact that she taught keep-fit pole dancing helped a lot, too.'

Connor winced. 'And we can keep that little gem quiet next Thursday, can't we, Jem? I mean, I'm all for it, of course, but Mum might not quite see it the same way . . .'

'Dear heavens and all the little gods, Connor,' – Jemini hugged him – 'stop worrying. That piece of my past will stay between us and my spectacularly toned abs and thighs. As will all my other sordid secrets. I promise not to upset your parents, or jeopardise your inheritance, in any way at all.'

'I don't care about my bloody inheritance!'

'Oooh, you're so easy to wind up!' Jemini chuckled, reaching for the baklava and adding figs and yoghurt in a bowl for Teddy. 'I know that. If you were, we wouldn't be together. Figs or baklava or both, for you?'

Kitty's phone signalled a text. So did Jemini's.

'Someone trying to sell something? Someone who knows us both? A marketing hit aimed at our demographic?' Jemini shrugged. 'Shall we look now or leave it until later?'

'Look now, because otherwise we'll only wonder and then eat pudding too quickly and get indigestion,' Kitty said, putting down bowls of yoghurt for the dogs, and then picking up her phone. 'Oh . . . it's . . .'

'Amy!' Also looking down at her phone, Jemini finished the sentence.

They stared at one another. Then at Apollo and Connor, who of course had heard a great deal about Amy and Miss B's Girls. Then everyone simply raised their eyebrows; the dogs carried on slurping up yoghurt; the Beatles happily warbled 'Yellow Submarine'; and Teddy banged her spoon to the back beat.

'One of you read it out then,' Connor said, his suspended spoon dripping fig juice. 'It might be exciting.'

'It'll be a deadly boring message about meeting up,' Kitty said. 'Jem and I thought recently that we hadn't had one of Amy's three-line-whip messages for a while. OK, here goes . . .'

'Hello girls!'

'Girls!' Kitty snorted. 'We're all marching swiftly towards forty! Amy probably still goes to school in plaits, and still reads Angela Brazil by torchlight under the duvet.'

'Amy is still at school?' Apollo frowned.

'She's a teacher.' Kitty chuckled. 'Head of English. Posh girls' school.'

'And Angela Brazil is an author of school stories. They're quite ancient,' Jemini explained. 'Amy has always been a fan. Right – crack on, Kit . . .'

'I hope you're all well and happy. For some reason we seem to have been very quiet since we last met. We've clearly all been extremely busy, meaning very little has been posted on our online groups . . . and so I've decided it's time for another real-life Miss B's Girls' catch-up.'

'As we suspected,' Kitty said. 'And some of us,' – she looked meaningfully at Jemini – 'have been busier than others.'

Jemini snuggled even closer to Connor. 'I have no idea what you can possibly mean. Just get on with Amy's address to the nation.'

'Now this next part may come as a surprise because you all know that I am a stickler for tradition, but I'm going off-piste (this is a joke!) here . . .'

126

'Someone's stolen Amy!' Kitty laughed. 'She's made a joke – well – sort of.'

'Kit – just get on with it!'

'And am going to suggest that we meet up again at Firefly Common.'

'Holy crap on a cracker!' Jemini's eyes were like saucers. 'Seriously? Or is that another joke?'

'No joke,' Kitty said. 'And not funny at all.'

'She doesn't know we live here now, does she?'

'No, and I've no intention of telling her.'

'So, she thinks you're still in Reading with James and being corporate in his dad's business – which wasn't even true last time, was it?'

'And that you're being a good Asian wife somewhere in the posh bit of the Midlands.'

Jemini nodded. 'Knowing nothing of you working and living in a kebab shop in the less-salubrious part of Reading – or me, a single mum, in a bedsit, working supermarket shifts.'

'And teaching pole dancing.'

'For exercise.'

'Oh, yes, of course . . .'

'And now we're both here – living in the very place she introduced us to.'

'And she isn't going to know that, either. We don't want to have to invite her back here for tea or anything, do we?'

'God, no.'

'We all managed to get there easily last time, didn't we? Miss B is in her final resting place there which makes it even more apposite, and I know we all thought what a pretty little spot she'd chosen to live out her autumnal years. However, as it was November, we clearly didn't see Firefly Common at its best, so therefore, if you're all in agreement, I'd like to suggest we meet again on Sunday August 30th, at midday, for lunch in that lovely little sea-view pub we went to after the memorial service.'

127

'Bloody hell!' Kitty sighed. 'She wants to meet at the Mermaid – again.'

Jemini shrugged. 'I guess she would. There's nowhere else really, is there? And she knows that we all know how to find it. Apollo – are you working that day? You can serve us lunch!'

'That'll make a change for the poor bloke.' Connor laughed. 'He waits on you two all the time as it is.'

'He does not! Well, yes, maybe . . .'

Apollo flicked quickly through his phone.

'I'm not working on the Sunday shift, no. It's August Bank Holiday, so they have asked me to do all day on the Monday instead. Pity – it would have been fun to meet your Miss B's Girls.'

'Believe me it'll be anything but fun,' Kitty said darkly. 'Thank your lucky stars you're well out of it. And Bank Holiday coming up already . . . the end of August – we'll be almost homeless by then. Time's going too quickly.'

'Depressing.' Jemini sighed. 'Homelessness *and* Amy to look forward to.'

'I hope this will be acceptable to you all, please let me know by return, and once I have the numbers I will make the necessary arrangements at Firefly Common. I'm sure we can't wait to see one another again and no doubt we all have lots of lovely and exciting news to impart – I know I have! With best regards, Amy.'

'Wow!' Jemini laughed. 'She's found a man? She's married and pregnant?'

Kitty shook her head. 'Nah. Amy wasn't interested in men – or women. Only school and dead writers. My guess is that she's been promoted.'

'Or eaten her Neon Tetras.'

Both Connor and Apollo looked confused.

'Amy keeps tropical fish,' Kitty said. 'She told us all about her new – um – shoal of Neon Tetras last time . . . She loved them.'

'OK, not fish. Headhunted then? Moving on to pastures new?

Oooh, maybe it's somewhere really famous like Roedean or Cheltenham Ladies'?'

'No doubt we'll hear all about it. Many, many times. So – are we up for it?'

'Yeah, why not?' Jemini laughed. 'It'll be great to see the girls again – even Amy.'

'So, are you replying or shall I?'

'We'll both have to text her back, won't we? Or she'll know we're together.'

'Blimey, yes. Good thinking.' Kitty nodded. 'You're clearly way ahead of me in this keeping-secrets game.'

Jemini looked across at Connor and winked. 'Yep, I think maybe I am.'

Chapter Eighteen

The wheels on the bus were certainly going round and round. Ad infinitum it seemed to Kitty. Because once they were all aboard the coach, and settled, and tiny backpacks had been stowed safely in the overhead lockers, and everyone had been head-counted and instructed in triplicate, Ruby's Nursery Magical Mystery Tour was underway – and everyone started singing.

They chugged along Firefly Common's High Street, singing and waving wildly at Angelica and Mr H and Netta and Noel and a dozen other familiar faces. Kitty, sitting across the aisle from her two miniature charges, checking every few seconds that they were still strapped in, sang along with gusto and began to think this may not be the worst day she'd ever spent.

The song had taken quite a long time. It seemed vitally important in the democratic toddler scheme of things to include a verse for every child, every parent, every minder, and the bus driver.

Then suddenly 'The Wheels on the Bus' had been taken over by 'Bouncing Along on a Little Red/Blue/Yellow/Every-Colour-of-the-Rainbow-and-Then-Some Tractor' and 'Bringing in the Apples, Pears, Strawberries, Mangoes . . .' Kitty was amazed how many colours there were and how many fruits the kiddies seemed to know. Clearly they were being well-reared and getting way more than their five a day.

Imogen, Kitty's co-charge for the day, was sweetly pretty with huge brown eyes and a cascade of blue-black hair. She and Teddy were clearly destined to be BFF the way they hugged one another, whispered secrets and exploded with mutual laughter.

It was, Kitty thought, as the coach trundled away from Firefly Common along the pretty Hampshire B-roads and out amid the glorious heather-purple fringes of the New Forest, all rather lovely. If only there wasn't the issue of Vinny . . . not to mention Amy . . . oh, and being homeless, to get in the way.

She'd continued to adopt Destiny's positivity methods, much to Angelica's delight, but still hadn't seen Vinny and had almost given up hope. If he really was a drifter, then he may well have drifted off to pastures new . . . and it was still, whatever Destiny said, all her fault. Kitty stared out of the window and watched the beautiful forest scenery slide past and wondered how Connor and Jemini would get on today with their networking lunch. There might just be something available to rent for peanuts, surely? Even maybe as house-sitters? If only something, anything, local would turn up, because how on earth could they bear to leave all this now?

For almost half an hour, the songs continued, no one felt sick or needed a toilet break, and Kitty was beginning to relax and simply enjoy being trundled through the delights of another gorgeous summer's day. So, it came as a bit of a surprise when the coach slowed, and turned down a narrow shingle track, all sand dunes and salty air and apparently in the middle of nowhere.

Once the coach had stopped, Ruby turned from her seat next to the driver. 'Children! And mummies and daddies and minders! This is our first stop! We'll be having lunch here, so bring your backpacks. I hope you've all remembered to pack a towel as well because we may be paddling.'

Several children clapped. Everyone else was pretty sure they'd packed a towel . . . probably.

Kitty was amused that all these coastal-living children were getting roaringly excited about being by the sea.

'We're only a couple of villages along, actually,' Ruby said more quietly to Kitty. 'But it's one of the smaller beaches and very retro, so not so many people come here from Firefly Common. Most people go in the other direction towards Bournemouth, so this is always a treat for the children. Welcome to Thrift Drift Cove.'

'Thrift Drift? Funny name . . . sounds like the sort of place you'd go to lose all your money. Or an Enid Blyton adventure venue.' Kitty frowned, then grinned. 'Oh – duh! It's because of the cliff plants, isn't it?'

'Well done, Alan Titchmarsh!' Ruby chuckled. 'Yes, there's masses of pink thrift everywhere here – along with campion and sea holly. It's really pretty. We usually get the kids to do a spot-the-flower. Haven't you ever explored here or anywhere else along the coast?'

Kitty shook her head. 'Not really. I think we were all so spell-bound by Firefly Common and the beach there – we all came from landlocked cities previously – that we just thought we'd found paradise and we've never really bothered to look any further.'

'Yeah, well, all these little places along here are pretty cool – you wait until we get to the next stop on today's trip, Heartbreak Bay – and that one's origin is a whole other story.'

'Blimey, yes – that sounds like pure Victorian melodrama. Abandoned serving wenches, cuckolded bridegrooms, and des-pondent jilted brides all hurling themselves from the cliffs with heartbroken cries of anguish?'

'Yep, and so much more!' Ruby grinned. 'But we don't tell the kiddies any of that. Ever. There are some cool places round here for sure, but when I go on holiday I want Marbs at least. Anyway –' Ruby clapped her hands and raised her voice. 'Have we all got our backpacks? Have we all got our sun hats? Have we all got our factor fifty?'

Everyone shouted 'yes Ruby', in a sort of high-pitched stag-gered roundelay. It was rather adorable.

'Good – well done. Now, children, Mrs Proctor and Miss Wil-liams will get off the coach first. When I say so, you can all file off the coach. Mrs Proctor and Miss Williams will then show you where to stand. You must hold hands with your pair-mate. You remember we've practised all this?'

They all nodded fervently. Kitty almost did the same. It was a bit Pavlov's dog.

'Good. Then you wait until your mummy or daddy or minder has also got off the bus and Mrs Proctor and Miss Williams will make sure you're all with the right people. Do we all understand?'

Everyone nodded. Including Kitty. But goodness, how involved and complex was this child-minding business?

Once off the coach, Kitty looked at the row of Ruby's tiny charges with fond amusement. Dressed almost uniformly in shorts, T-shirts and canvas shoes – as she was – and with their ubiquitous sun hats and brightly coloured rucksacks on their backs, they looked like a miniature army of Everest Sherpas. Then, like cogs in a well-oiled machine, the matching of children to adults took place without too much confusion at all. Ruby, Kitty thought, had everyone very well trained.

It was another delightfully warm blue-sky summer's day as, with Teddy holding one hand and Imogen holding the other, Kitty fell into line and followed the gaudy procession along the narrow winding path towards the sea.

'Wow!' She blinked in surprise when they reached the end. 'How fabulous is this? It's like time travel . . . and we thought Firefly Common was retro.'

Thrift Drift Cove was a tiny curved bay, with smooth golden sand, a little promenade fronting an ice-cream shack, a beach hut selling buckets and spades and postcards, the clearly much-needed toilets, and a very small selection of post-war children's fairground rides. It was also practically deserted.

'Everyone who needs to use the loo, put up your hand,' Ruby called.

Kitty didn't, but Imogen and Teddy did. Along with most of the others.

'Form an orderly queue!' Ruby chuckled. 'Always best to get the pee and poo out of the way before lunch, I find.'

Kitty pulled a face and joined the queue.

Sometime later, when everyone was loo-sorted and hands had been washed, Ruby announced that they'd be having their packed lunch on the promenade picnic benches before the next part of the day's adventure.

It was all very jolly, as the contents of the lunch boxes were examined and swapped and declared better than what their mummy/daddy/carer had made – just as it always had been. Kitty, sitting between Teddy and Imogen, ate small triangular sandwiches, a cereal bar and a banana with some nostalgia and even a slight touch of broodiness.

She smiled at Imogen and Teddy, and across at all the other children, and thought they were cute, gorgeous, fun – but feeling broody? Her? Nah . . . surely not? It was just her biological clock ticking amid all this cuteness overload. Wasn't it?

Anyway, Ruby gave her no further time to dwell on that anomaly as she clapped her hands and announced once the rubbish was all safely stowed in the litter bins and hands and faces were wiped, they'd be making their way down to the beach – in their pairs and holding hands with their grown-up – and turning left. Did they all know left? They didn't. Ruby pointed left and everyone nodded.

Ruby, Kitty thought, was a loss to any paramilitary organisation.

All orders obeyed, they marched neatly down to the beach, turned left and – Kitty's jaw dropped. Blimey!

Punch and Judy!

'Towels down on the sand in nice neat rows . . . we've done nice neat rows, haven't we?' Ruby raised her voice above the shushing of the waves on the shore. 'Good! The show is about to start.'

A proper Punch and Judy show! Narrow striped canvas tent, red-and-yellow ornately carved proscenium. The full works. The children – these twenty-first century screen-savvy children – looked on in wonder.

Kitty, like everyone else, dropped down onto the beach with

Teddy and Imogen wide-eyed in front of her. Ruby counted heads, made sure everyone was where they should be, then sat beside her.

'Punch and Judy?' Kitty said. 'Really? Are you sure it's suitable these days? I mean, it's pure violence – or is this the updated, sanitised politically correct version?'

'God, no.' Ruby looked askance. 'This is the original version. We've been coming here for a few years now and the kids love this. I mean – what's not to like? They know this is a show and just for fun. They know these are rather exaggerated puppets. They've been brought up on AI – this is the real deal. It's colourful, it's noisy, it has sausages and a crocodile and it's funny. They love the dog and the baby – and there's audience participation, and the good guys win and then they all end up happily ever after and take their bows – alive and kicking. I've not had a traumatised kiddie – yet.'

Nor did they on this occasion. The children were all completely awe-struck and laughed and shouted and cheered and booed in all the right places and applauded loudly at the end. The adults all clearly enjoyed it too.

Pure nostalgia, Kitty thought, taking charge of Teddy and Imogen again and wondering why her parents had never taken her on proper seaside holidays. Festivals, yes. Holidays, no.

'Children! Yes – carry on! Running up and down for a while to work off that lunch is a very good idea!' Ruby shouted, as most of the children chased one another pretending to be crocodiles. 'Then we'll go up to the esplanade and you can have one go on either the roundabout or the swinging boats if you wish. Then toilet and back on the coach for our next adventure.'

And in a whirl of wiping sandy feet, further toilet-escort duty, several breath-holding moments of terror as Teddy and Imogen soared into the stratosphere on the ancient wooden swinging boats, screaming with laughter as they clutched the crossed ropes, a head count and a further application of factor fifty, everyone was back on the coach, singing 'Five Little Speckled Frogs', and heading for Heartbreak Bay.

Kitty looked out of the window and thought anxiously about Jemini and Connor and if they'd manage to schmooze enough at the Lowe's garden party to find another home for all of them. And then she thought wistfully about Vinny.

And wished she hadn't.

Chapter Nineteen

At the very moment that Kitty was thinking about them, Jemini and Connor were networking like mad.

The Lowe's stunning, extensive and expensively landscaped garden was awash with men and women in their smart-casual summer best. Glasses of Pimm's were clutched, and plates, piled high with every delicacy the caterers could provide, were balanced carefully, as people circulated and smiled, all the time watching from beneath their Ray-Bans to make sure a rival wasn't stealing a march.

Jemini, sashaying around in her prettiest, floatiest, floral frock and stilt heels, absolutely loved it.

Deirdre and Lester Lowe had welcomed her with – well, if not actually open arms, then the warm and smiley equivalent. And they'd introduced her as not only a valuable member of the Lovell and Lowe family but also as Connor's girlfriend – which made her feel like a teenager and was pretty cool – and also sang her business-acumen praises to all the estate-agency clones they met on the velvet, emerald lawns.

Either Deirdre had had a frontal lobotomy or Connor had had 'a word'. Whichever it was – Jemini was very happy with her change of heart.

Fleetingly, she wondered how Kitty was coping with Teddy and Imogen. But only fleetingly. Teddy loved Kitty, Kitty loved Teddy, Kitty was sensible – and of course Ruby, scarily organised Ruby, was in charge. No, they'd all be fine and having a fab day out. Now, it was down to her, to discover if – and where – there might be a property suitable for them all to move into within the next few weeks.

Connor, working the crowd on the other side of the lawn, looked across and grinned. Maybe, she thought, that grin meant he'd found somewhere. Although . . . Jemini paused. How could there be anything half as wonderful as Sandcastle Cottage?

She took a deep breath and zig-zagged her way through the milling throng towards him.

Connor, rather too man-at-M&S in his chinos and pale-blue Oxford shirt for Jemini's liking, winked at her. 'Jem, this is Peter Marlow-Smith. Peter, this is Jemini, my partner. Jem, Peter owns Marlow-Smith's – they have a chain of offices further along the coast – you know?'

'I do.' Jemini smiled and held out her hand. 'Nice to meet you, Mr Marlow-Smith.'

'Peter, please.' Peter Marlow-Smith gripped her hand in a rather clammy squeeze and pumped it energetically up and down. 'Lovely to meet you, Jemini. We've heard so much about you.'

We? Had they? Jemini looked round for maybe a Mrs Peter or a Marlow-Smith contingent. There appeared to be neither. Perhaps Peter – middle-aged, puffy-eyed, hair too black to be natural, very overweight and sweating profusely – was channelling his inner Margaret Thatcher? Or Queen Victoria? He certainly looked the type.

She simpered. It wasn't deliberate. It just went with the territory and happened naturally before she could stop it. 'Have you? All good, I hope?' Then she groaned. Welcome to cliché city, Jemini . . . She looked at Connor. 'And what have you boys been chatting about?'

Boys! Dear god! What was wrong with her?

Connor looked as if he was trying hard not to laugh. 'Well, actually, Peter here deals with the sort of properties that we at Lovell and Lowe rarely see.'

Jemini frowned at Connor. Now he was talking like his dad

did when he was trying to impress a buyer. This was all very bizarre. Still, maybe she should just follow his lead and simper a bit more?

'Does he?' She raised her eyebrows, then turned her smile towards Peter. 'And what sort of properties are they, Peter?'

'Large, expensive properties – left empty following a death – either waiting for probate, or for inheritance tax to be sorted.' Peter glistened damply beneath the relentless sun. 'Or sometimes, just left empty while the families of the deceased owners decide amongst themselves if they want to sell or share or redevelop.'

'We certainly don't see many properties of that size in Lovell and Lowe, no,' Jemini said, slightly baffled by the turn of the conversation. 'They must be the devil to shift – if the family wants a sale of course – especially in the current climate.'

'Oh, they, are, Jemini! They are!'

'Which is why,' Connor added, 'Marlow-Smith deal with short-term lets on these properties, so that the inheritors can earn at least something from the houses, while their future is in limbo, so to speak.'

The penny dropped. Jemini grinned. 'Ah, yes . . . right. So, large houses suitable for multiple occupation – for temporary rental?'

'Yes,' Peter looked slightly dubious. 'Well, in theory. I mean – homes in multiple occupation has a bit of a – well – and I'm not a snob, but . . . well, not-quite-our-residential-area ring to it, if you get my drift?'

'Oh, I get your drift perfectly.' Jemini counted to ten. 'All a bit NIMBY for Marlow-Smith, I guess? HMOs – I mean.'

Peter wriggled a bit and then managed a patronising smile. 'We at Marlow-Smith have always prided ourselves on being all-encompassing. We have an all-inclusive ethos. However, we have to draw the line somewhere with the allocation of our larger houses. We have the other property owners in the same environs to consider, of course.'

'Oh, of course.'

Several people in the little networking groups around them, stopped talking, turned and lifted their Ray-Bans in ill-concealed curiosity.

'Jem . . .' Connor said quickly, sensing one of her left-wing rants about to escape, 'what I've been discussing with Peter is the likelihood that something of this nature, a large rental property, also short-term and affordable, may come his way, say, from September onwards, and if so, if he'd be kind enough to give us first refusal . . . because *we have a family on our books who might be interested*.'

'Ah, yes . . .' Jemini twigged. And much as she loathed every inch of the slimy Peter Marlow-Smith, this wasn't the time or the place to let rip. 'The – um – Appleby family, wasn't it?'

Connor nodded. 'That's right. They're currently renting in Firefly Common, Peter – have been for some time. We actually arranged the original lease and rental for them. They've been model tenants, haven't they, Jem?'

'Model.' Jemini nodded. 'Couldn't wish for better. Rent paid each month on the dot, no quibbles about dripping taps or squeaking floorboards, liked by the neighbours, pillars of society . . .'

She stopped. Maybe that was a touch too far? It seemed not.

Peter was beaming. 'They sound ideal. And they're looking to move on? May I ask as to why?'

'You certainly may, Peter.' Connor was matching him in the obsequious stakes stride for stride. 'The owner of the property has been travelling abroad but is now returning home to Firefly Common in September. The – um – Appleby family are very keen to remain in this area, they all work locally, so if anything suitable crops up on your radar . . .'

Connor tapped the side of his nose. Jemini looked at him in horror.

Peter tapped his nose back. 'Say no more, old chap. You'll be the first to hear.'

They both guffawed in a very false manner. The watching groups, sensing a deal being struck, became even more avid.

'One additional piece of information, Peter,' Jemini said. 'The Appleby family have a pre-school-age child and two dogs. I trust this won't be a problem?'

Peter looked momentarily as if it might be a monumental stumbling block, but managed to smile. 'I'm sure it won't be, dear lady, I'm sure it won't be. Some home owners always state if they're not willing to rent to – um – families who have either children or pets – so we'd not be able to accommodate the – um – family you've mentioned in one of those homes, obviously, of course . . . but, yes – there will be others, I'm sure, who won't object too strongly. Either way, it's good to have all the relevant info at my fingertips.'

Connor looked a bit downcast. 'So, the child and animals may mean our – um – yes, our search on behalf of the Applebys may be even more difficult?'

'It's a restriction they may possibly want to consider, yes.' Peter Marlow-Smith wiped his face with a hankie. 'If there was any way you could suggest to them that they might, well, dispose of the dogs.'

'Holy crap on a cracker!' Jemini exploded. 'Those dogs are like family! *Are* family! Dispose of them? *Dispose*? And the child? Shall we tell them to dispose of her too? For pity's sake, Peter – what kind of man are you?'

Peter blinked. Connor bit his lip and looked at the ground. His shoulders were shaking.

'Oh, er – well . . .' Peter stuttered. 'Of course, I didn't mean . . . um . . .' He quickly gained his equilibrium. 'That is – no, dear lady, of course I wouldn't suggest anything of the sort – and I must say you're a little firecracker, aren't you? I do love that in a girl. I could do with one just like you.' He smiled pudgily. 'May I ask, where did young Connor get you from?'

Jemini was, for once, momentarily dumbstruck. She simply stared at him. Then frowned. 'Sorry?'

'I just wondered where you'd come from,' Peter bared his teeth in a leer. 'And if there were any more like you there.'

Jemini was instantly torn between slapping his stupid jowly face and laughing. Deciding that hitting a prospective business partner on the manicured lawns of Lowe Abbey would be a step too far even for her, she laughed. 'I come from Slough via Edgbaston – and yes, there are several more like me back there. However, I'm not quite sure if that's what you want to know?'

'Slough! Edgbaston!' Peter brayed. 'You have a wicked sense of humour, my dear. No, what I meant was – where did Connor actually get you from?'

Connor stepped in. 'Peter – I didn't "get" Jemini from anywhere. Actually, I'm not sure I'm following you . . .'

Peter glistened even more and leaned forward conspiratorially. 'What I want to know, is, well, since Prudence left me for her fitness instructor, I've been very lonely and missing the companionship of a good woman, if you get my drift. I just wondered – well – with your Jemini being lively and outspoken, and a dusky maiden to boot, of course, if maybe she was one of those, well, mail-order ladies?'

'*Dusky maiden*? *Dusky-sodding-maiden*?' Jemini spluttered. 'I'm a brown British Asian, Peter. I. Am. Not. A. Dusky. Sodding. Maiden! Nor, you racist cretin, am I a bloody mail-order bride!'

The Pimm's glasses were rapidly emptied, the Ray-Bans removed altogether. The networking groups converged. This was entertainment of the highest order.

Peter held up his hands. 'No offence meant, Jemini. None at all. And I'm not a racist, goodness me, no – but a word of advice, my dear, maybe you should try to be a little more understanding of the English idioms and not be quite so defensive. Feisty may be good in the bedroom, but you're not helping Connor here in his business by behaving like a fishwife, you know.'

Even before Jemini could reply, Connor had grabbed Peter by the shoulder. 'Fuck off, Peter – take your racism and your misogyny and your innuendo and your snobby "homes for the rich" all-inclusive-bollocks ethos and stuff them – and please remove

Lovell and Lowe from your business contacts. We, as a firm, want nothing more to do with you.'

Jemini had never loved him more than at that moment.

The networking watchers didn't even pretend to be discreet any more. They were riveted. Estate Agency garden parties were usually such dull affairs. They all tucked their empty Pimm's glasses in the crooks of their arms and clapped like seals.

'Well, young Connor,' – Peter puffed himself up and slowly turned purple – 'oh, how you're going to regret this. You have no idea how much power I wield in our circles. You have just committed corporate suicide – and you and your parents and their partners will lose so much business when this gets out!'

'Actually, Peter, I don't think we will.' Deidre Lowe, in all her glory, elbowed her way through the rapt crowd, radiating red-hot anger. 'There are enough people here, people in our business, who have listened to every disgusting, racist, boorish word you've just uttered and will recognise you for what you are. Now, I suggest you apologise to Jemini, and to Connor, and please remove yourself from my hospitality and my premises immediately and permanently.'

Apologising seemed to be the last thing on Peter's mind. Huffing and puffing and muttering veiled threats of imminent estate-agency bankruptcy, he turned and trundled away.

The garden party crowd bellowed their approval and applauded even more loudly.

Deirdre, an avenging angel in turquoise shantung, watched him go, made sure he'd vanished through the electronic security gates, then turned to Jemini and Connor. 'Unspeakable man. It's people like him – dinosaurs – who make us, our profession, a standing joke along with tax inspectors and second-hand car dealers.' She turned to the avid crowd. 'Now, everyone else, that little show is, thankfully, over, so please go and refill your glasses and help yourself to more food. Although, if you agree with Peter Marlow-Smith, then of course you can all piddle off as well – don't let me stop you.'

There was much laughter and no one piddled.

'Oh, god – I'm so sorry!' Jemini looked at Deirdre. 'I've ruined your party. I should never have—'

Deidre held up her hand. 'Not another word. The man's an oaf. Connor – these people seem to all have empty glasses and plates. I've suggested they have refills, so do the decent thing and find them a wine waiter – or, better still, get them refills yourself – and feed them. We've paid enough for the food, and they're our guests after all. Jemini and I have things to talk about.'

Oh, my god, Jemini thought, I've wrecked it now. Deirdre's going to kill me in private and bury my body somewhere in the herbaceous border. There'll be no more Connor, no more job, no more anything at all . . .

And, with a last helpless look over her shoulder at Connor, Jemini found herself linking arms with Deirdre and being hurried away in the direction of Lowe Abbey.

Away from the partying crowds, Deirdre steered Jemini into a massive Victorian-style conservatory, complete with an Italian-tiled floor, real grapevines, lemon trees, deep-cushioned rattan sofas and blissful air-con.

'Please sit down.' Deirdre indicated one of the sofas. 'We shan't be disturbed here.'

Jemini sat nervously on the edge of a down-filled cushion, wondering if anyone would hear her scream and then deciding probably not.

'Mrs Lowe . . . Deirdre . . . I'm so very sorry . . .'

Deidre shook her head and sat opposite Jemini. 'Shush. No need. The man, as I said, is an oaf. You were absolutely within your rights to be as outraged as you were. I'm amazed you didn't slap him. However . . .'

There was always going to be a 'however', Jemini thought dismally.

'However,' Deidre continued, 'that isn't why we're here.'

'It isn't?'

'No. Firstly, I want to apologise to you. No family member,

employee, friend or guest of mine should ever be spoken to in that manner. I'm so very sorry that it happened to you. Here in our home. People like Peter Marlow-Smith are an anachronism, and however useful he may have been to us in business, he is clearly not the sort of man any right-minded person would want to be associated with. And I'm not surprised in the slightest that his poor downtrodden Prudence decamped with her fitness instructor.'

Jemini ventured a smile. This was going OK. So far.

'And,' Deidre continued, 'I owe you an apology, too. I possibly haven't been very friendly towards you – and this is remiss and unfair of me. I know how much Connor loves you – yes, *loves* – he's told me – and how much Lester likes and admires you, both as a person and as an employee. Oh, this is difficult, but I was just a bit – well – jealous.'

Jemini gulped. Exactly what Kitty had said. Wow.

'You don't have to . . .'

'No, please let me finish. Connor is my baby. My only child. I'm a possessive mumma bear, as they say. When Connor said you were his girlfriend I was prepared not to like you from the outset, with you being older and divorced and a mother, but I was wrong. I've got to know you, I like you, and I respect you. I can absolutely see why Connor loves you and why Lester says you're the breath of fresh air the business needs, and I do hope we can be friends.'

Jemini, now happy that she wasn't going to be strangled, slapped, or sent packing like Peter, exhaled with relief. 'Of course we can be friends – we *are* friends – and thank you for being so honest. I absolutely understand your concerns – but I love Connor very much. I would never, ever, do anything to hurt him – oh, and just in case you had any worries on that score, I'm not a gold-digger, either.'

Deidre laughed. 'No, I never thought you were that.'

'Phew.' Jemini smiled. 'But I still feel I may have been a bit too – well –– hasty, in my reaction to Peter just now. Perhaps I should have been grown-up enough to ignore him.'

Deirdre crossed her legs and leaned forward. 'If I'd got there sooner, we could have tackled him together and made him wear his balls as earrings.'

Blimey! Jemini blinked, making a mental note to never, ever cross Deirdre.

'Because,' Deirdre continued, 'he'd already insulted me, in a very similar way.'

'No! Really? What did he . . . ? I mean . . . of course, if you don't want to tell me . . .'

'I'd put a business proposition to him. Something I've been thinking about for a long time. I want to have an online portfolio simply called Sea Views. You know how lucky we are, living here on the coast, and how much it's the dream of so many people to have that – a home with a sea view . . . and of course, prices are usually sky-high – but not always, there are some hidden gems out there, and I wanted to build a group of south-coast estate agents who could find them.'

Jemini nodded. 'It sounds great. An amalgamation of local businesses working together, especially now, when things are difficult . . . perfect.'

Deirdre shook her head. 'I wanted Peter to add Marlow-Smith to the list – so that we had agents from both ends of the spectrum supplying the information.'

'Still perfect. All bases covered. And a cut for everyone, when a property is sold?'

'Exactly that!' Deidre beamed. 'You're a woman after my own heart, Jemini.'

Goodness, Jemini thought. High praise indeed. 'But Peter didn't want Marlow-Smith involved?'

Deidre frowned. 'Not only that. He patted me . . . he actually *patted* me – the bastard! And said I shouldn't bother my pretty little head – he actually said that! Um – yes, that I shouldn't bother my pretty little head about a business I clearly didn't understand.'

'Holy crap on a cracker! What did you say?'

'He gave me no time to say anything at all – just steam-rollered on, telling me to stick to being a typist and to leave the new-fangled ideas to the men, who, after all, were the ones with the brains.'

'Nooo!'

'Yes, indeedy. And then he said – and he laughed – that my idea was nonsensical and I would make Lovell and Lowe a laughing stock if this got out, and I just ought to stay where I belonged – the kitchen and the bedroom – like all women.'

'No way! He can't have said that? No way on earth. No bloke has said that for a million years!'

'He did. And then he laughed again and said "only joking" – but he wasn't.'

'The bastard!' Jemini leaned across the rattan divide and gave Deirdre a sisterly hug. 'The absolute bastard!'

'I know!' Deidre returned the hug, then wriggled herself free and stood up. 'God, I feel better for telling you all this. So, after we've both been slimed on by Mr Racist-Misogynist, I think we deserve a drink – and not the prosecco and Pimm's doing the rounds out there.'

Jemini watched her walk across the conservatory to a tall, pale-green cabinet which was, it turned out, a massive American fridge. A massive American fridge filled with champagne.

'Moët and Chandon, Bollinger, Veuve Clicquot . . .' Deidre smiled at Jemini over her shoulder. 'Although, on this occasion, I think it really ought to be Cristal, don't you?'

'Oh, yes,' Jemini agreed, not having a clue.

Deidre fetched flutes from a small pale-green Shaker cupboard next to the fridge, opened the Cristal with all the panache of an upmarket sommelier, and poured two glasses, then handed one to Jemini.

'To us. The Lowe women.'

'Er – yes . . . the Lowe women,' Jemini said, still in shock. 'To us.'

They clinked flutes. And drank bubbles.

And then they looked at one another over the crystal and the Cristal and giggled.

Chapter Twenty

The wheels on the bus were now trundling happily towards Heartbreak Bay on the second stage of the day-trip. Teddy and Imogen were showing no signs of flagging. Nor were any of the others. The singing was as loud and badly timed as ever.

'We try to give them about an hour at each place. That's enough for most of them,' Ruby had said. 'Most of them are past the afternoon-nap stage, but we usually manage to have tired them all out by home-time.'

Kitty reckoned that, even with the singing, given the fresh sea air at Thrift Drift Cove, the gentle rocking motion of the coach and the warmth of the sun through the windows, she'd soon be snoring gently.

She wriggled in her seat and looked at the scenery to keep herself awake. Another gorgeous fern-and-gorse-filled single-track road, another glimpse of wide forest pathways disappearing beneath centuries-old trees, dappled shadows dancing across purple heather, wild ponies cropping scrubby grass, little sandy streams cutting through the broom . . . and the air, as always, warm with the scent of pine trees and the sea.

Then a higgledy-piggledy half-hidden wooden signpost: Heartbreak Bay ½ mile.

'Right, children – and grown-ups.' Ruby stood up, rocking slightly. 'We'll be at our next stop in a couple of minutes. You won't need your backpacks for this part. I will have bottles of water if anyone needs a drink. You will need your sun hats, and make sure you've got your factor fifty on. The same rules apply this time, to keep us safe and all together when we get off the bus. We all know what they are, don't we?'

They all did. Loudly.

'Good,' Ruby continued. 'Then, when we're all off, you stay with your parent or carer and hold their hands because the cliffs here are very high, and then Mrs Proctor and Miss Williams and I will lead the way down to the beach.'

Everyone applauded and cheered.

The coach stopped then, and amid the cacophony of a busload of excited children, Kitty helped Teddy and Imogen with their seat belts.

Ruby clapped her hands. 'Now, who knows what we're going to see here?'

No one did. Kitty looked mystified.

Ruby laughed. 'We're going to see some sandcastles! Who likes sandcastles?'

Everyone did. Kitty again thought this sounded a pretty lame excursion for kids who had the beach on their doorsteps.

'And,' Ruby continued, 'who on this coach lives in a house called Sandcastle?'

Teddy screamed with delight and waved wildly. 'Me and Kitty do! And Mummy and 'Pollo and Connor and Honey and Zorro! We all live in a sandcastle!'

'Well, done, Teddy!' Ruby laughed.

Kitty smiled fondly as, for a moment, Teddy was the awe-struck envy of all her peers.

Yes, we all do live there, she thought – but for how much longer?

Once they were off the bus, Kitty held hands with Teddy and Imogen as they followed the nursery leaders and the crocodile of children carefully down the set of wide wooden steps cut into the cliffs to the beach. 'Right – here we go for the sandcastles then,' she said. 'Are we excited, girls?'

It seemed they were. Kitty sighed, hoped the next hour would pass quickly, and wondered how Jemini was getting on.

'OK,' – Ruby had stopped at the foot of the steps and looked up at them all – 'now you can look at the sandcastles, but you can't touch. Do we all understand?'

They did. Kitty thought it sounded even more boring now and wondered just how much the nursery parents were coughing up for this.

They reached the bottom of the steps. Teddy and Imogen squealed with delight. Kitty just stared.

Wow!

The entire curve of Heartbreak Bay's beach, sheltered from the winds by the cliffs, was covered in hugely ornate sandcastles that towered above the children: fabulously intricate sandcastles with moats and turrets and minarets; solid foursquare sandcastles with crenellated towers and battlements; fairy sandcastles with lights and darting rainbow figures; garrison sandcastles with marching soldiers.

In fact, every kind of lavish and elaborate castle it was possible to imagine. And they all had working parts, flowing water in the moats and fountains, lights in the windows, and ethereal music playing.

The children were mesmerised. So was Kitty.

There was even a miniature village with shops and schools and houses, all built from sand – with tiny people and cars and even a little railway station that, as far as Kitty could see, looked a lot like Firefly Common Halt – and it was all mechanised and moving and was quite incredible.

Further along, there were larger single sand sculptures of animals – real and mythical – slumbering on the beach, and of people playing and picnicking and sunbathing, and a scale model of the New Forest, complete with ponies and cows and sheep and deer, all carefully and delicately carved in sand.

Kitty was absolutely blown away.

'Clever, isn't it?' Ruby said. 'The kids love it – and I must say, I never get tired of seeing all this – although, of course, once the winter weather hits, most of the sculptures crumble or are washed away – but the Sandman comes up trumps with a new set of designs each summer and, tides permitting, we usually get a good six months' worth of viewings here.'

'The Sandman?' Kitty frowned.

'Yeah, he's a pretty famous sand sculptor apparently. Anyway, he does all this himself – so, a really talented guy.'

'He certainly is.' Kitty looked around in amazement. 'And his work is clearly very popular.'

The beach was crowded with tourists, locals and visitors, all following the roped-off one-way system round the stunningly artistic creations, phone cameras flashing as they went.

Kitty, holding on tightly to Teddy and Imogen, followed the crowd. The girls stopped at each towering castle, each tiny house, each fire-breathing dragon, and stared in awe and pointed and shouted in delight at each new discovery. Kitty just marvelled at the intricacy, the hours of work, the sheer creative complexity of the sculptures.

This place was incredible. She'd have to tell the others about it and come back here as soon as possible – without the dogs, of course. And to think she'd thought it was going to be boring.

Ruby caught up with them. 'All OK here?'

'God, yes!' Kitty nodded. 'I feel like a kid again, myself. This is all so mind-blowing, isn't it? I've seen sand sculptures before, but nothing on this scale or of this degree of brilliance. I could stay here for hours, just looking. Each time you look, you see something new. So clever.'

'It really is. Sometimes the Sandman is actually here, and he has a little chat at the exit, or answers questions. The children love that. I don't think he's here today, which means we should be out of here in about half an hour. Oh, and we give each child a little book with some pictures of the sandcastles in, along with a few crayons, so they can colour the pictures in on the way back to Firefly Common.' Ruby laughed. 'It makes for a mercifully quiet ride home.'

Kitty laughed as well, and watched Ruby move on through the ranks of the nursery children, checking that everyone was OK.

'Look!' Teddy pointed across the top of a towering multi-pinnacled princess castle. 'Kitty! Look! Down there!'

'What?' She stooped down to Teddy's eye-level. 'What, poppet?'

'It's Honey and Zorro. In the sand. Down there! Look!'

Kitty looked down, then laughed at the two small sand-sculpted dogs playing with a strand of obviously real seaweed on the edge of a moulded shoreline. 'Oh, yes – it does look like them – but it isn't really.'

'It is, Kitty. And there's me an' you an' 'Pollo.'

'Oh, sweetheart, I don't think so. It could be any family by the sea, and any dogs. Come on, poppet – let's go and have a look at the model village.'

With a last look, Teddy reluctantly allowed herself to be led away.

It was painfully slow progress, the sand sculptures were clearly very popular and the crowds all seemed to want to stop and stare at every exhibit, but eventually Kitty managed to manoeuvre Teddy and Imogen right to the front of the model village's viewing area. A village, Kitty thought again, that looked remarkably like Firefly Common.

Teddy and Imogen, children who had been brought up with the most sophisticated of animations and amusements were, as they had been with Punch and Judy, entranced by the little cars crawling along the tiny roads and the train chugging up and down on the branch line. It gave Kitty a warm glow of everything being all right with the world.

Just for a fleeting moment.

Because that was when she saw him.

Vinny was on the other side of the diorama.

Vinny, looking totally, absolutely, stunningly gorgeous in a pale-blue T-shirt, faded jeans, and with his dark hair falling into his eyes as he spoke to . . . who? Kitty couldn't quite see through the crowd.

Her heart thundered under her ribs and her mouth was dry. She swallowed. Oh, what a cruel trick of karma – after all the times she'd hoped to see him alone on the beach – to find him here with – his family? Well, no, presumably not, because he'd said he'd lost his only child . . . so – his wife? Girlfriend? Partner? Her children?

Kitty closed her eyes and hoped he'd have moved on before he noticed her.

Which he might well have done, if it hadn't been for Teddy.

'Vinneeeeeeeeee!' Teddy screeched happily, waving madly across the model village. 'Vinneeeeeeeeee!'

He looked up. Looked across. Frowned. Looked startled. And smiled.

Kitty, wishing she had something more substantial than Teddy and Imogen to hang on to, giddily managed to smile back.

Then he'd gone again, swallowed up in the snaking crowd.

Wondering if she'd just imagined him, and trying to remember all the things Destiny had told her about breathing in and breathing out and letting go, and still being aware that she was in charge of two small girls, Kitty managed to drift dazedly round the rest of the exhibition and try not to peer hopelessly at every tall, dark man who flitted through the milling crowd ahead of her.

Mercifully – for her, if not for the rest of the party – the tour was soon over and the nursery contingent was gathering by the exit ready for the upward cliff climb to the coach. Kitty was dismayed to still have a racing pulse and wobbly legs. No matter how many times she silently instructed herself to grow up, it seemed she wasn't listening.

Ruby was counting heads. 'All present and correct. Right, the toilets are at the top of the cliffs, so anyone who needs a wee tell Mrs Proctor and she'll organise the queue. The rest of us – all back onto the bus, and I've got colouring books and crayons for everyone. Let's go!'

As they climbed the steps, Kitty simply couldn't resist one last glance over her shoulder. Just in case. But there was no sign of Vinny. He must have already left with . . . she sighed . . . well, whoever he was with.

153

As soon as they reached the top, the children split into bus or loo factions. Teddy pulled Kitty towards the bus, while Imogen said she need the toilet and was tugging Kitty towards Mrs Proctor's queue.

'Help?' Kitty looked hopefully at Ruby.

'Ah, the universal joy of having more than one child. Don't worry, I'll take Teddy and strap her in,' Ruby said, 'and get her started on her colouring – you stay and wait for Imogen.'

As Mrs Proctor seemed to have the toilet queue moving at a steady pace, Kitty stood on the clifftop and stared out over the sea. The colours changed from silver-grey to iridescent blue and back again. There was a ship on the horizon gliding slowly from left to right. The motion of both the sea and the ship was hypnotic.

She took deep, deep breaths. Destiny would love this, Kitty thought, beginning to relax with the wind in her hair, the sound of the distant rhythmic cry of the gulls and the sun warm on her back. She closed her eyes, feeling the onshore breeze lift her mass of red-gold hair away from her face – exactly like Princess Merida, she thought, and giggled to herself.

The she heard his voice.

'Kitty?'

The giggle died. The meditative moment splintered. She turned and stared at him. Goodness, he was so beautiful. Goodness, she was probably going to say something stupid.

She took a deep breath. 'Um . . . hello.'

Vinny smiled at her. 'Hi.'

They just looked at one another. Kitty was absolutely convinced that he could hear her heart still beating its rapid tattoo against her ribs.

'Um . . .' she started again, really not knowing what to say. Knowing what she'd rehearsed for just such a moment. Knowing that she'd mess it up. Knowing she just wanted to hurl herself into his arms. Knowing she couldn't.

He raised his eyebrows. 'Such a surprise, seeing you here. I

154

couldn't believe it was you earlier – I tried to catch up with you to say hello, but you'd vanished in the crowd.'

'Snap.'

'But weren't you with Teddy?' He looked around. 'Where is she? Are you with Apollo and – er – Jemini, as well?'

'No. I'm escorting Teddy and her friend on a nursery day-trip.' This was easier. God, he was gorgeous. 'Teddy is back on the bus. Her friend is in the loo.'

'Right.'

'Um . . . Vinny, about – well – the last time we met. I'm really sorry.'

'No need to apologise. It was your decision. But I've missed seeing you on the beach.'

Kitty frowned. Her decision? Was it? To walk away from him? Well, yes, it was . . . but . . .

'Mmm, well I've been down there most days – swimming, walking the dogs, playing with Teddy . . . our – er – paths don't seem to have crossed.'

Dear god! What the hell was wrong with her? She was babbling – again.

'No, they don't, do they? Maybe . . .'

But whatever the 'maybe' was going to be, she'd never know.

Because fate, damn fate, chose that moment for Mrs Proctor to emerge from the toilet block and return a very whey-faced Imogen to her with the news that 'she'd been a bit sick', and for a stunning-looking woman in tight jeans and a pink vest, her long, sleek black hair falling almost to her waist, to appear at the top of the cliff steps, shielding her eyes.

'Vincent! Vinny! Come on! We're waiting!'

Wanting to scream and stamp her foot and have an all-out tantrum, Kitty simply cuddled the very pale Imogen against her, then looked at Vinny and forced a smile. 'Ah . . . you're clearly needed. Um – it was – er – nice . . . I – er – have to go, anyway. The bus is waiting to leave. Bye.'

Vinny shrugged and sighed. 'Yes . . . I guess – right . . . see you around, maybe . . .'

He turned to the drop-dead gorgeous woman at the top of the steps. 'OK, Tilda, I'm on my way.'

And with a final sketchy smile in Kitty's direction, he loped away towards the woman and the cliff steps.

Tilda, Kitty thought angrily, was a bloody stupid name. Like rice.

Tilda, the Rice Queen . . .

But my god, she was gorgeous – they were gorgeous together. Why did I ever think I stood a chance? Sod it. She hugged Imogen. 'OK, poppet – let's get you back to the bus. Do you feel a bit better now?'

Imogen nodded as they headed towards the coach.

'Good, then you can do some colouring-in . . . or maybe not.' Kitty remembered her own violent bouts of motion sickness as a child. 'Perhaps have a sip of water . . . anyway, we're not far from home. Oh, bless you, you're smiling now. Do you feel properly back to normal again?'

'Not really,' – Imogen shook her head and giggled – 'but you're really funny, Kitty. Your hair is all standing up on end. You look just like Beaker in the Muppets.'

Chapter Twenty-One

The following morning, in the kitchen of Sandcastle Cottage, Jemini and Kitty were sitting on either side of the big farmhouse table, gesticulating wildly with coffee mugs, and talking at the same time.

'. . . so then he said . . .'

'No way! Then what . . . ?'

'Dire Deidre did *what* . . . ?'

'Blimey . . . and was she stunning . . . ?'

'Yes . . . that's what I thought . . .'

'No sign of any suitable houses to rent . . . ?'

'. . . yep, Tilda, the sodding Rice Queen . . .'

'God knows what'll happen now . . .'

'. . . didn't you ask him . . . ?'

'. . . and all the time I looked like Coco the damn clown . . .'

'. . . at least you weren't mistaken for a mail-order bride . . .'

Apollo, clearing up Honey and Zorro's feeding bowls and putting down fresh water for them, listened to the shared stories of Kitty and Jemini's previous day's adventures with some dismay. From the bits and pieces he could gather, it sounded as if neither of them had had the greatest time.

He sighed. And it also seemed they were no nearer finding a new home.

So, while Teddy ate her breakfast in front of yet more adventures of Peppa Pig, and Connor drifted around somewhere in his boxers with coffee in one hand and a slice of toast between his

157

teeth, Apollo decided that escaping the house and taking the dogs for a long walk before everyone went to work, was probably a good thing.

Having fastened their leads to their harnesses, Apollo was tugged towards the open door by Honey and Zorro, whose claws scrabbled excitedly on the tiles.

'*Antío*, ladies,' he called back into the kitchen.

Neither Jemini nor Kitty answered. They were still talking. They probably didn't even hear him. He sighed.

He was naturally optimistic, but recently everyone had been edgy and unhappy and, well, down. And who could blame them? Soon this gorgeous summer would be over, they'd be leaving Sandcastle Cottage – and then who knew what the rest of the year held in store for any of them?

With the dogs panting on their leads, he headed away from the cottage and out towards his favourite walk and thinking place – on the bench beneath the tall pine trees in Firefly Common's recreation ground.

'*Kalimera*, Apollo!'

He groaned and turned round, fixing his best smile. 'Good morning, Angelica.'

She bounced up beside him, dressed as usual at this time in the morning in one of her many pink designer jogging outfits. 'Glorious morning again, isn't it? I'm going to try and do my five miles before it gets too hot.'

Apollo nodded. 'Impressive. You are an inspiration to us all. Please, don't let me delay you.'

'You won't.' Angelica jogged on the spot. 'How's Kitty?'

'She's OK, I think. Why?'

'I hoped she was keeping up with her meditation and relaxation and mindfulness, that's all. Destiny asked me how she was doing.'

The dogs took advantage of the unscheduled pit stop to investigate a new scent buried deep in the ferns at the side of the road. There was a lot of snorting and snuffling and wagging of Staffie tails.

Apollo watched them with love, and smiled. Then he remembered Angelica's question. 'Ah, sorry. Yes, the mindfulness. I think Kitty has a lot of that right now.'

'Oh, good. I'll tell Destiny. Oh, by the way, have you heard anything from Mavis Mulholland?'

'Who? Oh, the lady who owns Sandcastle Cottage.' Apollo's heart sank. 'No, why? Have you?'

'Not directly, no, but on the grapevine – it seems she's on her way back to the UK right now.'

Apollo nodded. 'We were aware that she would be back to reclaim her home in September. We've not heard anything definite.'

'According to the WI gossip – and they're rarely wrong – her cruise ship is due into Southampton in the first week of September. This is only a month away – goodness knows where the summer has gone. I don't know all the details about Mavis coming home, and I don't know what this will mean for you and the others, of course. Mind you, I guess Lester Lowe must know all about it – as he rented the cottage to you in the first place. Still, I'm sure you'll be able to work something out. Ah, well – mustn't stop. *Antío!*'

'Yes, *antío* . . .' Apollo said dismally, as Angelica trotted purposefully into the distance. He pulled the dogs away from their foraging. 'Sorry, guys. We need to be walking. I need to be thinking.'

The thinking wasn't going too well, and he and the dogs had navigated the High Street and just reached the entrance to the recreation ground when Netta and Noel, striding out with their Nordic walking poles, fetched up beside him.

'Good morning, Apollo and doggies.' Netta gave him the full benefit of her bared-teeth grin. 'Just the chaps we needed to see, eh, Noel?'

Noel, all knee-length khaki shorts, Aertex shirt and rucksack – a mirror image of Netta's outfit – nodded. 'I'll say. We wondered where you'd all be moving on to, now Mavis Mulholland is coming home.'

Netta peered at Apollo. 'Oh, you've gone quite peaky. Oh, have we been indiscreet? Have you not been told?'

Apollo sighed heavily.

Honey and Zorro, who were industriously investigating Noel and Netta's hiking boots, stopped and looked up enquiringly, heads on one side.

'Angelica has just told me that she's heard, via the village gossipy mill, that Mrs Mulholland will be back earlier than we'd thought. Now, right at the beginning of September. Is this what you have also heard?'

'From the WI? Yes.' Netta and Noel nodded in sync.

'We have enjoyed having you as neighbours, very much so.' Netta looked sad. 'We'd hoped you'd be staying on. It seems this isn't to be. So, where will you all go?'

Honey and Zorro abandoned the hiking boots for something rather gruesome that had been squashed into the pavement.

'We don't know,' Apollo said sadly. 'We will need to find somewhere very quickly, I think.'

'We'll keep our ears to the ground,' Noel said, also baring his teeth in a good-humoured grin. 'We'll be sorry to lose you.'

'We'll be very sorry indeed to leave,' Apollo said with feeling. 'But it is Mrs Mulholland's home. She will need it back. Now,' – he removed the dogs from their gouging – 'we must go. Goodbye.'

'Cheery-bye,' Netta and Noel chorused. 'And good hunting.'

Good hunting? Huh? Apollo slumped down on his favourite bench and unfastened the dogs' leads. This morning, not even his beloved heavy-metal bands could cheer him, and he left his headphones in his pocket.

Zorro and Honey did their usual trundling hither and thither, sniffing, rolling, smiling. Apollo watched them with sadness. They'd loved it here, too. So different from when he and Kitty had lived in the Reading flat, and the dogs had known only city streets and regimented parks, and nothing of this glorious freedom.

He sighed. And now, what would happen to them all if they had to go their separate ways? For years, he'd looked and failed to find the love he'd lost: his girl, May. He was resigned to that being a lost cause. He wasn't a fool. But to lose the companionship of Kitty and the others – and maybe not be allowed to have the dogs living with him . . .

Oh, he put his head in his hands. It was too much to bear. There must be some solution to this, surely?

Honey and Zorro, sensing his mood, waddled up on either side of him and licked his hands.

'Ah, my moros. My dear little ones . . . whatever happens, I won't lose you.' He scratched their solid bullet heads. 'I've lost so much in my life – but I won't lose you. This I promise you.'

As the dogs slobbered happily between his fingers, he only hoped that it was a promise he would be able to keep.

Chapter Twenty-Two

After the events of the previous day, Kitty thought her Friday-lunchtime shift at the Silver Fish Bar might just bring back a little normality into her life.

With the holiday season in full swing, fish and chips, either eaten in or taken out, still seemed to be high on the Firefly Common visitors' must-have list.

And as usual, it being a traditional Fish Friday for the locals, they were very busy. As well as Kitty, Mrs Gibby, Rhonda, and two teenage girls from the nearby High School who had been looking for holiday jobs and who had been immediately taken on as extra waiting staff, were all working. There was hardly time to breathe, let alone think.

Concentrating on fish and chips and hungry customers, Kitty decided to push all thoughts of Vinny and his stunning partner, Tilda the Rice Queen – not to mention Jemini and Connor's failure to find even a sniff of a new home – completely out of her mind. At least for the time being. Having another Scarlett O'Hara moment, she told herself she'd think about it all tomorrow.

Right now, the only things occupying her were constantly having to dash from the kitchen into the restaurant with loaded trays, collecting the empties, wiping tables, making sure everyone had what they'd ordered, and that those waiting for a table knew exactly how long their wait would be.

It numbed both the feet and the brain.

Even the usual compliments from her lovely regulars like Jessie and Norm couldn't lift her spirits today. She was tired and un-happy and out of sorts.

'You've got a face like a wet cod,' Mrs Gibby said cheerfully as the lunchtime rush intensified and she worked her magic, shovel-ling mountains of chips from one of the bubbling deep fat fryers and into the warming compartment on the long, sleek stainless-steel range. 'What's up, duck?'

'Nothing. Everything. Just ignore me.'

'Not easy when you look like you're about to burst into tears.' Mrs Gibby slapped pieces of cod and haddock through a bath of batter mix, drained them and dropped them expertly into another bubbling vat of oil. The resulting hiss and the rise of steam was almost pyrotechnical. 'Do you want to take a break? Are you feel-ing ill? You've worked like a Trojan every day since you've been here, Kitty, and I always worry that I work people too hard.'

'I'm fine,' Kitty said. 'I just made a bit of a prat of myself yes-terday, which is the story of my life, sadly – oh, and we still need to find a new home before September. And I'm trying really hard to be upbeat and positive, but at the moment I'm crumbling a bit.'

'Well, I'm not sure I can do anything about either of the first two things, but we can't have you crumbling in front of the punters – it'd be bad for business.' Mrs Gibby chuckled. 'So, why don't you pop out into the yard with a can of Coke from the fridge and sit down for ten minutes? As you know, it's nice and shady round the back there – and quite picturesque, as long as you ig-nore the empty oil drums and the smell of fish.'

Kitty laughed. 'Ta – I will, if you're sure. I didn't sleep well last night. But just for ten minutes. No longer.'

'Man trouble . . .' Mrs Gibby whispered knowledgeably to Rhonda as Kitty headed towards the cold-drinks cabinet. 'You mark my words.'

The tiny yard at the back of the fish-and-chip shop where the staff took their breaks when the weather was fine, was, as Mrs Gibby had said, shaded, but hardly a place of beauty. However, the wooden table and trestle benches were tucked away against the trunk of a massive chestnut tree and were clean and cool, and Kitty sank down gratefully, opened her can of drink and closed her eyes as the ice-cold bubbles trickled down her throat.

Bliss.

She stretched her legs out under the table, opened her eyes again and watched the leaf shadows dance. There was a distant hum of traffic and footfall and voices from the High Street on one side, and the even more distant shush of the sea on the other. It was wonderfully soothing and soporific.

'Is anyone sitting here?'

The voice – his voice – made her jump. Had she dreamed it? Imagined it?

She stared at him. 'What . . . ? What are you doing here . . . ? I mean . . . ?'

Vinny smiled. 'Well, is there? Anyone? Sitting there?'

'No – and this is part of the Fish Bar. You shouldn't be here.'

He sat on the bench opposite her, and slid his long legs under the table. His black T-shirt said that he'd been at Woodstock in 1969. She knew he hadn't.

He lifted his own can of Coke in salute. 'Now, as for whether I should be here or not – just now, when I went in to the chippie and asked if you were working today, the lovely lady behind the counter said that if I was the reason you looked like a wet cod then I was to take a cold drink and get my arse out here pronto. If it turned out I wasn't the reason, then I had to go back in there and tell her so.'

'Oh my god.' Kitty shook her head. 'I'm really sorry.'

'You said that yesterday, too. And the last time I saw you on the beach. I didn't know why, then, either. So, should I stay or should I go, as the Clash so succinctly put it? Not,' he said quickly, 'that you look anything like a wet cod, by the way.'

'Thank you.' Although yesterday, I apparently looked like a Muppet. I'm clearly holding all the aces, looks-wise, she thought. 'And you can stay.'

'Good.'

He smiled at her, and her world somersaulted in a cascade of rainbows and rose petals. Then she remembered Tilda the Rice Queen. Damn it.

They sat in silence for a moment. Companionable, not awkward.

'Yesterday . . .' Kitty said slowly. 'I wanted to apologise for the last time we met. I wanted to apologise for being crass about –' she stopped. She couldn't look at him. Couldn't bear to see the hurt. Then she remembered Destiny's mantra, took a deep breath and looked at him. 'Well, about the loss of your child.'

Vinny blinked at her. He had incredibly long dark eyelashes. She wondered why she hadn't noticed them before.

'About – *what* . . . ?'

'The loss of your child. I rambled on, like I do, about you building sandcastles for your own children and you said . . .'

Vinny put his drink down. Slowly. 'I guess I said something along the lines of one child, and not any more? Was that it?'

Kitty nodded. 'Yes. And I'm so very sorry. I had no right to pry. I really didn't mean to hurt you. It was such a stupid thing for me to assume, and then I realised that you had lost a child and . . .'

'I said one child, and not any more, because that's the truth. I have a son, Oliver, and he's eighteen – he's well past building sandcastles – and he lives in Australia, anyway.'

Kitty stared at him. 'Really?'

'Really.'

Oh. My. Word. She breathed a massive sigh of relief.

Then she pulled a face. 'But you don't look old enough . . . oh, god – no – what I mean is . . . eighteen . . . um . . .'

Vinny laughed. 'I backpacked round Australia and New Zealand when I'd finished school and before I went to college. I was nineteen when I met Cara in Sydney. She was a year younger than me. We thought it was love. I was back home when she phoned and told me about the baby. I was shocked and a bit scared – but she was a lovely girl, and we'd had a lot fun together, and I suddenly had responsibilities. I asked her to marry me. I said I'd fly over. Get a job. Support them both.'

Kitty was riveted. And more than a little jealous.

Vinny shrugged. 'She laughed at that. She told me she was way too young to get married, that we'd had a fling and I was a great guy but not the love of her life. She said she had a life to live and it sure as hell didn't involve being married at eighteen. She told me her parents were more than happy to help her out with the baby.'

Kitty fiddled with her Coke can. She was very aware that, had she been in Cara's position, her parents, despite their odd life-style choices, would have been anything but supportive and understanding.

'We were so young. Kids ourselves. But we had a baby depending on us,' Vinny continued, 'so, I told her I'd always make sure she had whatever she needed for Olly's upkeep, and asked her to let him know about me – and over the last eighteen years, I've managed to get over there more or less every year to see Olly – well, both of them – although Cara has been married for ten years now, very happily, and she and David have another couple of kids. Olly and I are good mates – Cara and David have done a great job.'

Kitty swallowed. 'I am such an idiot.'

'I'm saying nothing.' Vinny grinned. 'So, is that honestly why you vanished that day? Because you thought you'd just reminded me of my dead child?'

'Yes.'

'Jesus!' Vinny shook his head. 'I mean, if it had been true – which, thank god, it wasn't – then you rushing away because you felt upset and embarrassed would have made some sort of sense. But as I had no idea that you'd completely misinterpreted what I'd said, I assumed it was something I'd done to insult you. One minute we were laughing over the dogs having caused mayhem with that little girl, and then – *whoomph*! You were belting away from me up the steps – and until yesterday, I haven't seen you since. I had no idea what I'd said to offend you.'

'Whereas I knew exactly what I'd said to offend you. Or thought I did.'

They looked at one another. The extractor fans and generators at the back of the Silver Fish Bar, blew alternately hot and cold. The noise was an off-key rattle and hum. It was hardly the stuff of dreams.

'We've been pretty stupid, haven't we?' Kitty said.

'Yep.' Vinny sighed. 'You see, over the past few months of meeting and chatting on the beach, I thought of you as a friend. We were getting to know one another a bit more each time we met. I really liked you. You made me laugh. I'm a bit of a loner . . . a bit shy . . . but you were friendly and outgoing from the start – and then there was Teddy and the dogs and Apollo, and you told me all about them and you chatted about so many things which was great, and I thought we were getting on well. And then – you'd gone.'

'We *were* getting to know one another really well,' Kitty said sadly. 'I felt much the same as you. I always looked for you on the beach, and really missed you when you weren't there – oh!' The penny suddenly dropped. 'Through the months when you were missing – you were in Australia?'

'Yep. Mostly escaping the cold here and spending the spring or summer over there with Olly, and Cara and David's family . . . oh, and working some of the time, too.'

They sat in silence again.

'I should have tried to find you earlier,' Vinny said. 'Because I realised how much I missed you. But heck, I'm a bloke – you'd stormed away from me, you'd obviously had second thoughts, you clearly didn't want to be with me, and I wasn't going to risk having my head bitten off – so I tried to forget all about you and . . .'

And managed to forget me really well with Tilda the Rice Queen, Kitty thought sadly. And it's all my fault. Bugger.

'Well, once I'd plucked up the courage to try and find you and apologise for blurting out stuff without thinking,' – Kitty looked at him – 'I started practically haunting the beach – no, I'm not proud. I wanted to see you – and I couldn't . . . didn't . . . you weren't there.'

'Working,' Vinny said. 'I've been flat out at work recently. And yes, I could have come to see you here – or at Sandcastle Cottage, because you'd told me where you worked and lived – but I assumed that you didn't want to see me, and I do have a bit of pride and not a lot of confidence, so I backed off. Until now.'

Kitty sat and took all this in. 'But . . . so, why now? Why today?'

'Because seeing you yesterday made me realise just how much I wanted to see you again. To talk to you. To find out what I'd done wrong and if I could put it right and, well, to get to know you properly. You looked so lovely yesterday on the clifftop, unaware of anything but the sea and with your hair streaming in the wind – like a Pre-Raphaelite painting.'

'Seriously?' Kitty erupted with laughter. 'Apparently, I looked like Beaker!'

'Muppets Beaker?'

'Yep.'

'Yeah, well, maybe . . . yeah, I can see that, too.'

They grinned at one another.

'However,' – he surveyed her – 'you'll always be more Princess Merida with a touch of Julia Roberts, to me – but with an awful lot of very original Kitty, thank goodness.'

Kitty knew she was blushing. He'd actually taken that much notice of her? Wow.

He reached out to take her hand across the table.

Kitty shook her head. 'I need to say this first because, if we're going to be – well – friends, then I need to know where we stand . . . I'm not in a relationship. I haven't been in a relationship for a long time. But yesterday . . . you were with someone – Tilda?'

Vinny sighed. 'Yes, I was. But not in the way you think – god, no. Tilda is happily gay and happily attached to a marine biologist called Suzie. Tilda runs the sand sculptures exhibition at Heartbreak Bay – mercifully not anywhere else. She's a slave driver. She'd organised a talk for me . . . she'd come to get me.'

Although feeling very elated about Tilda, The Rice Queen,

and her happy relationship, Kitty still frowned. 'So – you're not seeing anyone at the moment?'

'No. Like you, I've been single for quite a long time. Once bitten – sorry – cliché – but you know what I mean?'

Kitty nodded. 'Only too well. But – OK – Tilda . . . yesterday at Heartbreak Bay . . . a talk? You? There? Why?'

'Because I'm the Sandman.'

'Holy crap on a cracker!'

Vinny laughed. '*What*?'

'Jem says it all the time – it just came out. It's appropriate, though. *You*? You build, design and make all those incredible sculptures? That's who you are? What you do?'

He nodded. 'I thought, because you were there, that you knew.'

Kitty didn't know whether to laugh or cry or hurl herself at him. She decided to just talk. For now. 'I had no idea. But you're a genius artist, then. Amazing. Incredibly talented. Just brilliant and clever and creative and – well – just wow. Vinny – are you blushing?'

'A bit. Like I said, I'm a bit of an introvert. I don't tell people what I do – I mean, "I build sandcastles" isn't the greatest work-related chat-up line, is it?'

'I think it's simply mind-blowing.' Kitty stared at him. 'And it's so much more than sandcastles, isn't it? You should be shouting it from the rooftops. How can you be – well – *him* – and people not know?'

'*You* didn't.'

'No – true – but then I'm a relative newcomer and I'd never heard of Heartbreak Bay until yesterday – let alone the sculptures and – well – you . . . but surely, people who know about the sand sculptures there must know you're the Sandman?'

'No, they honestly don't, because most of the time I'm simply in the background at any of my exhibitions, making sure the sculptures are looking as they should, with no damage, and I always step in with my little bucket of water and paintbrush to do running repairs if needed. So if anyone sees me, then they think I'm just the handyman or something, I guess. I'm invisible – by choice. Heartbreak Bay is the only local exhibition I do. The little Q&A sessions Tilda organises are only for the kids really, none of them know me from Adam when I'm out doing my shopping or walking on the beach or having a drink in the local café – which is how I like it.'

Kitty simply stared at him. 'So, if I hadn't been there with the nursery trip yesterday, or ever, and we'd met up again one day in the future, we wouldn't have had this conversation?'

'Not for ages. Probably not, no. I certainly don't talk about it – well, not until I know people pretty well. Anyway, like I say, people seem to think it's what kids do – or maybe vagrants?'

Kitty sucked in her breath. 'You know about that? You know that's what they call you?'

He grinned. 'Well, yes – let's face it, this is a pretty conservative area . . . people fit into boxes, or they don't fit in. I appear to be unemployed with no visible means of support, I walk along the beach, staring at the sand or the sea, I'm not fussed about fashion – jeans and T-shirts and my big 1960s charity-shop overcoat when it's cold – and I like my hair longish . . . so, yes, people judge.'

'I thought you looked fabulous – er, *look* fabulous – very rock-star arty.' She smiled at him. 'Don't blush! So, when you walk along the shoreline . . . ?'

'I'm thinking of ideas, designs, new sculptures – it's my think-ing place.'

'Yes, I get that. And so much you've said in the past makes sense now. But when you're not around, when you vanish – and not when you're in Australia – are you somewhere in a studio, con-juring up new designs?'

'No, there's no studio – I'm not that organised. If I'm missing, it's usually because I'm at a competition. They have sand-sculpture contests in Britain but also all over the world. I like to enter a few each year, it's good for the CV, plus there are monetary awards – it's a lucrative side of my work.'

'Blimey. I can see I've got a lot to learn. Sandcastle contests on a worldwide scale – who knew?' Kitty grinned at him. 'But, yes, I totally can see that you'd get endless inspiration from the coast – it's helped me a lot with most of my problems . . . they just seem so small and insignificant when you have the vast sky and the sea and . . .'

'That's why I liked you so much, right from the start. Why I enjoyed talking to you. Because I recognised a kindred spirit, who enjoyed the sea and the sky and the beach whatever the weather, and because you chatted to me as if we were friends. Unlike so many other people, you didn't judge me or ask me awkward questions –' he stopped and looked at her across the table – 'and OK yes, because I really, really fancied you.'

He reached out for her hand again and this time, she didn't move away. The touch of his skin on hers was electric. She curled her fingers round his, and they sat, holding hands across the faded ancient table, amid the Coke cans.

Kitty looked round at the scrubby grass, the stacks of empty oil drums, the crates and polystyrene boxes that had contained potatoes and fish and were now piled neatly against the wall, waiting for the recycling people to collect; at the scruffy once-white back wall of the Silver Fish Bar, at the extractor fans and the rusting grilles of the generator, and thought nowhere had ever seemed more romantic.

Vinny smiled at her. 'So, where do we go from here? Are there any other skeletons you'd like me to unleash? Or do you want to wash all your dirty laundry in public first?'

'Well,' – Mrs Gibby bustled out from the back door, carrying a tray – 'before either of you get down to that, I thought you'd need some refreshments.'

'Oh, goodness.' Kitty looked at her watch. 'I'm really sorry. I've been ages – I didn't notice the time. I ought to get back – you're so busy.'

'We're coping. You sit there, young Kitty, and you relax and enjoy yourself with this very dishy young man who has just given you back your sparkle.' Mrs Gibby beamed at them both. 'Warms the cockles of my heart, it does – you take as long as you like, my duck . . . you deserve this.'

'Oh, wow – thank you so much,' Kitty said, looking at the tray – with the Brown Betty tea-for-two set, and a large bowl of chips and a plate of bread and butter. 'I think I'm going to cry.'

'Don't you dare.' Mrs Gibby gave her shoulder a squeeze.

'Thank you. This looks amazing!' Vinny smiled at Mrs Gibby. 'You're very kind – and how much do I owe you?'

'Nothing at all. You just enjoy it, and keep making this young lady smile – oh, and invite me to the wedding, of course.'

And she was still chuckling as she waltzed back inside the fish bar.

So, in the scruffy backyard of the Silver Fish Bar, over cups of strong tea and deliciously thick chip butties, they exchanged phone numbers, and Kitty gave Vinny a short and relatively sanitised version of her life so far, and she discovered that his parents lived along the coast in Christchurch and didn't really approve of his lifestyle or his career choice and therefore the relationship was a distant one (something else they had in common); that Vinny rented a room in an old school friend's house in Hinton Chervils, the next village along, because everything about his profession meant no 9–5, no permanent job, travelling to competitions, and no steady income; that he'd studied at a London college of art; that he'd always been interested in sculpting with different materials – and because he loved the coast, the sand-sculpting had turned from a hobby into a career.

They also discovered they liked the same books – thrillers and police procedurals – and food – practically anything except offal – had very differing musical tastes, both enjoyed watching most sports, that they might tussle over control of the telly remote as their viewing habits seemed to differ, and although Vinny was an avid fan of sci-fi cinema and Kitty wasn't, they both loved old black-and-white films, especially Hitchcock.

That they had a shared love of summer days and the sea was a given, but it was pretty cool, Kitty thought, to find out that they also both loved rainy nights, snowstorms, real fires, and proper old-fashioned Christmases.

'We've wasted a lot of time,' Vinny said, stacking the après-tea-and-butty debris onto the tray. 'We should have had this conversation weeks ago.'

'We should.' Kitty sighed. 'Although I did try – but it always sounded as if I was trying to interrogate you.'

'And I probably clammed up, because I never know what to say when I'm asked about myself.'

'Thank goodness for Mrs Gibby, then – if she hadn't made me take a break and then sent you out here, none of this would have happened.'

'A sliding-doors moment.' Vinny grinned. 'A concept that always bothered me.'

'And me – the scary "what if".'

'So, let's sort that out straight away – are you free tomorrow?'

'I am.'

'Great. I'll pick you up at ten thirty.'

'In the morning?'

He laughed. 'Yes. And, I guess this always sounds sinister, but I do know where you live.'

'Oh, yes – something else I blurted out when I probably shouldn't have. However,' – Kitty sighed – 'there's one more massive elephant in the room.'

Vinny stopped stacking the crockery. 'Is there? You mean we haven't covered everything?'

She shook her head. 'The lease on Sandcastle Cottage runs out in less than a month. The owner is coming home to stay. And we have nowhere else to go. This could be the end of our time in Firefly Common . . .'

Chapter Twenty-Three

'Kitty's got a date! Kitty's got a date!' Jemini and Teddy held hands and skipped noisily round Sandcastle Cottage's kitchen the following morning. 'La-la-di-dah-di-dah! Kitty's got a date!'

Honey and Zorro joined in, bouncing up and down and barking excitedly.

Connor, who was just about to leave for work, and Apollo, who was on the late shift at the Mermaid but had been unable to sleep, sat at the farmhouse table with their coffees and watched with amusement.

Kitty, of course, was upstairs, getting ready, and missed all the fun.

'Nice to see some happiness,' Apollo said. 'I hope Kitty has a lovely time.'

Connor nodded. 'Me too. It's about time. Look, this morning, I'm going to have a word with Dad and see exactly where we stand on the lease here. The rental was always an odd one, and I've never seen the original paperwork – and we really need to know what it says. We also need to know if Dad's heard when Mrs Mulholland intends to move back in. Officially – and not from village gossip.'

'It would be good to know,' Apollo agreed, 'even though we may not like what we hear.'

They looked sadly at one another.

Apollo lifted his coffee mug. 'Still, with you and Jemini working in the estate agency, you could find a nice place for the two of you and Teddy, quite easily, I guess?'

Connor pulled a face. 'We could, of course. But it's not what either of us want. We all belong together. I know I was a bit of a latecomer to the party, but I can't imagine not living with all of you – and the dogs of course – anywhere else.'

'This is what Jemini feels too, I know. I asked her.' Apollo nodded. 'It's good to know that we all feel the same and want to stay together. Even if it turns out that we will have to split up before very much longer.'

They exchanged looks over the tops of their mugs and heaved a mutual heartfelt sigh.

At 10.25 a.m., Kitty paced up and down the veranda, hopped up and down the porch steps, rushed down the garden path, looked quickly in each direction along the lane and repeated the procedure. Because anything was better than just standing still and waiting.

Her butterflies had butterflies and she felt slightly sick. This was awful – like being a teenager all over again.

She had no idea what Vinny was going to be driving, or even from which direction he'd appear. Or even – she admitted to herself – if he'd turn up at all.

She'd showered at some ridiculous hour and washed her hair, leaving it to dry in the early morning sun, and had then tried to tame the curls into some tousled yet carefree clearly desirable Pre-Raphaelite look. The Pre-Raphaelites, she reckoned, must have spent half their day doing their hair and then not moving their heads an inch . . . Also, remembering the Beaker look and being careful to avoid a repetition, after ten minutes she'd given up trying to emulate Elizabeth Siddall and settled instead for what the influencers called a 'messy bun', with tendrils escaping all over the place.

After a slather of lip gloss, a fair bit of blusher, some kohl and several coats of mascara, along with the up-do, she was reasonably pleased with the result.

Along with the faded denim cut-offs, the pale-blue rosebud-sprigged vest and the ubiquitous sequinned flip-flops, Kitty hoped she'd achieved a sort of glam-casual amalgam. If Vinny arrived and told her they were going to have tea with his dowager great-aunt or something, she'd have to go and change, but for an informal first date she thought she looked OK.

Everyone else had thought so too, when she went downstairs – but they might just have been being kind.

Kitty, too nervous to stay indoors, and because the dogs were slightly worried by the pacing, leaned with what she hoped looked like casual nonchalance, on the garden gate.

'What-ho, young Kitty!' Netta and Noel, returning from their first Nordic walk of the day, stopped by the gate and chorused in unison. Netta did her bared-teeth grin. 'And you look a proper bobby-dazzler – that outfit's not for serving up fish and chips, I'll be bound.'

Kitty agreed that it wasn't, and explained that she was being taken out.

'Oooh, somewhere nice?' Noel asked.

'And,' Netta queried, 'by whom?'

Noel shook his head at his sister. 'That's not polite, Netta. One should only enquire using generalisations.'

'Still quoting mother's 1920s book of etiquette,' Netta muttered. 'He knows it off by heart.' She raised her voice. 'Very well, then, Noel – but because I want to know, I shall just wait here until the gentleman – or lady – arrives, and then I'll have the evidence in front of me, will no longer have to ask questions, and I'll know without upsetting Emily Post's biggest fan here.'

'Emily Post?' Kitty frowned.

'The absolute authority on all aspects of etiquette in the early to mid- twentieth century,' Noel said. 'Mother swore by her. I still do. Netta has gone a little rogue on manners latterly, I fear.'

Kitty felt she may have been about to learn even more about Emily Post, but was mercifully rescued by the appearance of Angelica and Mr H.

'We saw you,' Angelica said, 'from the front guest-bedroom

window. We said we thought you looked as if you were waiting for someone.'

'She is. She's being taken on an excursion,' Noel piped up. 'My instincts tell me she'll be escorted by a gentleman.'

Netta wasn't to be outdone. 'But we don't know by whom, and it's apparently rude to enquire, so we're waiting to see.'

Angelica raised her very recently threaded eyebrows. 'Ah . . . so, do I tell Destiny that her work here is done? Would I be correct in thinking that mindfulness and positivity have won the day?'

'Load of bollocks,' Mr H said, before Kitty could reply.

Netta and Noel looked shocked.

Angelica ignored the comment. 'So, anyway, Mr H and I popped down to see what was what. Who is he – as if I need to ask – and where are you going?'

Kitty looked at them all and laughed. God, she loved these people, who were the polar opposites of anyone she'd ever known, almost caricatures of themselves, but who had always been such good neighbours and become amazing friends.

She was going to miss them so much.

'I have no idea where we're going.'

'Is it a magical mystery tour?' Netta clasped her hands. 'We used to go on those with our nanny when Mummy and Daddy were too busy to take us out, didn't we Noel?'

Noel nodded, smiling beatifically. 'Happy days, Netta. Happy days. Ooh – Kitty – is this your young man now?'

Everyone stared and watched as an original dark-green 1960s Mini Cooper S trundled along the sandy track towards them.

Kitty could have clapped her hands in delight. Her own car, her beloved new-breed Mini in Oxford Blue, had gone the way of her home and everything else she owned, thanks to the vile James and his law-breaking father, and she'd not been able to afford a replacement since.

But what could have been more apt for Vinny, than this glorious piece of motoring history?

As the car came to a halt, Angelica, Mr H, and Netta and Noel all craned forward.

'Oh my word!'

'Surely not!'

'It's Vinny the Vagrant!'

'Netta – you mustn't say that! Emily Post says—'

'Stuff Emily Post, Noel – our little Kitty is being taken out by Vinny the Vagrant!'

Only Angelica smiled and hugged her. 'Well done, sweetie. He's absolutely smoking hot.'

He certainly was, Kitty thought happily.

Vinny was dressed, much to Kitty's relief, in jeans and T-shirt and trainers, so there was presumably no planned dowager-great-aunt visits on the horizon. He uncurled himself from the driving seat, smiled at Kitty, held her hands in his, and kissed her very gently.

'Hello.' He gazed at her. 'You look gorgeous.'

'Thank you,' Kitty said dazedly, through the cascade of rainbows and bluebirds and celestial trumpets. 'So do you. Oh, and we've just shared our first kiss in front of an audience.'

'So we have.' He kissed her again. Slowly. 'Not bad for two shy introverts, eh?'

'Not bad at all.' She sighed happily, hoping that her legs would stop shaking long enough to hold her up.

Then she looked towards Sandcastle Cottage. Jemini, Apollo and Teddy were standing at the top of the porch steps, laughing and waving. Honey and Zorro had padded down the garden path and were standing at the gate, tails on full-whizz, Staffie smiles at their widest. At least Connor had already left for work, Kitty thought, so not quite a full house.

'My almost-family, who you already know,' she said to Vinny. 'And my neighbours, who you don't.'

Vinny waved at the Sandcastle Cottage contingent, leaned down to pat the dogs, and then grinned at everyone else. 'A welcoming committee – fabulous.' He held out his hand. 'I'm Vincent Cassidy.'

One by one they shook his hand and introduced themselves.

'They were worried that I might have fallen into bad company,' Kitty explained.

'Which of course, you have,' Vinny said cheerfully, trying to extricate his hand from Angelica's clutches and beaming at them all. 'But I promise to have her home safely by midnight.'

He opened the passenger door and she curled herself into the lovely worn-leather and polished-wood interior. As he slid into the driving seat, he leaned across and kissed her again. 'Well, here we are, then.'

'Here we are,' she agreed happily. 'I'm not sure I believe it – after all the false starts and faffing.'

'There was a lot of faffing.' Vinny nodded, steering the Mini carefully round the neighbours who had now been joined on the road by the entire Sandcastle Cottage posse. Everyone clapped as they passed. Kitty waved. 'On both sides, although, obviously, I tried more to be aloof and enigmatic.'

'No, you didn't!' Kitty laughed. 'You admitted yesterday, you were just monosyllabic and non-committal.'

'You make it sound almost endearing.' Vinny chuckled as they moved steadily into the traffic on the High Street. 'Whereas, as I recall, you asked questions with all the ferocity of Jeremy Paxman – only you had better hair. And were prettier, obviously.'

They laughed. Together. And Vinny reached across and took her hand, holding it under his on the steering wheel.

'This car is fabulous,' Kitty said, as they drove past Firefly Common's recreation ground and headed beneath the colonnade of pine trees towards the New Forest road. 'It's very you.'

'What, old and unfashionable? Cheers.'

'Cool and original and classy.'

He grinned at her. 'Yep, OK – I'll take that. And the car . . . yes . . . not ideal for someone tall with long legs, but I was willing to make the sacrifice. I've had her for years and years and she probably costs me more now annually to keep roadworthy, than she would have done to buy new, but I'll never part with her. Do you drive? What car do you have?'

They were halfway through the New Forest, past the miles of open heathland covered in scrubby broom and gorse and heather, and into the avenues of ancient woodland with ponies grazing, by the time Kitty had finished telling him all about the demise of her beloved Mini and what had led up to it, and a few other details which added depth to the slightly sanitised life story she'd given him the previous day.

'Bloody hell!' Vinny looked at her. 'You've had a tough time.'

'I thought so at the time – but not so much any more. I was so angry about losing the car and the house and everything I'd worked for and paid for. And then once I'd met Apollo and my life had changed radically, I realised they were just things. And things really, really don't count.'

'This is true. But we've become an increasingly materialist society. Things – new, bright shiny things – seem to matter an awful lot, to an awful lot of people.'

'Not to me.'

'Nor me.' Vinny chuckled. 'Otherwise, I'd have become the architect my parents always wanted me to be, and be designing multi-million-pound houses for people with more money than taste. Plus, I'd be driving the latest top-of-the-range car, and living in Sandbanks luxury, surrounded by – well – new, bright shiny things.'

'I'm so glad you're not.' Kitty smiled. 'I've learned a lot by losing everything. I know what's important now. But the bad bits – well, it's just life, isn't it? Apollo and Jemini have had some rotten deals too – no doubt everyone has. There are good times and bad times and you just have to make the most of it.'

'Very philosophical. And true. And one of the reasons I've tended to keep people at arm's length, I guess – any cock-ups in my life are then simply down to me, and I have to sort them out.'

She looked across at him. 'So, you're taking a huge risk with me, then?'

'Massive.' He smiled. 'In fact, this is the biggest gamble I've taken since I put a tenner on Bournemouth to top the Premier League in 2015.'

She giggled. She loved him.

And then there was the signpost: the higgledy-piggledy, half-hidden wooden signpost: Heartbreak Bay ½ mile.

'You're taking me to work?'

'I am. Fair's fair. I shared your work experience yesterday. Today, I'm returning the compliment.'

Today, the car park at the top of Heartbreak Bay's cliff was empty. The wicker gate across the steps that led down to the sand sculptures was closed. Kitty scrambled from the Mini and smiled to herself. What a difference a day or two made . . . as the song so aptly almost put it.

'We don't open to the public until one,' Vinny said, locking the Mini. 'We've got an agreement with the tourist board, so that all the various attractions on this stretch of the coast can accommodate visitors at staggered times. We have such small beaches along here, and we're all trying to make a living – and the locals know where and when to visit, but the holidaymakers don't – so we open here from one until four, most days.'

'And are you always here? No – you can't be – you've been on the beach back home during the afternoons.'

'I'm only here if I'm working on a new sculpture, or if Tilda has arranged a chat session, or if the weather has been bad and I need to do running repairs. She rings me if she needs me.'

They stood on the clifftop, staring out to sea. The air was summer-warm and sweet-scented. It was very quiet. Vinny pulled her against him and traced her lips gently with his fingers. She shivered. Was this all too much, too soon? She'd never ever felt like this before. How badly broken was her heart going to be if – when – this ended?

Kitty stared out at the horizon where the sea and the sky merged – it was endless and unfathomable, and would go on forever. But they wouldn't. Whatever the risks, it was so important to make the most of this – of the happiness.

181

She sighed and turned to face him. 'I'm not sure I believe this. I was so unhappy when I was here before.'

'Me too. I was pretty sure I'd messed up any chance I'd had of actually ever asking you out – like a normal person – on a date . . . Then – there you were. With Teddy. Here. I thought I'd found you again, and I'd have the opportunity to talk to you and sort out whatever the problem had been – and then you'd gone. Again. And I hadn't said any of the things I'd been meaning to say.'

'I'd rehearsed a speech, too,' Kitty said. 'I doubted it would ever come out right if indeed I ever saw you again, but I had the words ready, just in case. Mercifully for you, I never had to use them. They were rubbish.'

He laughed. She slid her arms round his neck. And this time the kiss was no longer gentle.

'Well,' – the voice came from somewhere a million miles away – 'I do hope this means you'll now stop moping like a sulky teenager, Mr Cassidy. And I also really hope that this very gorgeous female was the cause of the moping?'

Slowly, reluctantly, Vinny and Kitty parted, then turned and stared at the stunning Tilda.

'Kitty – meet Tilda. Tilda, yep, right on all counts. I was just going to show Kitty round some of the sculptures and try to explain that what I do is slightly more than just building sandcastles.'

'It's just building sandcastles,' Tilda said, straight-faced. 'Stop showing off.'

Kitty giggled and decided Tilda could become a good friend.

'You so know how to dent a boy's ego.' Vinny grinned. 'And god – please don't tell me you've arranged a talk group for today?'

'No, I haven't.' Tilda shook back her cascade of long black hair. 'And even if I had, I'd cancel it. You know me – a hopeless romantic – I never stand in the way of true love.' She laughed. 'Fabulous to meet you, Kitty, and so glad you two have finally got it together. He's been a right pissy misery to work with lately. Enjoy the sandcastles, children – but remember to be away from here before the hordes arrive. And I'll be in my little hut if you need me.'

'Tilda's little hut is where the real magic happens,' Vinny said as, hand in hand, they walked down the steep cliff steps. 'She's an ace animator.'

'Isn't that something to do with cartoons?'

'It is, yes,' Vinny said as they headed into the exhibition, 'but it's also used in the world of model-making. Tilda has an electronic set-up that would baffle most aerospace engineers. She's the one that brings all this to life – her bells and whistles make everything move, make the water flow, smoke rise, music play. All the magic. She makes my sculptures come to life.'

Kitty nodded. 'I was certainly impressed by it all – and it seemed to be happening – well – naturally. I couldn't see any strings, or wires, which obviously I wouldn't, now I know there aren't any to see. She's very clever. And does she come with you to your Sandman competitions?'

'She has done. The ones in the States, anyway. They're much bigger on animation over there. But usually, most sand-sculpture contests are simply that – sand sculptures.' He looked at her. 'Are you bored now?'

'What? Are you kidding? Now I've got the chance of an exclusive viewing, and I'm not being buffeted by hundreds of holidaymakers, I'm going to walk all round everything with a critical eye.'

'Christ!' Vinny winced. 'Not too critical, I hope. I'm a shy introvert with zero confidence, remember? Seriously, I'll feel less awkward about it if you walk round on your own and ask me questions afterwards. I'll be over there on the dunes if you need me – but be gentle with me.'

Kitty laughed, and while Vinny sat back on one of the sandbars amid the spiky, coarse sea grass, she walked slowly round the castles and the now-stationary and silent model village and the soundless roaring dragons and slumbering dinosaurs, seeing the sculptures with fresh eyes, picking out so many details she'd missed, still in awe of his talent.

She stopped and looked across at him. He had his knees drawn up to his chin, and his hair had fallen forward in the onshore breeze. He was watching her and smiling. God, she thought, he was so gorgeous.

She called across to him. 'Um . . . Vinny, this one . . . the family-at-the-seaside sculpture here. Teddy was fascinated by it. She said the dogs were Honey and Zorro – and that the little girl was her, and the grown-ups were me and Apollo. I told her she was mistaken. But now I've looked at it properly, she wasn't, was she?'

'No. She was right. I added you all in here not long after I first met you. You intrigued me right from the start – but obviously, at that time I thought you were a family. I simply thought you were beautiful – and I thought Apollo was a very lucky man.'

'I'm blushing now . . . but I wish you'd told me all this earlier. I'd fancied you for ages . . . right from when we first moved into Sandcastle Cottage at Christmas and I saw you walking on the beach.'

'Doing my Vinny the Vagrant act?'

'Yep.'

'And you still fancied me?'

'Like you'll never believe.'

'Bugger!' Vinny sighed. 'We've wasted a lot of time by being scared of being hurt and both attempting to be a bit foolishly enigmatic, haven't we?'

'We have.'

Kitty looked at the miniature sand sculpture of herself, right down to the halo of wild curls, and thought no one could ever pay her a greater compliment.

'So – what do you do when it rains?'

'I usually find a pub or a café until it stops.'

'Idiot. I mean to the sculptures.'

Vinny uncurled his legs and stood up. 'If it's just a shower, we wait until it passes, then I can whip round repairing any minor damage. If it's a long-term heavy storm, we close the exhibition and pray that there's still something left at the end. We did try having tarpaulins on a sort of framework to cover it all up, but it didn't work. It really is in the lap of the gods. So, this summer – scorching hot, no rain – has been perfect for me and this.'

'OK, next question . . . when you build a sculpture – you have an idea, a picture in your head, and you start putting it together, I can understand that. But then how does it stay together? I've built sandcastles on the beach, and no matter how hard you pack the sand in, they're still flimsy things that crumble and collapse. So, are your sculptures built with other things added, not just sand?'

'Wash your mouth out!' Vinny laughed. 'There are purists in the sand-sculpture business who'd have a fit of the vapours at that remark. And now, it really depends on whether you think our new-found relationship can withstand what happens next.'

She blinked. 'You're just going to tell me something weird, aren't you? You have a fetish?'

'No, I don't. Well, no . . . only sand. Which is what I'm now going to bore you with. The Talk.'

'The kiddie's version?'

'The shortest I-don't-want-to-bore-the-most-beautiful-woman-I've-ever-met-rigid-too-soon version.'

'Righty-ho, you smooth-talker, I should be able to cope with that.' She looked at her watch. 'Go!'

Vinny laughed. 'OK – the day when I built that sandcastle on the beach for that child . . .'

'Nirvana.'

'Yes, Nirvana. I used mostly wet sand on the shoreline and whatever beach sand she'd shovelled into her bucket. It held together because of the wet sand. However, as soon as the sand dried out, there would have been nothing to hold it together and the castle would have collapsed – even without the tide coming in and washing it away.'

'Just as well we'd cluttered off by then, then,' Kitty said. 'Bearing in mind the mighty temper of mamma bear Charlene-Louise.'

'Was that her name?'

'It was . . . OK, so, dry sand crumbles and wet sand dries out. Next.'

'So, this is one of the main reasons why my exhibition is here and not on the beaches at Firefly Common or Thrift Drift or Hinton Chervils . . . Heartbreak Bay has something none of them have – something that's vital for sand-sculpting to work.'

'Am I supposed to guess, here?'

'Not unless you want to.'

'I don't. I actually can't imagine . . .'

Vinny looked over his shoulder. 'Over there, just on the other side of the furthest exhibit, the cliffs are split into a minor chasm and there's a gully that runs through it, flows down across the beach and forms a little freshwater estuary into the sea. It's called Heartbreak Bunny, by the way.'

'Cute, I think . . . or not that type of Bunny?'

'Not. Anyway, the constant little stream of fresh water trickling through the cliffs from the River Chervils, brings with it huge deposits of river sand.'

'Which is different to beach sand?'

'Exactly. Beach sand is like a zillion tiny rounded-edged particles, washed to smoothness by the movement of a gazillion tides.'

'And river sand is more ruffty-tuffty altogether?'

'It is. It has jagged edges and a consistency which, when it's mixed with beach sand, makes it all stick together like glue. Although, we in the trade don't call it river sand – we call it . . .'

'Fluvial deposits.'

'Bloody hell!' Vinny stared at her. 'You know this stuff?'

'Of course – doesn't everyone?' Kitty arched an eyebrow. 'No, actually, once I knew you were the Sandman I didn't want you to think I was a complete nermal, so I looked you up.'

186

'Bugger.'

'It was fascinating – lovely pictures on your website, by the way – and I learned stuff, but none of it was as interesting as this. Please go on . . . once you've got the right amounts of beach sand and fluvial whatsits, then what?'

'Then we mix it with either tap water or sea water – nothing else – and start building. And that's it really. You have a design in your head, and lay out the foundations quickly, then just build it up, layer by layer, firming it down . . .'

'Tamping.' Kitty grinned.

He sighed. 'Yes, tamping. You can tamp by hand, but usually on the bigger sculptures you might need a—'

Kitty put up her hand, trying not to giggle. 'Tamper?'

'Gold star, Miss – um – good god, Kitty, I'm really sorry, but I don't even know your surname.'

'Appleby.'

'Thank you. Yes, a tamper . . . after that, it really is just building it up, layer by layer, shaping and compacting, working quickly so it doesn't dry out before you've got the right shape. Then, once you've got your foundation, you just start adding the twiddly bits, all the details, which is the fun part. And that's it, basically.'

'That's it? That's all there is to it?'

'Yep.'

Kitty said nothing for a moment. 'And just one of these – one of the castles, or the houses in the village, or the huge animal sculptures – must take you for ever. It's hours and hours of delicate, painstaking, back-breaking work that isn't even permanent – and you can say "that's all there is to it"?'

Vinny shrugged. 'I've been doing it a long time now. I do get peed off when it rains heavily – or if people let their kids clamber all over the sculptures and break them down – and yes, we've had a fair bit of mindless vandalism, but like any job, if you love it enough, however hard it is, it doesn't seem like work.'

'Are you misquoting John Lennon?'

'Mark Twain, actually.'

'Show-off! I knew that really!' She grinned. 'Miss B wasn't all Austen and Brontë and Dickens, she was also very hot on Twain – and Steinbeck.'

'Miss B?'

'Our sixth form English teacher . . . I was in this little clique of literature nerds, and Amy, who was the biggest nerd of all and dead bossy, called us Miss B's Girls . . . oh, god – don't look like that. Yes, it was a bit swotty and everything – Jem and I were probably the least nerdy, and actually we – Miss B's Girls – still all get together from time to time . . . and I think you're glazing over a bit.'

'I promise I'm not.' Vinny laughed. 'Well, OK, maybe a little bit. But then I've just probably bored you to death with the minutiae of fluvial deposits, so I reckon we're quits.'

'Maybe – although I did nothing with English . . . you at least channelled your creativity into being a genius artist – and all this is quite amazing – and your parents must be so proud when they see what you've created, surely?'

'My parents have never seen anything I've ever made. They have no interest, quote, in a beach-bum who wastes his time building sandcastles.'

'Bastards,' Kitty hissed. Then, 'Oh, god – sorry – they're your parents.'

'Not as you'd notice, and that's a very apt description – and far milder than they deserve, in my opinion.' He smiled at her. 'And are yours proud of you?'

'No! Mind you, I haven't yet told them I've climbed the fast-food ladder from kebabs to fish and chips.' She smiled. 'Not that they ever had any interest in what I wanted to do – which is probably why I had no career plan at all, and why I was so easily sucked into James's family life and business so early on. My parents don't even know where I live any more. They selected their alternative lifestyle and it didn't include a kid who would have loved a dad who made her laugh, and a mum who read her bedtime stories.'

Vinny pulled a face. 'We got the parental short-straws, didn't we?'

'Seems very much like it, yes.'

'And now, we've thoroughly depressed ourselves,' – he pulled her closer – 'maybe we should go and find somewhere for a romantic lunch?'

'Not the chippie?'

'No.' He laughed. 'Not the chippie. Not today. Glorious as it was, and will be again, I've booked somewhere completely different for today, it being our first date and everything. Have you ever been to the Chewton Glen Hotel?'

Chapter Twenty-Four

'He told everyone he'd get you home by midnight,' Jemini said haughtily.

'He did,' Kitty said happily. 'He just didn't say which midnight.'

'And you didn't take an overnight bag or anything – and you didn't leave here in those clothes.'

'We went shopping for essentials.'

'We were worried.'

'I texted you. And Apollo. And Mrs Gibby.'

'Yes, OK, but even so – you've been gone for three days . . . *Three whole days!*'

'I know.' Kitty sighed. 'It's been absolutely amazingly lovely.'

'I should flipping think so – three days in the Chewton Glen Hotel . . . *on a first date?*'

'We thought we'd wasted enough time . . . we had a lot of catching up to do.'

'And have you?' Jemini grinned. 'Caught up?'

'Oh, yes.'

'And where are you off to now?'

'Bed. To catch up on my sleep.'

The following morning, as soon as everyone had given her the third degree – again – and Zorro had finally stopped slobbering her to death after her being missing for *three whole days* – again – and Connor had vanished to open up the estate agent's, and Jemini had vanished to get Teddy ready for nursery and herself ready for joining Connor later in the morning, Kitty managed to get a few minutes to herself and sat on the top step of the porch, nursing her coffee.

The sun skittered through the trees, the warm smell of the sand paths mingled with the ever-present tang of the sea, and everywhere was silent, save for the birdsong and the distant rush of the waves on the shore.

And she had never felt so absolutely, totally, blissfully happy.

Apollo came and sat down beside her. 'Tell me to go away, if you just want to sit and dream and smile.'

'I'd never tell you to go away. Are you OK?'

'Happy for you, Kitty. So happy. Falling in love is never easy. Falling in love and then not being with the person you love is painful beyond bearing.'

She squeezed his arm. 'Oh, you should be with someone, Apollo. You have so much love and kindness to give.'

'But no heart, Kitty. I have no heart to give. I lost that many years ago. This is why I'm glad you and Vinny have managed to be truthful with one another at last. I could see how you felt – and how he felt, also.'

'You could? You should have told me.'

'You'd have laughed. You never have the belief in yourself. You never have known what a beautiful and lovely woman you are. Vinny could see this. I'm very happy for you both.'

'Thank you. We're very happy too. Although, what the future holds, I have no idea. He belongs here . . . his life is here . . . his work is based here . . . so, if we have to leave Sandcastle Cottage . . .'

'He has a home? You could go to his home to live? He loves Zorro, so you could take him too – that wouldn't be a problem?'

'No,' – Kitty shook her head – 'not a problem at all – but Vinny only rents a tiny box room in his friend's house, with no room for me and Zorro. He probably earns more than we do, but his work is seasonal and his payments aren't regular. Which means he can't get a mortgage – and like for the rest of us, rental prices round here for anything bigger than a bedsit are way out of his range.

Anyway, as we've all said before – you and me and Jem and Connor – and now Vinny, we're not going to split up. Never. Ever. We've come through so much – we must be able to find a way to stay together now.'

'You are the optimist in love.' Apollo stood up. 'Stay that way, Kitty. Life's too short . . . now, I'll take the dogs to the recreation ground before Angelica catches me.'

'I think she fancies you. I think she waits for you to leave, and then she jogs out just in time to catch up with you.'

Apollo pulled a face. 'I hope not. She's a nice lady, but she's married. She shouldn't be fancying me if she's married.'

'I suppose she can always look but not touch,' – Kitty grinned – 'and you should be flattered. But, seriously, *I* should be taking the dogs out this morning. It's definitely my turn.'

Apollo shook his head. 'You sit there and smile and daydream for longer, Kitty. I like the recreation ground. I think there. And listen to Metallica.'

Kitty laughed. 'An odd choice of meditation music – maybe you should mention it to Destiny, she's always looking for the weird and the wonderful from the little I experienced . . . No, I'm joking. Whatever it takes. Just enjoy it.'

Whistling to the dogs, fastening their leads and heading out of the gate took Apollo slightly less than five minutes, Kitty reckoned. It took Angelica a mere thirty seconds longer to appear.

'Has Apollo gone?' Jemini poked her head out of the door.

'Yep, with the dogs, to the recreation ground – hotly pursued by a jogging Angelica.'

'Seriously? Do you think she . . . ?'

'I think she simply needs someone to tell her she's attractive, and to take an interest in her. I'm guessing Mr H isn't too hot in that department.'

'Like most men, probably, then. Apart from ours – of course.'

Kitty giggled. 'Oh, of course. But even if Angelica *was* after Apollo for more – um – carnal reasons, we both know she'd be wasting her time. Apollo is dead straight, so a married woman would be out of the question anyway, and of course, he's a one-woman man . . . and that ship has clearly sailed long since. So sad.'

'It is.' Jemini sat on the step beside her. 'But not for you. Which is fabulous, because Vinny's drop-dead gorgeous – and it's about flipping time that you found a decent man. So – when is he moving in?'

'I think it might be a bit soon for that,' Kitty said. 'We might have done a lot of – er – catching up on our first date, but . . . oh, hell, who am I kidding? If I had my way, he'd be here now, if we weren't being evicted in a couple of weeks.'

'Well, we do have a bit of news on that score,' Jemini said. 'Oh, nothing really good or positive or anything – don't look like that – just that Connor's dad has dug out all the original agreements with Mavis Mulholland, and he's bringing them over this afternoon so we can go through them and see exactly where we stand.'

'Out in the road with all our belongings in about ten days' time,' Kitty said, 'would be my guess.'

'Oh, shush, Kit. Mind you, Apollo is being right downbeat about it, too.'

'Of course he is – we've all been through this before – and now we've lived here, built a life here, and love living here, losing all this will be a million times worse.'

'Cheer up. We haven't lost it yet. And we still have Amy and the Miss B's Girls fiasco to look forward to next week, haven't we?'

'Heaping gloom upon gloom,' Kitty said. 'Bring it on.'

Jemini hugged her. 'Shut up. Think about Vinny – I mean – well . . . no, maybe don't – you go all gooey and glazed when his name's mentioned. You'll be spilling chips over the pensioners, come lunchtime . . . Righty, I'm off to take my precious child to Ruby's, and then see what joys the world of estate agency has to offer today. Are you just working the one shift?'

Kitty nodded. 'Mrs Gibby was so excited by what she considers the success of her matchmaking, that she said I could have the whole week off if I wanted. Which I don't.'

Jemini stood up and yelled for Teddy to leave Peppa and get a hurry on. 'OK, Kit – so, you'll be home this afternoon sometime, and if these Mulholland papers turn up anything even slightly hopeful, I'll text you. Bye.'

Kitty sat for a little longer, smiling because of Vinny, but holding out no hope at all about Sandcastle Cottage. Because Mavis Mulholland hadn't written to her. Because she'd written before to tell Kitty of her plans – surely if she intended to delay returning again, she'd have said so by now?

Her phone pinged. She smiled.

Good morning. I've missed you. I love you. I'm a bit besotted. I've got to work today. The Rice Queen (I'm so glad you told me that in an unguarded moment of lust and laughter – there were a lot of those, weren't there?) has arranged a kiddie chat. Are you still OK for this evening? I love you – have I already said that? Is this too teenager-in-love for words? Love you for ever and always. V x

She giggled and texted back.

Of course still OK for this evening but missing you so much. Also very much a teenager-in-love here. I've already scribbled your name all over my pencil case. I love you, too. Bad luck on the kiddie chat, good luck with the fluvial deposits and don't tell Tilda about the Rice Queen thing – I like her – I want her to like me. I'm working, too – will try and have got rid of the cod-and-chips aroma by the time we meet. See you later. Love you for ever and always too. K x

Don't shower! Vx
Idiot! Kx

She was still giggling when the postman scrunched up the gravel path.

'Morning, Kitty. Running well behind this morning. The van broke down just as I'd left the sorting office. Had to wait ages for a replacement . . . usually home and finished by now. Here you go, duck.' He handed her a pile of envelopes. 'I'll be lucky to be home before dinner at this rate. Have a nice day.'

'You too,' Kitty said vaguely, staring at the blue airmail letter with her name written in a familiar scrawl on top of the sheaf of post in her hands. 'You too.'

Chapter Twenty-Five

In Lovell and Lowe's High Street branch, Jemini and Connor, along with both Deirdre and Lester Lowe, spread the papers out across the desk.

'I've printed off copies of all correspondence we've had from Mavis Mulholland and/or her solicitors,' Lester said. 'Right from when she took over the deeds of Sandcastle Cottage, after her husband died.'

'And I traced all our dealings with her by phone or email, in case we've missed anything,' Deidre added. 'We also have quite a bit of info about the house prior to that – when it was run as a B&B etcetera – but honestly that's all archive stuff and doesn't add anything relevant.'

Lester Lowe shrugged. 'Since Kitty became the leaseholder of Sandcastle Cottage, Mavis has been in touch, by email, to update me on her whereabouts and to ask how things were going at the house. Until the last few months, I've sent her email updates by return to reassure her that you are all looking after Sandcastle Cottage and have made it your home. She's always seemed happy with what I've told her. But – like the rest of you – I haven't heard from her now since the start of the summer . . .'

Jemini sighed. 'So, she's about as enigmatic here as she appears to be everywhere else?'

Connor nodded. 'Although, over the years, since she's been widowed, she has been in to see us a couple of times . . .'

'Really?' Jemini interrupted. 'So, you've actually met her, have you? You never told us that – Kitty and I have been wondering what she looks like ever since we moved in – bloody hell, Connor! What are you like? We asked you about her and you were rubbish. You could have saved us all those hours of trying to find out something about her – she has no online presence at all – and all the time you knew . . .'

'Jem – hold your horses! I only saw her once very fleetingly.' Connor laughed. 'You and Kitty asked how old I thought she was and I told you I had no idea. No, when I said she came in to see *us*, I mean to the business – but she always used to come in to see Dad in the other office – not here. The day I saw her we more or less passed in the doorway – I have no real recollection of her at all.'

Jemini looked at Lester. 'Right, OK – so *you* know what she looks like – I mean, Kitty and I had a theory at one time, that she might already be back here in Firefly Common and sort of keeping an eye on us.'

'Covert surveillance?' Lester Lowe laughed. 'Hardly Mavis's style, I'd have thought. I don't know what to say about her – she was – well – ordinary, I suppose. Friendly, outgoing, straight-talking, easy to deal with . . .'

'What did she look like, though?' Jemini asked impatiently. 'Goodness, you men are all the same – honestly, I'm just curious about her.'

Deirdre shrugged. 'Don't look at me, Jemini. I never met her. She always saw Lester.'

Lester pulled a face. 'Yes, she came in a couple of times, to discuss either selling or renting the house, because she always felt, once she was on her own, it was far too big for her, but, both times, she decided against it because, well, because Sandcastle Cottage is, as we all know only too well, unique and very special, and Mavis never felt the time was right to let it go. But as to what she looked like – tallish, dark-haired, attractive, middle-aged, I think . . . sorry, Jem – that's about as much as I can remember. I'm not good on people – just houses.'

Jemini sighed. It didn't sit well with the bleached-blonde, cuddly, Beryl Cook-type lady, she and Kitty had imagined. And Lester's vague description could fit anyone, anywhere.

'Anyway, not long after she'd been to see Lester the last time, she won the lottery jackpot,' Deirdre said. 'And it gave her the freedom to travel that she'd always craved. Which is why you and Kitty and Apollo got the house for such a nonsensically cheap rental figure. Money was no longer a priority for Mavis. No one in the village seems to know an awful lot about her. I've heard she and Clive Mulholland met online – he was much older than her, of course, and had lived alone for some time following the death of his first wife. There was some speculation that Mavis had been round the block a few times, so to speak, but even if that was true, she seemed to make Clive Mulholland very happy in his last years.'

'And copped for the lot when he died?' Jemini said.

'Well, yes.' Lester laughed. 'But there was no one to dispute his will. He had no children, there were no distant rellies all baying for a share of the house – and, as I understand it, he was property-rich but relatively cash-poor in comparison, so with Sandcastle Cottage being as huge as it is, Mavis had a bit of a millstone round her neck, financially.'

'OK' – Jemini nodded – 'so winning the lottery meant all her problems were over and she could – well – carry on cruising?'

Deidre laughed. 'Very aptly put, Jem. And yes, this is exactly what she's done.'

Connor frowned. 'But we're no nearer knowing when she intends coming home, are we? Last time, she sent us a letter informing us, as her letting agents, plus a personal one to Kitty – that hasn't happened this time, has it?'

Lester Lowe shook his head. 'No. And, of course, the original rental papers that Kitty signed were only for a six-month period. Mavis extending the lease in a letter would never have stood up as a legal document. Not that that matters now, of course.'

'Which means,' – Jemini ran her fingers frustratedly through her hair – 'that there's nothing in this lot of paperwork to stop us all being kicked out of Sandcastle Cottage in the very, very near future . . . sod it – I'll go and put the kettle on. Who wants tea? Coffee? And as we're all a bit depressed, I'll get the biscuits, too. A sugar-rush carb-hit is possibly what we all need right now. Won't be a sec . . .'

'There is one piece of good news,' Deidre said after they'd all got drinks and the biscuit tin was in reach, and they were sitting round in the armchairs reserved for special clients – the ones with large cash deposits and no chains attached to their current properties. 'Not that it makes any difference to the will-she-won't-she Sandcastle Cottage conundrum, but I've had a taker on my Sea View portfolio – and the details have only been up online for a few days.

'That's great,' Jemini said. 'So, is this a genuine enquiry do you think?'

'Very much so.' Deirdre sipped her tea. 'A Mr and Mrs Gandolfo. A retired couple. Cash buyers. Very interested in that fisherman's cottage out on the cliffs overlooking Thrift Drift Cove. It's been completely renovated and brought bang up to date – all mod cons and then some. I've arranged for them to pick up the keys and have a look round whenever it's convenient. I'm just waiting to hear back. If it goes through, it'll get the Sea View plan rolling, and everyone who signed up for it will make some money. Exciting, no?'

'Yes, very!' Jemini smiled. 'And one in the eye for Peter Marlow-Smith.'

'Oh, yes. Abso-bloody-lutely,' Deidre said, laughing. 'Any more custard creams going over there?'

In a moment of déjà vu, Kitty went to work with the airmail letter, unopened in her pocket. It wasn't that she was scared to read it – well, OK, she admitted, she really was – but because, when she'd received Mavis Mulholland's previous letter, Vinny had been there. And tonight he'd be with her again – although, she thought happily, under completely different circumstances. But, months ago, she'd thought of him as her talisman, and that if he was around when she opened the letter, the news would be good, and she was superstitious enough to not want to risk hexing it this time round.

She'd keep the letter and read it later. With Vinny.

Glad that the decision was made, Kitty shoved the letter in the pocket of her tabard and set off for the Silver Fish Bar.

Of course, Mrs Gibby and Rhonda – as well as Grace and Jade, the two High School girls who were temping as waitresses – wanted to know the details of her first date with Vinny. She didn't tell them all of it. Obviously. However, what she did tell them had them all sighing happily and resuming their fish-and-chip duties with soppy smiles and starry eyes.

Mrs Gibby took every opportunity to hug her and say how thrilled she was to have kick-started the romance of the century. Oh, and how bloomin' darn sexy Vinny was – not unlike the late lamented Mr Gibby had been in his prime, apparently.

Kitty, pretty starry-eyed and happily sighing herself, flew through the lunchtime session, thinking about seeing Vinny later and not about the letter in her pocket. Even the fact that Jemini hadn't texted her, and therefore there was obviously no good Mavis Mulholland news forthcoming, didn't manage to faze her. Not today.

But, at the end of her shift, when Mrs Gibby, no longer all teasing and jolly but now wearing her serious face, suggested they 'pop out the back for a couple of minutes for a little chat before you go home', her heart sank.

They sat, as she and Vinny had done, at the trestle table. Mrs Gibby had brought out mugs of tea. The rattle and hum of the extractor fan and the air-con and the generator was a cacophony today. The smell of fish and empty oil drums made her feel sick.

The magic had gone.

'Right,' Mrs Gibby said. 'I've been meaning to have this little chat with you for a while now. But the time never seemed quite right – especially when you were so down and depressed.'

Oh, god, Kitty thought. She's going to sack me . . . Let me go . . . Can't afford me any more . . .

'But now you're all loved-up and bushy-tailed with your gorgeous young man,' Mrs Gibby continued, 'the time seemed perfect. Therefore, I wondered if you'd be kind enough to pop in and see me tomorrow evening, about six-ish? After we've closed . . . yes, I know you're working tomorrow until four – but I need to talk to you and Rhonda together, and she's going to have to get over here from the Christchurch shop tomorrow.'

'Oh . . . yes . . . of course, but . . .' Kitty mumbled and stumbled over her words. 'Please, can't you just tell me whatever it is, now? Not tomorrow – not in front of Rhonda . . . please . . .'

Mrs Gibby shook her head. 'I'm doing it this way because it's fair, Kitty. I've always been fair to you, haven't I?'

'Yes, of course you have, but . . .'

Mrs Gibby raised her mug. 'Tomorrow, Kitty – oh, and I've asked Rhonda to bring her hubby, Raymond with her. I'd like you to bring that very handsome Greek boy you live with, please.'

Fleetingly thinking Apollo would be thrilled to be referred to as a boy, let alone handsome, Kitty frowned.

'Apollo? You want me to bring Apollo? We've never been – well – a couple or anything . . .'

'I know that.' Mrs Gibby nodded. 'And I have my reasons. I think if Rhonda and Raymond are both here, then, being absolutely fair, you should have Apollo. Drink your tea, duck, it's getting cold.'

Kitty didn't want her tea.

'But – why not Vinny?'

'Because Vinny Cassidy is divine and will no doubt be with you for ever and a day, but for this meeting I want someone who is capable of – oh – Kitty, let's just leave it until tomorrow.' Mrs Gibby stood up and collected the mugs. 'I'm sorry to be so vague – but until I can talk to you and Rhonda together once the chippie is shut, then it isn't fair on either of you. Go home now and have a lovely evening with Vinny. Tomorrow is another day, as someone far more famous than me once said.'

'And you have absolutely no idea what she wants to see you about?' Vinny drew her towards him. 'She didn't give you any clue at all?'

'None,' Kitty said, leaning her head against his chest. 'All I can think is, she can't afford us both, and because Rhonda is family she's going to sack me and give my hours to Rhonda – and I think she wants us both to have a man with us in case we have a cat fight or something.'

'Seriously?'

'No – maybe – oh, I don't know. I have no idea what's going on any more or why she wants Apollo to be with me. Maybe it's because Apollo and I go back a long way and – god, who knows? Anyway, Apollo has said he'll be there, and he's been brushing up on employment law via Google ever since I told him, just in case.'

They were sitting side by side on the top of the beach steps. It was another deliciously warm and gentle evening. The beach itself was almost deserted, and Honey and Zorro, given their freedom, were tearing up and down on the shoreline, attacking seaweed, shells, and the odd seagull with gay Staffie abandon.

'Surely, though, if Mrs Gibby was going to let you go,' – Vinny kissed Kitty's bare shoulder – 'she'd have just done it – and she'd have to have a good reason – and anyway, she struck me as a really lovely lady.'

'She is.' Kitty, in white jeans and a black vest, drew her knees up to her chin. 'That's why it's all so odd. Oh, life's a bitch, isn't it? I mean – here we are,' – she looked at him – 'hopefully . . . properly together, at last . . . and now, I'm not sure if I'll have a home or a job.'

'And now,' Vinny said, 'having seen Sandcastle Cottage tonight, properly, for the first time, I can quite see why you're all so unhappy about leaving there. It's a dream home.'

'I know. It is. However,' – she smiled at him – 'if someone says

I have to lose home, job or you, and that I can only have one out of the three, I'll hang on to you, I think.'

'A little more conviction there might have helped.' Vinny laughed, standing up and hauling her to her feet. 'And don't count your chickens, Miss Appleby, because you went against my express wishes and no longer smell of cod and chips.'

'But it's Black Opium now,' Kitty said. 'Far more enticing, surely?'

Vinny kissed her. 'Oh, yeah, that's almost as good . . . and it makes me feel a bit – ah, sod it, the dogs seem to have vanished. I think we ought to get down there and keep an eye on those two canine reprobates before they disappear from view and end up in the middle of Bournemouth or somewhere even further south.'

Dogs, huh? No idea of timing, Kitty thought, as she and Vinny pulled apart, and they called and whistled to Honey and Zorro, who eventually stopped in their tracks and looked over their shoulders, tails wagging.

'Stay!' Kitty yelled, her voice whisked away on the dancing breeze. 'Just hang on and stay there! Both of you!'

Holding Vinny's hand, she skittered down the remaining steps, and they managed to get the dogs to turn round and trot back safely in the direction of the Mermaid where, once they reached the bottom of the jutting cliff, it meant they could go no further.

With Honey and Zorro now prancing through the shallows ahead of them, as Vinny skimmed flat stones for them to chase across the surface of the silver-blue ripples, Kitty decided the time had come.

She pulled the airmail letter from the back pocket of her jeans and sat on the sand. White jeans – damp sand . . . what the heck.

The dogs, tired of gulping mouthfuls of salty water and not catching a single stone, turned their joint attention to digging massive holes, hurling clouds of sand out behind them as they excavated, tails wagging and snuffling happily.

Vinny dropped down on the beach beside her.

'This,' – Kitty waved the airmail letter – 'came this morning. It's from Mavis Mulholland – I recognise the writing.'

'Ah, OK.' Vinny nodded. 'But – I remember that other airmail letter – that was when we first met, wasn't it? I caught the letter . . . I think I fell in love with you then – but I could see how important the letter was to you, and I assumed – yep, don't laugh – that it was from your boyfriend, partner, or husband, who might be in the forces and stationed overseas, and . . .'

'Dear lord!' Kitty laughed. 'You should be writing romantic fiction. But, yes, that was the first time we spoke – and the letter wasn't the bad news I'd been expecting – so, I thought, when this one arrived, that maybe . . .'

'I'd be your lucky four-leafed clover again?'

'Yep, something like that.' She opened the letter, her hands shaking. 'OK, here goes . . .'

My dear Kitty, no formal Ms Appleby this time. I feel that we are friends now, even if this friendship and correspondence is, by necessity, a little one-sided. I love you for looking after Sandcastle Cottage so well. Is love too strong a word? I don't know, I hope not. My life changed with my lottery win. I understand from Lester Lowe, that your life changed when you found Sandcastle Cottage. This is the sort of happy symmetry that I love. I'm delighted that you continued to live there for those extra months and have been enjoying it throughout the summer – with your extended family. Yes, Lester Lowe has told me all about them, of course – and again, I'm so thrilled that the many rooms in that beautiful house are now filled with happiness and people and animals and children all turning it into a home. This is how it should be. However – yes, of course there's a however – I'm now on my way back to Firefly Common. I'm enjoying every minute of the luxury that this most luxurious of cruise ships can provide. But I am coming home at last. This time I haven't told Lester Lowe of my plans because I think they are more important to you in the first instance. They affect you personally and yes, OK, legally (which is where Lester Lowe will be informed), but I still think you should hear them first. And not in one of my rambling letters. I will come and see you at Sandcastle Cottage and talk to

you in person as soon as we've docked at Southampton and I've got myself
sorted. All being well, and if everything runs on time, this will be very early
in September. In the meantime – please stay put. I don't want to rock the
boat! I am very much looking forward to meeting you. Yours affectionately,
Mavis.

They looked at one another.

'Well –' Vinny sighed. 'It seems I've been a pretty rubbish talisman this time round, doesn't it?'

Kitty shrugged. 'Not your fault. Obviously. It was just me being a bit superstitious, which is nonsense anyway. But it was always worth a try. Just in case.'

'So, what the actual fuck – sorry, but honestly. What the hell is that letter actually supposed to mean?' Vinny frowned. 'It's all airy-fairy nothingness. What are you supposed to understand from that?'

'God knows.' Kitty exhaled. 'But now we know she's definitely coming home. That she'll want the house back. And that she'll come and tell us so in early September – which is merely days away now, really.'

'But that she doesn't want you to move out yet? Why?'

'No doubt because she's spent all her lottery winnings on every conceivable form of luxury item and travel there is, and now our piddly bit of monthly rent is all she'll have to keep her going, and if we hang on into September then that's another month she'll get out of us.'

'And are you going to tell the others? About the letter?'

'Yes, but not tonight.' Kitty sighed. 'Tonight is only our second date. I want it to be special. I don't want the whole evening to be ruined by questions and recriminations and anger and possibly tears.'

'I promise I won't cry.'

'Not you, idiot.' Kitty laughed in spite of everything, and kissed him.

Vinny kissed her back, and they tumbled backwards into the sand.

'This is just perfect,' he said eventually, sitting up and shaking sand from his hair. 'Proper teenager-in-love stuff. Snogging on the beach.'

'And this, too,' Kitty said, drawing a heart in the sand with 'KA <3 VC'.

Then, laughing, she scrambled to her feet and whistled to the dogs. 'Come on – let's go and have a drink or several in the Mermaid and forget all about Mavis Mulholland and Mrs Gibby and all the other crap for now.'

'OK.' Vinny stood up and slid his arms round her waist. 'But what happens if I have far too much to drink, and am unable to legally drive home to my lonely bed in my lonely room in Hinton Chervils tonight?'

'That, Mr Cassidy –' she laughed – 'is the whole point of the exercise. Race you to the steps – and the loser buys the first pint!'

Chapter Twenty-Six

The following afternoon, at just gone five thirty, Kitty and Apollo made their way across the common's rutted sandy tracks towards the High Street. They didn't speak, and for once, Kitty found that the familiar scent of the waist-high ferns and the sweetness of the tangled gorse, failed to enchant her.

She'd finished work less than two hours earlier, and Mrs Gibby had still refused to be drawn on what this meeting was about and why it had to be held both after the shop closed and with Rhonda there as well – not, of course, to mention Apollo and Raymond.

She and Apollo had given up speculating on what was happening. And even Vinny, who, the previous evening in the Mermaid, after a fairish intake of beer, had tried to convince Kitty it was anything from Mrs Gibby having been taken over by an alien invasion, to her having decided to turn the chippie into a health bar for hipsters, had admitted defeat.

Added to this, Kitty had told Apollo, Jemini and Connor about the rather confusing contents of the letter from Mavis Mulholland that morning, and the current atmosphere in Sandcastle Cottage was less than euphoric. Everyone had looked like it was root-canal day. Apart from Vinny, of course, who had been amused to find that sharing her bed also involved sharing it with a large and snoring Staffie, and was still smiling.

'Here we are, then,' Apollo said as they stood outside the Silver Fish Bar. 'Although, what we are actually doing here remains a mystery to me.'

'And me,' Kitty said dolefully, 'although I'm pretty sure it's not going to be good news. Oh, well, let's get it over with. We'll have to use the back door, this one's alarmed.'

'It must feel like I do, then. No, sorry, Kitty, not really the time for a joke, is it?'

Kitty led the way down the alley at the side of the shop and across the scrubby, scruffy outside area with the trestle table and benches, and knocked on the back door.

Mrs Gibby pulled it open straight away, almost as if she'd been waiting for them. 'You didn't have to knock.' She smiled at them both. 'Come on in. Rhonda and Raymond have just arrived. We're through here.'

She ushered them into the restaurant. The tables were empty now, obviously, but still had their red-and-white gingham cloths and their cruet sets neatly placed in the centre.

'It's lovely to meet you.' Mrs Gibby shook hands with Apollo. 'Thank you so much for coming.'

'Very nice to meet you, too, although I'm mystified as to why you have invited me here,' Apollo said gravely. 'But Kitty has said much about you. She likes you very much.'

'And I like her,' Mrs Gibby assured him. 'Also, very much. Now, Rhonda, Raymond – this is Kitty, as you know, and Apollo.'

Everyone smiled and nodded and shook hands with everyone else, in what was almost a madcap version of 'Auld Lang Syne', only without any music or singing.

Mrs Gibby indicated the largest table at the end of the restaurant. 'We'll sit there, I think. More room.'

They sat.

Mrs Gibby rested her plump elbows on the table. 'I've pondered long and hard about how to do this, and eventually I've decided this is the only way to do it fairly, because you, Rhonda, and you, Kitty, are equally important to me, plus I didn't want to have to go down the legal route before I'd spoken to you.'

She paused. No one spoke.

'I'm giving up the Silver Fish Bars.'

'Nooo,' Kitty said. 'Are you ill? You can't . . . I mean . . . No!'

'What Kitty said!' Rhonda shook her head. 'Please don't say you're ill.'

'I'm not ill!' Mrs Gibby chuckled. 'I've recently had my annual MOT and I'm fine, for my age. But that's it: for my age. I'm well past retiring age, I've dished up fish and chips all my life, and my feet are tired, my knees are knackered, and quite honestly, I want to enjoy some of my old age before it's too late.'

They sat in silence for a minute.

'So, is that just this shop – or all of them?' Rhonda said. 'The end of the Gibby era?'

'This one and yours in Christchurch,' Mrs Gibby said. 'The others are all out on franchise anyway, now, and various family members are involved on the periphery, but the Firefly Common and Christchurch Silver Fish Bars are the only two originals that I still own outright.'

Kitty suddenly wanted to cry. She remembered that cold, wet, dark day when she'd first come to the village and been so unhappy, and looked through the window of the Silver Fish Bar and seen the gingham-clothed tables and the fat Brown Betty teapots and the lovely fish-and-chips-only menu cards, never dreaming that one day she'd be actually working there.

'So,' Raymond said in a deep, slow voice. 'That's the end of it for our Rhonda and young Kitty here, is it? That's what all this cloak-and-dagger nonsense has been about, is it?'

Kitty felt she couldn't have put it better herself.

'Actually, no, it isn't.' Mrs Gibby chuckled. 'All this cloak-and-dagger nonsense, as you call it, has been very carefully thought out to make things better and fairer for both Rhonda and Kitty. I know your circumstances are very different, but I wanted you both to have first refusal at the same time.'

No one spoke.

'Goodness me!' Mrs Gibby sighed. 'Am I going to have to use words of one syllable? I'm offering you, Rhonda, and you, Kitty, the chance to buy the respective shops.'

'Bloody hell!' Raymond said. 'That's an offer and a half . . . What do you reckon, Rhonda? Can we do it?'

'I don't know, Ray . . . we're not that flush . . . we could re-mortgage the house, I suppose . . .'

Kitty shook her head. Rhonda and Raymond might be able to buy the Christchurch shop – but she knew buying this Firefly Common one was an impossibility for her.

'I can't,' Kitty said quietly. 'Thank you so, so much for the offer – I would love to own this place and run it – it would be a dream come true for me, but I have nothing. Nothing at all. Not even anything to offer as collateral.'

Mrs Gibby smiled round the table. 'I'm very aware of all this. Of Rhonda and Raymond having a large family and many other demands on their money . . . and you, Kitty, I know what drove you here, to Firefly Common, and I know your circumstances, too. This is why I wanted Raymond to be here with Rhonda, and also I asked Apollo to be with you. My idea is that you should be joint owners . . . Rhonda and Raymond in Christchurch – Raymond could have his name on the papers and help out in the shop when needed, but still carry on working as a self-employed plumber . . . and then you and Apollo can both work here – Apollo as head chef, and you, Kitty, in the role you've excelled at – absolutely everything else.'

'But I have nothing to give you, either,' Apollo said. 'Some very little savings. Not enough. My shop in Reading was compulsorily purchased. They gave me peanuts. Even that has all gone now – my wages from the Mermaid are not great . . . oh, but this would be such a wonderful place to own – for me and for Kitty, we did so well in Reading together with the shop . . . but now, we have nothing to give you.'

Mrs Gibby sat back. 'Which is exactly what I expected you all to say, and why you're here. It is far more important to me that the two shops, founded by my grandparents – so, back in the dark ages, obviously – should be run by people who love them. So, as I own them outright and I have neither the need or the desire to sell for the money, my solicitors have drawn up agreements which would make it possible for you – both couples – to take over ownership immediately, and pay for the privilege as and when . . . If the shops don't make money, as they most likely won't through the winter months, then so be it, and if you decide that full ownership isn't for you, then that can be dealt with, too. I just think, for both of you, it'll be the ideal opportunity to start your own business, while at the same time I can retire happily, knowing that you are taking care of the business I love.'

'Wow,' Kitty said. 'Just wow.'

'What Kitty said, again!' Rhonda smiled. 'So – if we say yes, then we don't have to find any money upfront or anything? We can sign that paperwork your solicitors have drawn up, and all the legal ownership papers, everything like that – and we will own the shop? Just like that?'

'Exactly like that,' Mrs Gibby said. 'But I need you to think about it tonight – and let me know as soon as poss. Then I'll get everything drawn up legally – and I can start my retirement plans for the end of September.'

'That quickly?' Kitty said. 'My head's still spinning – oh, but – the end of September . . . we might have nowhere to live by then. You know what the situation is like with Sandcastle Cottage.'

'I do, my duck, I do. Only too well. And, well, there is a flat upstairs here which would be yours, too, if you needed it. There's a small kitchen, living room, two bedrooms, bathroom . . . usual things. My old man and I used to crash out here in the early days, then, after he'd gone, I rented it out for a while. It's been empty for a bit. But if you agree to take over the shop, then the flat is yours, too.' Mrs Gibby smiled at Rhonda and Raymond. 'Same goes for you with the Christchurch shop, of course. Flat above it is all yours – could be a nice little bit of extra income if you got a tenant in.'

They all looked at one another.

Apollo broke the silence. 'This is all too wonderful – and, of course, this is how Kitty and I lived above the shop in Reading – but we have dogs. If we lost Sandcastle Cottage but bought here and lived in the flat, would we be allowed to have dogs?'

Mrs Gibby laughed. 'Apollo, my love, if you go ahead and take up my offer then the flat is yours. You can have whatever and whoever you like living with you.'

Apollo and Kitty stared at one another. Rhonda had got out her phone and was doing some mathematical calculations.

'Now,' – Mrs Gibby hauled herself to her feet – 'I'm going to get a bottle of fizz from the fridge and we can all have a glass and drink a toast to – well – what will be will be.' She stopped and smiled at them all. 'But I do hope you'll all say yes, of course, and make an old lady very, very happy.'

Chapter Twenty-Seven

The glorious summer was coming to an end. The last days of August were blue and golden and warmly honey-scented. But the evenings were noticeably shorter and the mornings misty.

Apollo and Vinny had taken the dogs down to the beach. Apollo was now clearly feeling safe from Angelica's unwanted attention, with Vinny as a bodyguard. Kitty decided not to tell him that Angelica also fancied the pants off Vinny and may try a two-for-the-price-of-one seduction stalking session instead. Connor had already left for work, and Teddy was chuckling away at Daddy Pig having made a prat of himself – again.

Kitty and Jemini were nursing coffees on either side of the kitchen table.

'So, you and Vinny and Apollo and the dogs could all snuggle up in your little flat over the chippie,' Jemini said, looking as if she was going to cry. 'And me and Connor and Teddy could find a nice little ticky-tacky new-build to rent on some massive toytown estate miles away called Badger's Fart. And this would be the end of us and Sandcastle Cottage and all the fun and being together. This is so not what we signed up for.'

'I know – and it won't ever, ever come to that . . .' Kitty said, jumping up and hugging her. 'Apollo and I will take up Mrs Gibby's offer to lease/buy and run the Silver Fish Bar at the end of September, obviously, we'd be mad not to – but we also intend to fight to stay here. We belong together, and we'll stay here even if we have to – oh, I don't know, squat or barricade ourselves in or, well – do whatever it bloody well takes.'

Jemini laughed. 'OK, yes, I agree! But then, it is Mavis Mulholland's house – she does have a perfect right to want it back, damn her.'

'Maybe she could move in with us?' Kitty said. 'There's plenty of room, still.'

'God, no – that would be like having your nan living with you, watching your every move, telling you to put a vest on and eat your greens and all that crap.'

Kitty giggled. 'Righty-ho – we won't ask Mavis to move in, then. Maybe she could be a lodger with Netta and Noel, or Angelica and Mr H – they've both got massive houses and only themselves in them, if you know what I mean.'

'Sort of,' – Jemini drained her coffee mug – 'but that was shocking syntax for one of Miss B's Girls.'

Kitty groaned. 'Don't remind me – the meet-up is this Sunday, isn't it? Oh, joy . . . It never rains but it pours – as my nan never, ever said.'

August Bank Holiday Sunday broke all the British Bank Holiday Rules – and dawned, as had the rest of that scorching summer, not only dry but sunny, warm and growing rapidly warmer. Firefly Common was packed with holidaymakers and day-trippers, all desperate to grab that last bit of seaside sunshine before the children went back to school and autumn set in.

Despite all the ongoing turmoil on the domestic front, Jemini and Kitty had put on their best floaty summer frocks, and their best sparkly flip-flops, and promised not to even think about anything but Miss B's Girls today . . . and just to get the get-together over without Amy – or any of the others, really – getting a sniff that Firefly Common was now their home and had been for some time.

Vinny, Connor and Apollo had already laid bets on which one would give the game away without thinking, and at what time this would take place.

Before they'd left, Kitty and Jemini had attempted to explain to Connor and Vinny why they had to pretend to Amy and the rest of Miss B's Girls that they didn't live in Firefly Common.

'One reason,' Jemini had said, 'is because the life we have here, now, is, as you know, perfect. We don't want anyone else to know about it. We've left the crap behind and rebuilt our lives and we're happy – more than happy – and Amy and the rest of the girls are great, in small doses, but they belong to the past and the lives Kit and I used to have – not the ones we have now. And also because we've lied to them – a lot.'

'It's a bit complicated.' Kitty had nodded. 'Apollo knows all this – but when we, Miss B's Girls, first came here to Firefly Common, all arranged by Amy to meet up for Miss B's memorial service, we, Jem and I, were both going through a really rough time, but pretended we weren't, because, well, everyone else was doing OK and we didn't want to admit just how bad our lives were, even to each other. Oh, and we only met up once or twice a year at most, and so it was just easier to pretend that things were rosy . . . and once you start telling those sort of untruths, you just end up having to tell more, until you know you can never go back and say "sorry – none of that was true" – because it's all too massive.'

'And,' Jemini had butted in, 'yes it was all a lie – but it didn't matter. As far as we knew that day, we – and the rest of Miss B's Girls – would never see Firefly Common again. Until, of course, Kitty wandered into Lovell and Lowe while she was waiting for her train.'

'And I assumed she wanted to look at Sandcastle Cottage with a view to renting.' Connor had grinned. 'And the rest, as they say, is . . .'

'One big fat secret, as far as Miss B's Girls are concerned.' Kitty had grinned. 'And that's how it's going to stay.'

'Good job Amy said she'd booked a table,' Kitty said as they scrunched across the Mermaid's shingle car park at lunchtime. 'It looks rammed in there.'

'Bound to be – where else are people going to eat? The Silver Fish Bar is closed on a Sunday – which is pretty short-sighted these days, and something I'm sure you and Apollo will alter asap – and Nellie's Café only does breakfasts and snacks.'

'Mrs Gibby is really winding down now,' Kitty said, in defence of her much-loved employer. 'She needs one day off a week, at least – she's ancient. Right – now, where have we left our cars?'

'Huh?'

'Our mythical cars, in which you drove from Brum and I drove from Reading this morning. Have we left them out here – or back on one of the side roads?'

'Oh, right – god . . . this subterfuge thing is tricky isn't it?' Jemini sighed. 'Side road, I think, then we can sneak off home and pretend to be going to our cars.'

'Yes, good thinking.' Kitty linked her arm through Jemini's. 'Right – here we go.'

The Mermaid was, as they'd guessed, heaving. All the tables were fully occupied, the crowd at the bar was already three-deep, and the noise level was ear-splitting. They looked around for any sign of Amy or the rest of the girls, but it was futile.

'Nope. Can't see her – or any of the others,' Jemini said. 'But Amy must be in here somewhere. She's never been late for anything, ever, in her entire life.'

Their phones pinged in unison.

Buffeted by a tidal wave of sweaty vest-clad holidaymakers desperate for food and cold drinks, they stepped back outside into the car park and looked at their mobiles.

'Amy,' they said together. 'OK . . . let's see.'

Girls – the Mermaid is packed. Fortuitously, I've booked an outside table. Everyone else is here. Can only imagine you're both having trouble negotiating the A34 on Bank Holiday Sunday. Maybe you should have left sooner? We won't order food until you arrive. Will see you soon, we hope. Amy.

They looked at one another and laughed.

'The A34 is always a bugger on a bank holiday,' Kitty said as they headed round the side of the pub. 'It's taken me ages to even reach the motorway . . .'

'Me, too.' Jemini giggled. 'Although it's so long since I drove that I'm not sure I know how any more. And Kit, please kick me if I say the wrong thing . . . I can't even remember what I said I was doing the last time we all met up.'

'You were pretending you weren't divorced, pretending you didn't work in a supermarket, pretending you didn't live in a bedsit, definitely pretending that you weren't doing the keep-fit pole dancing, oh, and pretending that you didn't have Teddy either, as I recall.'

'Blimey, that's a lot of untruths to remember. And you?'

'Oh, I was pretending I was still Miss Corporate, living on our cosy-clone new-build housing estate, with James, of course, and enjoying all the trappings of a reasonably well-off young business-couple's life. Whereas I was actually living in a room in Apollo's flat with a rescue Staffie, over a kebab shop in the mean streets of Reading.'

They looked at one another.

'So,' – Jemini frowned – 'is that what we have to pretend our life is like today? The same as last time?'

'Um . . . yes, I think so.' Kitty giggled.

'OK – I just hope we both have good enough memories to pull this off.'

'Yeah – me too. But we can do this . . . hopefully . . . but, heck, Jem – when you think back to what we had – or rather, didn't – how we *were*, before we came here . . . how bad was our life then? And how fabulously good is our life now?'

'Perfect,' Jemini said with feeling. 'Apart from the fact we're going to lose Sandcastle Cottage, of course.'

'Which we're not going to talk about today – oh, look, there they are!' Kitty raised her hand and waved. 'Smile, Jem – and remember your lines – or your lies.'

Chapter Twenty-Eight

Miss B's Girls, as one, looked up from their perfectly placed table on the clifftop, with full sea views and sheltered from the sun's midday heat by a huge blue-and-gold striped parasol, and waved back with enthusiasm.

'Amy's had her hair cut!' Jemini hissed as, smiling, they made their way across the huge expanse of the Mermaid's beer garden. 'The plaits have gone! She has a bob! She looks twenty years younger!'

'And she's lost weight,' Kitty, also smiling, hissed back. 'And holy hell, she's wearing jeans – and a cold-shoulder vest thing.'

'She's got a man!' Jemini whispered, still without losing the smile. 'Either that, or she's discovered Slimming World and online shopping.'

'Maybe both? All three?' Kitty laughed. 'She did say she had something to tell us, didn't she?'

'Girls!' Amy rushed towards them, enveloping them in a very uncharacteristic hug. Amy was so not a natural hugger. 'How wonderful to see you! And how clever of you to manage to coordinate your journeys and arrive here together.'

Jemini and Kitty exchanged 'looks'. They hadn't thought that one through at all.

'Oh, er, yes . . . funnily enough, we both stopped at Tot Hill services at the same time – we couldn't believe it,' Kitty improvised quickly. 'We've been in convoy ever since.'

'And you look fabulous, Amy,' Jemini said, clearly hopefully steering the conversation in a different direction. 'We hardly recognised you.'

'I've had a bit of a makeover,' Amy said. 'Because I've reached a new stage in my life and – well – plenty of time for the details later. Shall we order? I've got jugs of iced water on the table . . . come and say hello to the others – oh, this is fun – all being back together here again, isn't it?'

Kitty and Jemini hugged and smiled at Claire, Becky and Emma, and slid into the vacant seats. They only half-glanced at the Mermaid's menu – which they both knew off by heart – and quickly joined in the usual all-talking-at-the-same-time gossip.

'Right,' Amy said, the change of image having not stretched quite as far as her ingrained head-girl manner, 'if we've all chosen, I'll whizz up to the bar and order. And drinks?'

Remembering in time that they both had long and difficult return journeys back up the A34, Kitty ordered spritzers for her and Jemini. Claire was on orange juice because she was pregnant, again – farming in the fens, or wherever it was, must be pretty good for all-round fecundity, Kitty thought. Becky and Emma ordered a bottle of prosecco and one of lemonade 'so that we can share and water it down. We still haven't decided which one of us is driving home yet.'

Amy, still with the razor-sharp memory that made her an A-star pupil all the way through school, didn't need to write down any of the food or drinks order.

They watched her go.

'Right.' Kitty leaned across the table. 'What the hell has happened to Amy? Has she discovered men at last?'

Claire, Becky and Emma were, however, disappointingly as much in the dark as Kitty and Jemini.

Speculation ran the gamut from yes, a man, or maybe – from Becky and Emma – a woman, to possibly just the thought that being forty wasn't that far off the horizon and maybe it was time to make more of herself.

'Mind you,' Claire said, looking across the table, 'you two look like you're doing OK. More than OK, in fact. You both look absolutely stunning and years younger than the rest of us. What's new with you two – I mean, obviously not men, because we all know you're both settled there, but work? Or what?'

'Er – just – um, work, yes.' Jemini floundered. 'Yes, um, Krish and I are doing well in the business. It's all going well up there.' She looked at Kitty. 'Same for you, Kit, isn't it?'

'Oh, er, yes. Work is manic. Everything's hunky-dory in my little world.'

'And you and James still not married?' Becky asked. 'I hope not – because it means our invitations got lost in the post!'

Everyone, except Kitty, laughed.

Claire beamed. 'And still no patter of tiny feet yet?'

'Er – no – um, James and I are still having too good a time to want to tie ourselves down.' Kitty closed her eyes, feeling decidedly uncomfortable. Lying on this scale didn't come easy. 'And marriage can wait a while yet, I think.'

'And are you and Krish not entering the joyous realms of parenthood yet either, Jem?' Claire asked. 'Surely you must want children?'

Clearly being a mother of twenty or whatever ridiculous number it was now, Kitty thought crossly, made Claire want everyone else to be in the same state of broody breeding bliss.

Jemini looked startled for a moment. 'Ah – no, goodness, no – er – like Kitty and – um – James, Krish and I are still busy building an empire. Babies can wait.'

'Well, you shouldn't leave it too late,' Claire, the earth mother, said. 'You're both already going to be elderly primigravidas as it is.'

'Elderly *what*?' Jemini frowned.

'First-time mothers,' Emma put in. 'Don't you remember your Latin?'

'No, thank god,' Jemini said.

'Thanks, Claire.' Kitty forced a smile. 'That makes me feel a whole lot better about getting older.'

'Oh, I didn't mean . . .' Claire flapped her hands. 'Ignore me. I've got baby-brain-itis.'

'Probably a permanent fixture,' Jemini muttered, as she and Kitty exhaled and exchanged 'looks' again.

By the time Amy returned with the tray of drinks – 'they said they'd bring them out to the table, but I could see we'd be waiting for ever so I just grabbed the tray; food will be about twenty minutes,' – the remainder of Miss B's Girls had caught up on most of the gossip.

Jemini and Kitty both wondered if they were the only ones who had just completely invented everything they'd done since the last meeting.

'I got here early and took flowers from us all to Miss Bowler's grave,' Amy said, dishing out the drinks in exactly the same efficient way as she had the dinners at school. 'Her friends here have kept it all very neat and tidy. I think she'd be happy that we're all back together here because of her, don't you?'

Everyone agreed.

Kitty and Jemini exchanged yet another 'look'.

The food arrived and was fabulous, as the Mermaid's food always was – only, Jemini and Kitty agreed, not quite as fabulous as it would have been had Apollo been on cheffing duty that day. Kitty was actually very glad that he wasn't, as Amy had insisted on barging off into the kitchen 'to compliment the chef' and she knew how much Apollo hated being the centre of attention.

Once Amy had returned, and the drinks had been replenished, and she'd worked out who owed what, and the bill – and a healthy tip – had been settled, everyone had sat back and gazed out over the glorious view of the Solent and the misty outline of the Isle of Wight on the horizon.

Amy chinked her glass with a spoon. 'Well, I think we'll all agree that this has been another super meet-up. I'm sure Miss B would be delighted that so many years on, we're still all happy to be together. And we've obviously all had a lot of things to catch up on, and incredibly fascinating it's been – but I'd like to share my news with you all now.'

221

'It's a man,' Jemini muttered darkly. 'It's got to be a man.'

'I've left Elphinstone High.'

'Which isn't a man, but could so easily be a song by the Eagles,' Kitty whispered.

'You all look surprised – and I must say, so was I, when I decided this year to spread my wings a little,' Amy continued. 'After all this time, I'm leaving the Berkshire countryside behind and have been offered a new post – well, Head of English, obviously – but at a new school.'

Everyone looked pretty amazed. Because being Head of English at Elphinstone Girls' High School in the Royal County of Berkshire was Amy's raison d'être, and it been indelibly stamped right through her, like – well, Kitty thought – like a stick of rock. So much so, that when Amy had finished university she had returned to their alma mater as a member of staff rather than a pupil.

Everyone oohed and aahed a bit and waited expectantly for the follow-up.

'Was she pushed or did she jump?' Jemini hissed.

'I left Elphinstone at the end of last term, and decided then to take a little time to update my appearance before starting my new post at the end of September.'

Everyone took the bait and said how lovely her new hairdo, new figure, and new clothes looked, and to ask where on earth was she going?

'Ah,' – Amy attempted to look coyly mischievous and almost pulled it off – 'this is where the big surprise comes in. My new post is at Hinton High School for Girls – it's just down the road from here, on the edge of the New Forest, between Hinton Chervils and Hinton Lacey. And I'm hoping to find a lovely little house and make my home in Firefly Common – just like our beloved Miss B. What do you say to that, girls?'

Kitty, her hand clapped over her mouth, was too horrified to say anything.

Unfortunately Jemini wasn't quite so lucky.

'Holy crap on a sodding cracker!'

'. . . And that wasn't even the worst thing . . .' Kitty, curled on Vinny's lap, said, trying not to laugh. 'Then – then she said – oh, well if you want to find somewhere decent to live in Firefly Common, I work with my partner, Connor, in his family's estate agency on the High Street here. We'd be delighted to try and find you your perfect new home.'

'By then I'd totally forgotten which lie we were on and it just slipped out,' Jemini said. 'In my defence.'

They were all sitting in the garden of Sandcastle Cottage, enjoying drinks in the balmy evening warmth. Teddy was playing on her tree swing and both the dogs were eating crisps in the paddling pool.

Apollo, Connor and Vinny all looked at one another.

'I had Jem,' Connor said, 'at four-ish.'

'Mine, I think.' Vinny grinned. 'Two-thirty.'

'Excuse me,' – Apollo leaned forward – 'Vinny, you had *Kitty* at two-thirty. However, I had Jemini at two forty-five. Which I think, gentlemen, makes me the winner. Hand over your money.'

Vinny and Connor pulled mock angry faces and parted with a fiver each.

'You bet on me – us – not being able to keep up the pretence?' Jemini squawked indignantly. 'That's disgusting!'

'It was gambling on what we'd all agreed was a dead cert,' Apollo grinned. 'And I won.'

Jemini shook her head, laughing. 'Men! Huh!'

'Anyway,' Vinny continued, 'so, after Jemini had blown her cover, presumably all the rest of the pretence had to be unveiled?'

'It did,' Kitty said miserably. 'It took forever. Everyone was riveted and gobsmacked, and now everyone knows we've not only lied about one lifestyle but two, and that puts us firmly into Billy Liar territory as far as they're concerned.'

Jemini nodded. 'And now Bossy Boots Amy will be coming round here some time soon to collect all the lovely property details that I've found for her – and will no doubt bore us all rigid with tales of her Neon Tetras.'

'And she'll probably clash with the arrival of Mavis Mulholland clutching the eviction notice,' Kitty said dismally. 'Oh, lucky us – we've got so much to look forward to.'

They all looked at one another, and sighed.

Chapter Twenty-Nine

Three days later, the start of September showed no inclination to turn into full-blown autumn. It was still warm in the mornings, once the mist had cleared, and hot in the afternoons, and with no sign of rain. The grass was bleached to straw, gardens had wilted, and Firefly Common flagged.

Apollo and Kitty had signed Mrs Gibby's paperwork – as had Rhonda and Raymond – had already advertised for staff to start in October, and had, during a meeting with the solicitors, been informed that they could do exactly as they wanted with the premises as long as they intended to continue to use it as a restaurant and takeaway business. So Apollo was going to get his wish . . . the chippie would be known as the Silver Fish Bar *and* Golden Kebab House. It was all a dream come true . . . oh, and they'd decided to leave the upstairs flat empty for the time being – just in case.

And then there was Vinny . . . Kitty smiled blissfully to herself with the undiluted joy of the ecstatically wonderful early throes of Being In Love.

She sang along with Radio Two as she whizzed round Sandcastle Cottage's living room with the hoover – just in case Mavis Mulholland turned up today – oh, yes, Vinny was now practically a permanent fixture, only returning to his Hinton Chervils room for clean clothes and to collect his post.

He fitted in with everyone so well – just like Connor had done – and had become part of the family practically overnight.

And of course, Kitty thought, jabbing the pointy bit of the

vacuum cleaner under the corner sofa, Vinny was not only the most incredible man she'd ever met, but he really, really didn't mind sharing the bed with Zorro.

So, on this particularly gloriously sunny morning, Kitty was on housework duties, the dogs were in the garden, Apollo had gone into Bournemouth to see a man about a vertical rotating spit for the newly planned kebab area, Teddy was at nursery, Jemini and Connor were at work, and Vinny had been called out by Tilda to do running repairs at Heartbreak Bay after the fire-breathing dragon had been subjected to a lot of unwanted attention from an unleashed cockapoo.

Therefore the 'coooeee' through the open door, just as Kitty had switched off the hoover and had decided to have another coffee before whizzing round with the duster, was less than welcome. She sighed.

'Come in, Angelica . . . I'm in the kitchen.'

'Er – I'm not Angelica, and I have no idea where the kitchen is.'

Kitty frowned – not Mavis Mulholland either then – and hurried out into the hall.

'Amy! This is a surprise!'

She hoped upon hope that her welcome sounded – well – welcoming.

Amy, still looking far less Amy-ish in jeans and a pretty broderie anglaise top, her bobbed hair glossy and even wearing a touch of make-up, smiled. 'I did mention I'd come and find you here and collect the property information Jemini said she'd leave for me. I know I could have called into the estate agent's, or even browsed Rightmove, but it was kind of her to offer to help – and I do appreciate people being kind.'

Kitty hoped her face had stopped looking shocked. 'Er – yes . . . yes, of course – oh, please come in . . . I know Jem said she'd sorted out details of the modern flats and one-bed houses you were looking for – all within a reasonable radius of the school, of course . . . so much easier for her to sift through it all first rather than you having to go into the estate agent's and . . .'

For pity's sake, Kitty told herself, stop babbling. Just get the brochures, offer her a cup of coffee – and stop babbling. 'It's – um – lovely to see you – please come on through – would you like coffee?'

'Is it decaff?'

'Er – we have decaff . . . I think – yes.'

'Then, I'd love one – and this,' – Amy looked round her in astonishment – 'is an absolutely gorgeous house.'

'We love it.' Kitty led the way into the kitchen. 'Oh, please sit down. I'll put the kettle on. We – me and Jem – were stunned at your news, by the way – very brave of you to make that move.'

Amy looked at her. 'Maybe, but not as brave as you and Jemini have been. You should have shared all that awfulness with us, you know, we'd have understood and maybe been able to help. It's what friends do.'

Is this really Amy? Kitty thought as she reached for the coffee jars – hoping that Amy was going to be OK with supermarket instant – and not for the first time, marvelled at the change.

'Thank you for saying that.' Kitty put milk and sugar and sweeteners on the table. 'It means a lot. Maybe we should have been honest but, well, you – and the others – were always so to-gether and sorted and organised – we felt like total failures. And I was far too ashamed of what had happened to me, to even begin to admit it to you.'

The kettle boiled. Kitty made coffee.

Amy nodded. 'I can understand that. I'm aware that my life has been pretty smooth and maybe I've not always been able to see why other people's haven't run on the same lines. I mean, I was a spoilt only child of rich and doting parents, had everything I ever wanted given to me without asking, did well at school, did well at university, went straight back to Elphinstone – and, well, here I am.'

'And your parents?'

'Are living out their well-heeled pension years in a luxury apartment especially provided for the elderly healthy wealthy in the wonderfully cushioned-from-the-real-world depths of the Home Counties. Yours?'

'Living an alternative lifestyle in a yurt on an island somewhere north of Shetland as far as I know.'

They exchanged grins.

Kitty pushed the coffee mug across the table to Amy. 'So, seriously – why all the massive changes, now?'

'Because my parents decided to sell the house and decamp to their retirement home – at last. It meant I didn't have to be their little girl, at home, going to Elphinstone every day.'

Kitty blinked. 'You did that for your parents? You stayed as Amy, Head Girl, Swot, Miss B's Darling, long after we'd grown-up – for your parents?'

'I did. I was entirely biddable. I was programmed to be eternally grateful for what they'd given me – and given up for me, too – I think. You've said your parents weren't very warm or interested or kind, well mine went the other way. I was smothered, and I felt I owed them everything. I did exactly what they wanted me to do, because it was easier and didn't upset them. But, as a result, I was in danger of wasting my entire life . . . There are so many ways to ruin a child's life, aren't there?' Amy sipped her coffee. 'This is good – thank you.'

Kitty wanted to hug her.

'So, do you know where you want to live?'

Amy smiled. 'Well, obviously Firefly Common – but truthfully, if I can't find a house here, then anywhere local. All the villages are gorgeous. Somewhere nearer the Hintons? One of the little New Forest hamlets?' She looked around the sunny kitchen. 'This house is simply wonderful, Kitty. You're so lucky.'

'We know. It's a bit of a Tardis, too – it used to be a B&B so there are loads of rooms, but, of course, sadly we're probably going to have to leave it soon because . . .'

Over a second coffee, Kitty told Amy all about the Sandcastle Cottage saga and Mavis Mulholland's imminent return.

Amy was suitably shocked and suitably sympathetic. And then

Honey and Zorro, having belatedly sensed an intruder, scrabbled their way into the kitchen and pounced on Amy with their usual over-enthusiastic Staffie welcome.

Kitty was horrified. 'I'm so sorry. They won't hurt you. They love everyone. I'll just get them to go outside.'

'Please don't!' Amy's voice was Staffie-muffled. 'They're fabulous. I love dogs – animals – would have loved to have pets . . . but my parents didn't approve, didn't like animals, and didn't like the mess.' She laughed as Zorro attempted to clamber onto her lap and Honey licked busily between her bare toes in her flip-flops.

'Well, if you're sure you're OK.' Kitty smiled. 'They can be a bit full-on – we rescued them, so they're a bit spoilt now.'

'They are wonderful!' Amy managed to fondle both of their solid heads at the same time. 'I still have my Tetras of course, but once I'm settled, I must see how many rescues I can rehome.' She looked at Kitty. 'This probably sounds insane to you, but I feel like I've been reborn. It's just fabulous . . . oh, um – sorry – but can I use your loo?'

Kitty pointed her in the direction of the downstairs cloakroom and chuckled at Honey and Zorro. 'You now have another fan – and a friend for life. Well done.'

With the dogs both trying to scramble onto her lap, Kitty sat, drinking the dregs of her coffee, gazing out of the kitchen window, mulling over Amy's revelations and thinking how bizarre life was.

And then Amy screamed.

The dogs flattened their ears and stared. Kitty rushed from the kitchen into the long passageway that lead to the downstairs cloakroom. Was there a spider in the loo? Was Amy phobic? Was . . . ?

Amy was standing in the hall, leaning against the wall, shaking.

Bloody big spider, Kitty thought, hurrying towards Amy.

'What on earth's the matter? Are you OK? Goodness, you've gone pale . . . come and sit on the bottom stair for a moment . . . shall I get you a glass of water . . . ?'

Amy allowed herself to be led to the staircase. She sat down, still trembling violently.

Kitty sat beside her. 'What happened? Was it a spider? In the loo?'

Amy shook her head. 'The loo was fine . . . it's – it's that . . . I was desperate for the loo, so didn't notice it on the way in – but then, just now, on the way out . . .'

Amy pointed to the wall.

Kitty frowned. A spider on the wall? Not that she could see. Anyway, the wall was covered in photo tiles. They'd all decided that they took millions of photos on their phones and had stacks of real photos in boxes from pre-digital days, so they'd take advantage of a junk-mail offer, and have some of their most precious pictures made into wall tiles.

They were an eclectic mix and filled the not-inconsiderable length of the passageway between the kitchen and the rest of the house.

Kitty knew they'd all have to go before Mavis came home.

However, why they'd freaked Amy out was a total mystery.

Amy stood up, shakily, and walked over to the wall, pointing to one of the tiles.

'This . . .' her voice was little more than a whisper. 'Where on earth did you get this?'

Kitty peered, couldn't see what she was looking at, and so crossed the hall and looked over Amy's shoulder.

'Oh, that one – that's a not-very-good picture of Apollo and the love of his life – his girl, May.'

'Apollo . . . you know Apollo?' Amy still stared, transfixed, at the tile.

'Yes, he lives here and . . . why? Do you know him, too?'

Kitty frowned – had Amy been a secret kebab-buyer in Reading? Had Angelica got a stalking rival?

'He lives – here? Apollo? This . . .' Amy's finger shook as she pointed. '*This* Apollo?'

'Yes – he's just gone into Bournemouth . . . in fact, as the dogs have just belted out into the garden, I would say he's just arrived home and . . .'

Amy swayed.

'Kitty!' Apollo appeared in the hallway. 'I've got a great deal on the rotisserie! Nice people! We can do much business there, I think! All installations included in the price – will be ready by the beginning of October and . . .'

He stopped and stared at Amy.

She stared back.

Kitty still hadn't got a clue what was going on.

'May . . . ?' Apollo whispered. 'May . . . ?'

Amy nodded . . . and burst into tears, and then Apollo rushed across the hall and bundled her up in his arms, with Honey and Zorro dancing round them joyously, then he kissed her and smoothed the tears away from beneath her eyes with his fingers.

'Don't cry, *mou* . . . angel . . . Please don't cry . . . My girl, May . . .'

Chapter Thirty

'. . . So,' Kitty said, later that evening after everyone had returned, and they were all in the garden on the sunloungers, so she didn't have to go through it more than once. 'It turns out that Amy is Apollo's long-lost love . . . torn away from him by her over-protective and rather unpleasant parents . . . they had no time to exchange details . . . Apollo has loved her all his life, as we know – and she has never looked at anyone else.'

They sat in silence.

'Wow. But what are the chances?' Vinny said, swinging his long legs across Kitty's lap on the sunlounger.

'About a trillion billion to one, I reckon,' Jemini said. 'With a bit of Firefly Common magic thrown in.'

'But his girl was called May?' Connor said, cuddling up to Jemini. 'And she's Amy . . . so . . . ?'

'Oh, they were trying to explain that – both talking at once, not keeping their hands off each other – it was wonderful! Oh, and Angelica is going to be so gutted.' Kitty chuckled. 'Anyway, I sort of gathered that he'd misheard her say Amy: it sounded like May. The first time they met, there was this ancient song playing on the equally ancient badly tuned radio in Apollo's family taverna – Dion and the Belmonts were singing "My Girl the Month of May" and it all just fitted, and it became their song and she loved that he called her May and never corrected him.'

'Apollo told us some of this at Noel and Netta's party,' Jemini said. 'It was when we realised how much in love he'd been.'

Teddy and the dogs chose that moment to create a tidal wave in the paddling pool. There was a lot of giggling and barking and mess.

'Oh, god, I'm going to miss this if – when – we have to leave here.' Connor sighed. 'Anyway – so, where are the happily reunited couple now?'

'Walking along the beach, catching up on the last twenty years,' Kitty said. 'Sooo romantic.'

Vinny kissed her. 'Have we been out-romantic-ed, do you think?'

Kitty shook her head. 'Goodness, no.' She kissed him back. 'We're on an entirely different level of lust and love and laughter.'

'Oh, good.'

Jemini snuggled even closer to Connor. 'But how fabulous is this – and how lucky we all are. So, I suppose Amy – oh, gosh, or do we have to call her May, now? – won't be needing all the property info I dug out – and Lovell and Lowe will miss out on their percentage.'

'How come?' Connor frowned.

Jemini kissed him. 'Because, dear, sweet, toyboy of mine, there is no way on god's earth that born-again Amy won't be moving in here with Apollo, is there? Even if we're all going to be out on our respective ears as soon as Mavis Mulholland hits dry land.'

'Ah!' Connor nodded. 'Yes. Of course she'll move in here. Although, we still might make a bit of a killing on one deal . . .'

They all looked at him.

'Mum and Dad have gone to a bit of a "do" in Winchester tonight. They'd arranged for Mr and Mrs Gandolfo to collect the keys for the Sea View cottage out at Thrift Drift Cove – but they, the Gandolfos, got delayed, so Mum asked me to bring the keys home here, and the Gandolfos will collect them, and sign for them, sometime this evening.'

'Very trusting of your mother,' Vinny said. 'Letting strangers have the keys just for a viewing.'

Connor nodded. 'Well, usually one of us goes with the prospective buyer, of course, but apparently, Mr and Mrs Gandolfo are one-hundred-per-cent sure they want the cottage – they've spoken to the previous owners, and the refurb builders, and had it all checked out – and they've already paid a substantial deposit . . .'

'Wow,' Jemini said. 'Well done, Deirdre and the Sea View idea. Should we be round the front, just in case, then? Do you know what time they'll be arriving?'

Honey and Zorro suddenly stopped splashing and started barking. Then, clambering wetly out of the paddling pool, they hurtled round the side of the house in Staffie tandem.

'Um – right now, I guess.' Connor laughed, uncurling himself. 'I've got the keys and the paperwork in the kitchen . . . I won't be long.'

He wasn't.

With the dogs doing their Staffie-tail-wagging best, Connor reappeared, only moments later, followed by a couple of total strangers.

Kitty, Vinny and Jemini sat up.

'Mr and Mrs Gandolfo,' Connor said, looking slightly bewildered. 'The new owners of the cottage at Thrift Drift. They – um – wanted to have a word with Kitty.'

The Gandolfos, Kitty thought, made a handsome couple. They were both suntanned and elegant in matching white-linen trousers and un-matching casual tops. Late middle-age, maybe . . . she was taller than him, with a fabulous Grace Dent-style soft up-do – still very pretty – and he was shorter and had a big, smiley face.

Kitty smiled at them. 'Hello . . . um . . . I'm not sure . . .'

Mrs Gandolfo smiled and clanked some rather gorgeous gold bracelets. 'Hello, Kitty!' She laughed. 'You have no idea how much I've been longing to say that.' And she laughed again.

Kitty just stared. She'd never seen these people in her life. Vinny squeezed her hand. Jemini was frowning. No one spoke. Even Teddy was silent. It was all very bizarre.

Mr Gandolfo was smiling beatifically, as if in on some massive joke.

'I'm sorry,' Kitty said, 'but I don't know who you are. Should I?'

234

Mrs Gandolfo held out her left hand. Diamonds and gold sparkled and glinted. 'Roland and I were married just a few weeks ago, on-board ship. It was wonderfully romantic.'

Mr Gandolfo smiled some more and nodded.

Kitty shook her head. 'Um – well . . . congratulations, but . . .'

'Before I became the third Mrs Gandolfo, my previous name was Mulholland.'

'Holy crap on a cracker! Jemini exploded.

Kitty just sat open-mouthed. 'No way . . . no way . . . you mean – you're—?'

'Mavis Mulholland, as was, yes.' Mavis beamed. 'And you, Kitty, are every bit as lovely as I imagined you'd be – and,' – she swept her arms round the garden – 'this – all of you – and that beautiful little girl and these gorgeous Staffies, are exactly as I imagined you would be – and it's all just so perfect.'

Knowing this was the moment she'd dreaded for so long, Kitty took a deep breath and stood up. Mavis Mulholland was home – and Mavis's home was Sandcastle Cottage.

Kitty blinked back tears, determined to be grown-up about this. 'It's lovely to meet you at last, too . . . and this . . . well, I never expected it to be like this . . . but . . . well . . . oh, now you want your lovely home back, don't you? Wow – we'll need some time to pack up and find somewhere else and . . .'

Mr Gandolfo continued to smile. Mavis laughed. Inappropriately, given the circumstances, Kitty thought.

'Actually, Kitty,' – Mavis stopped chuckling – 'as well as collecting the keys to our new local home – and yes, young Connor, your parents have been in on this last bit of subterfuge, it suited my sense of the dramatic to do it this way – I have something for you, if you want it . . . oh, but is there someone missing? Apollo? Is he not here?'

Connor seemed to be the only person not stunned into silence. 'Um – he's, er, gone for a walk, on the beach . . . with his girlfriend . . . he'll be back soon . . . probably . . .'

'As long as he's still living here, that's perfect – I wouldn't want to interrupt his love affair.' Mavis beamed at Kitty. 'So, my dear Kitty, Sandcastle Cottage has been a very happy home for me, but is clearly far more than that for you all, and I've always said it should be a proper family home – and now it is. And yes, Roland and I have bought the fisherman's cottage out at Thrift Drift – it'll be our pied-à-terre when we're here in the UK. But Roland and I have invested in other homes abroad – and we'll be travelling a lot – so . . . here you are . . .'

She handed Kitty a large padded envelope.

'You won't need anything else,' Mavis said, 'all the details of my legal people are in there, and they'll deal with all the boring stuff, there'll just be the hassle of changing names on the official bills and things . . . but otherwise – I hope you'll be very happy.'

Still not sure what on earth was happening, Kitty opened the envelope, pulled out a fat, chunky document and stared mesmerised at the cover page.

'No way on earth!' Her hands shook. She looked at Mavis in shock. 'The deeds – to Sandcastle Cottage . . . you can't possibly . . . ?'

'I can and I have.' Mavis beamed. 'You and Jemini and Apollo, as the original renters, are now the joint owners. I've wanted to be able to do things like this all my life, and the lottery win – and Roland – have made it possible.' She nodded to her new husband. 'Roly, love – go and get the champers from the car, there's a pet.'

Blinking back tears, Kitty clapped her hand to her mouth. 'Oh, my word . . . I don't know what to say . . . I have no idea what to say . . . thank you . . . I mean . . . well, thank you so so much. No, that's just not enough . . . I mean . . . Oh . . .'

'Give us a hug, duck,' Mavis said. 'And shut up. You have no idea how happy this makes me.'

Still clutching the envelope, Kitty flew across the lawn and into Mavis's arms. She was immediately wrapped in a glorious and expensive-scented hug.

'There,' – Mavis chuckled, standing back and surveying Kitty – 'all sorted – and don't you dare cry because you'll set me off if you do. Now, in a minute, I'm going to nip in and see Angelica and Mr H, and Noel and Netta, and bring them up to speed before we leave. But not until we've done this right and proper.'

Mr Gandolfo appeared round the corner then, escorted by Honey and Zorro, and bearing several bottles of champagne.

Vinny and Connor, still looking pretty stunned, rushed off into the kitchen for glasses and ice-buckets.

Just as they'd started pouring fizz into flutes, Apollo and Amy, hand in hand, drifted round the side of the house and stopped and stared.

'Far, far too much to go into right now,' – Kitty grinned at them – 'but come and meet Mr and Mrs Gandolfo, have a drink to celebrate, and we'll fill you in later.'

Roland and Mavis, having been introduced to everyone else, shook hands, handed out glasses, and Apollo and Amy, looking star-struck and bemused and clearly not sure that they weren't dreaming anyway, simply said 'thank you' and smiled some more.

Honey and Zorro lapped happily from the paddling pool.

Connor and Jemini, and Teddy – who'd been fished out of the pool and furnished with a Fruit Shoot – all cuddled up together in a haphazard and giggling group hug.

Vinny slid his arms round Kitty and kissed the top of her head. 'I'll have to be on my best behaviour, now you're my landlady, I suppose.'

'Too right.' She smiled up at him. 'I love you, Vincent Cassidy.'

'Good, because I kind of love you, too.'

Mavis beamed round at them all and, with a jangle of bangles, lifted her glass. 'To you all. To us. To a happy life. And to Sandcastle Cottage!'

They raised their glasses.

'To Sandcastle Cottage!'

THE END

Acknowledgements

Just a big thank you to all my lovely Facebook friends who have supported me and cheered me on from the sidelines throughout the writing of this book. I seriously couldn't have done it without you.

Also, a huge thank you to Sheelagh Rogers for being a lifesaver and whisking me off to lunch every time I flagged; to Jude Hughes for being simply the best – oh, and for Zorro of course; and to Patricia Lester for allowing me to nick her glorious superstar black Staffie, Beetle, and turn her into Honey.

And a special mention for my editor Rosanna Hildyard for being lovely, professional and kind; and Eloise Wood whose copy-editing was a dream, worked miracles and made me giggle. Thank you both for making me fall in love with writing again.

And to find out how Kitty and friends first found Sandcastle Cottage, discover . . .

Christmas
at
Sandcastle Cottage

*The **snowy short story prequel** to*

Summer
at
Sandcastle Cottage

Available now!

ACCENT

Addictive thrillers. **Gripping** suspense.
Irresistible love stories. **Escapist** treats.

For **guaranteed brilliant reads**
Discover **Headline Accent**

 @AccentPress

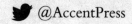

ACCENT